Praise for Mary Stewart's Merlin novels:

The Hollow Hills

"A reading adventure, an entertaining blend of history and modern imagination ... Stewart combines magic, intrigue, and violence to create a fascinating novel.... Merlin and Arthur are brought to life through Stewart's gift for storytelling."
—*Detroit Sunday News*

The Last Enchantment

"Mighty ... Climactic ... [The] action and suspense [are] constant, even harrowing."
—*The Wall Street Journal*

The Wicked Day

"Beautiful ... Brilliant ... One of the best!"
—*Detroit Free Press*

By Mary Stewart:

MADAM, WILL YOU TALK?*
WILDFIRE AT MIDNIGHT*
THUNDER ON THE RIGHT *
NINE COACHES WAITING*
MY BROTHER MICHAEL*
THE IVY TREE*
THE MOON-SPINNERS*
THE ROUGH MAGIC*
AIRS ABOVE THE GROUND*
THE GABRIEL HOUNDS *
THE WIND OFF THE SMALL ISLES
TOUCH NOT THE CAT*
THORNYHOLD*
THE STORMY PETREL*
THE PRINCE AND THE PILGRIM*

The Merlin Trilogy:
THE CRYSTAL CAVE*
THE HOLLOW HILLS*
THE LAST ENCHANTMENT*

The novel of Mordred:
THE WICKED DAY*

Poems:
FROST ON THE WINDOW*

For children:
THE LITTLE BROOMSTICK
LUDO AND THE STAR HORSE
A WALK IN WOLF WOOD*

Published by Fawcett Books

THE PRINCE AND THE PILGRIM

Mary Stewart

FAWCETT CREST • NEW YORK

A Fawcett Crest Book
Published by Ballantine Books
Copyright © 1995 by Mary Stewart

http://www.randomhouse.com

Library of Congress Catalog Card Number: 96-90776

ISBN 0-449-22443-0

This edition published by arrangement with William Morrow and Company, Inc.

Manufactured in the United States of America

First Ballantine Books Edition: April 1997

10 9 8 7 6 5 4 3 2 1

In this, the fiftieth year of our marriage,
this book is dedicated to my husband,
Fred,
with all my love.

Contents

ONE: Alexander the Fatherless   1
TWO: Alice the Motherless   37
THREE: The Knight-Errant   77
FOUR: The Pretty Pilgrim   127
FIVE: Alexander in Love   183
SIX: Alice and Alexander   243
Epilogue   295
The Legend   301
Author's Note   304

ONE

Alexander
the Fatherless

1

In the sixth year of the reign of Arthur the High King of all Britain, a young man stood on the cliffs of Cornwall, looking out to sea. It was summer, and below him the rocks were alive with seabirds. The tide, coming to the full, swept in over the pebbled shore to break in mild thunder on the base of the cliffs. Out beyond the foam-veined shallows the sea deepened in colour to the darkest indigo blue, with, here and there, fangs of rock where the water frothed in angry white. It was easy to believe—and of course the young man believed it—that the old land of Lyonesse lay drowned out yonder, fathoms deep, and that the people of that doomed land still walked—or rather floated, like the ghosts they were—among the buildings where fish swam, and where on still nights could be heard the muffled tolling of the drowned church bells.

But today, with the sun high and the sea as calm as the seas ever get on that cruel stretch of coast, no thought of the old lost kingdom crossed the mind of the watcher on the cliff. Nor was he conscious of the summer beauties round him. With a hand to his brow, he was straining, through narrowed eyes, to distinguish something far out to the south-west. A sail.

It was a strange-looking sail, which belonged to none of the ships he could recognise. Nor was it one of the rough-rigged craft used by the local fishermen. This was a foreign-looking rig, with a square, red-brown sail. And as it came clear to the sight there moved behind it another. And another.

And now the ships themselves were visible, riding long and low in the water. No device on the sails; no banners at the mast; but along the thwarts rows of painted circles glinting in the shifting sunbeams. Shields.

Unmistakable, even to him who had never seen a Saxon longboat before. And where certainly no Saxon longboat had any right to be. Then suddenly, as he watched, the ships—there were five of them—turned as one, the way a flight of birds turns at some unheard and invisible signal, to make for the shore and the narrow harbourage of the bay a bare mile to the north of where he stood. Even then the watcher paused, in the very act of turning to run with the news. It was just possible that the ships, so far west of the Saxon Shore, that strip of territory granted to the Saxons long ago, and now the home of a federacy of Saxon kingdoms, it was just possible that the little fleet had been driven off course, and was seeking shelter here for repairs and fresh water. But there had been no storm recently, and—he could see details now as the ships drew nearer—the vessels showed no sign of damage, and there as witness were those shields and the thicket of spears above them. So, five Saxon longships, fully armed?

He turned and ran.

The young man's name was Baudouin, and he was brother to March, King of Cornwall. The king had left

Cornwall some three weeks previously, to seek a conference with one of the petty kings of Dyfed, and during his absence the care of the kingdom had fallen on the younger man. Though the king had, of course, gone royally attended, he had not taken with him the main body of his fighting men, so when Baudouin rode out, as he did almost daily to check the kingdom's boundaries and visit the guard towers, he rode with an armed escort.

They were with him now. They had dismounted beyond a rocky bluff, out of the sea-wind, to rest the horses and share out the barley-cakes and thin ration wine. They were some fifteen miles from home.

Within minutes of the alarm the troop was mounted, and riding hard for the steep coomb that led down into a sheltered bay which the local fishermen used for harbour.

"How many?" It was the officer riding at Baudouin's side. His name was Howel.

"Hard to say. Five ships, but I don't know how many men one of their warships will take. Say forty to a ship, fifty, perhaps more?"

"Enough." Howel's voice was grim. "And only fifty of us. Well, at least we'll have the advantage of them as they try to beach and get ashore. What can they be planning to do, so far from their own borders? A quick raid, and then away? That wouldn't avail them much here. There's only that village half a league up the coomb, poor fisherfolk hardly worth their spears, one would think."

"True enough," said Baudouin, "but armed as they are, I doubt if they mean us well. I don't think they'll have come so far from their own Shore territories just for what pickings they can find in the villages along this coast. And I doubt if these are outlaws from the Shore. There are other possibilities. You must have heard the rumours?"

"Aye. Stories of landless men putting across from Germany and the far north, and perhaps not finding enough of a welcome on the Shore, and being driven to look for a footing elsewhere? You think that could be true, then?"

"God knows, but it looks as if we're going to find out."

"Well, but how to stop them?"

"We can try, with God's help. And His help on these coasts tends to be very practical." Baudouin laughed shortly. "They may have been hoping to come in with the tide, but by my reckoning it's just about on the turn, and you know what that means in Dead Men's Bay."

"Yes, by God!" Howel, who had lived all his life on that coast, spoke with fierce satisfaction. "They won't know those currents. Even our own fishermen won't try the bay when the tide's this way."

"That's what I'm counting on," said Baudouin, cheerfully, but before Howel could ask what he meant, they had reached the edge of the coomb, and pulled up their horses.

The bay was small, where a narrow river, little more than a stream, ran steeply down to meet the sea. As it widened out at the mouth it ran shallowly through pebbled sand, but with the tide high, as it was now, the sand was covered, waves washing right up to the turf. Out in the bay fangs of rock jutted up, each in its swirl of white water.

"Ah." It was a note of satisfaction from Baudouin. He was leaning forward in the saddle, peering down at the rough jetty of piled stones which served the fisherfolk for a landing-stage. Beached high and dry in its shelter lay four small boats. "As you say, all safe at home."

He turned to give swift orders. Three of the troopers wheeled their horses, and galloped off inland towards the village that lay higher up the coomb. The rest sent their horses slipping and scrambling down the steep bank to gain the narrow strip of turf above the tide.

The tide being just on the turn, and the breeze light and fitful, the Cornishmen knew that no sails would suffice to bring the longships in. But their oars could; they were powerful ships, and powerfully manned.

"So what's to do?" asked Howel.

Baudouin was already off his horse. "These are our seas. Let us use them." And presently, under his direction, the troopers had seized the four small boats that were beached there, and were manhandling them down from their safe moorings and into the edge of the tide. They were barely launched, half afloat, when the three men who had been sent to the village came down the little valley at their horses' fastest pace. On the saddle in front of each man was a bundle roughly tied in sacking. The leading trooper held a blazing torch high in one hand.

A man by the boats gave a shout and pointed. "My lord! There they come!"

Still far out, low in the water, the longships stole round the point. Their sails were furled, and oars flashed in the sunlight. One of the men gave a short laugh. "Hard work, that. Happen they'll be past fighting by the time they get ashore."

"They will be dead when they get ashore," said Baudouin calmly, and proceeded to give his orders.

So it was that the Saxons, rowing their armed fleet into the quiet-seeming bay, found themselves suddenly in the grip of a fierce current that threatened to sweep them straight out to sea again. The strength of the current took them by surprise, driving their ships off course and turning them sideways to the shore. As the rowers, bending to their oars, fought to bring the craft back again, and force them nearer inshore, a shout came from the Saxon lookout.

Out from the south side of the bay, where the rough jetty had hidden them from view, appeared a small flotilla of boats. They seemed to be unmanned. They bobbed away from the jetty, spun for a few moments aimlessly in the waves, then, as the outgoing current took them, they gathered speed and headed, as directly as if aimed, for the Saxon longships.

As they bore down on the vessels still helplessly wallowing in the tide-race, it could be seen that smoke was rising from the little boats, smoke which burst, suddenly and vividly, into flame. Then the Cornish boats, well ablaze, were in among the longships, driven against them and held there by the current, while the Saxons, abandoning their rowing, fought to fend them off with oars which flamed and charred and spat fire into their own ships. Three of the Saxon ships, tangled with the fireships into a blazing mass, caught fire and burned. Some of the men managed to scramble aboard the other vessels, one of which capsized. One longship only escaped the fire. Bravely, the men aboard her tried to hold her clear of the blazing wreckage, and pick up the struggling swimmers, but the heavy load and the driving current were too much for them, and at length the surviving ship, overloaded as she was, managed to fight her way back to seaward, and, leaving the smoking wreckage and the despairing cries for help in her wake, vanished once more beyond the point.

The Cornishmen, thigh-deep in the water, waited for

the rest. Barely thirty of them reached the shore, struggling to land only to meet the swords of the troopers. Of the survivors, the first three, by Baudouin's orders, were dragged alive from the water and bound, to be taken back for questioning. The rest were killed as they reached the shallows, and their bodies thrown back into the sea for the current to take. But first they were robbed of what valuables they carried, and this, too, at Baudouin's bidding. "For," said he, "we still have to face our real battle, with the fishermen whose boats I have just destroyed. So take what weapons there are, but set the rest of the takings aside—yes, here beside me. I shall see that none of you is the loser by this day's work, but the villagers must get their due. Believe me, the loss of their catch, for as long as it will take them to build new boats, will soon seem far more dreadful to them than the chance of a Saxon raid!"

"Chance! It was real enough!" said one man, pulling a broadsword from its scabbard. "Look at this! These notches! Every one a death, I've no doubt!" He handled the sword lovingly, but threw it, with its belt and gilded buckle, down on the pile.

"A thing is only real once it has happened," said Baudouin. He looked around him at the troopers who, some of them with outspoken regrets, but all cheerfully, were following suit. "And thanks to your speed and readiness, this did not." He laughed. "But let us hope that the villagers saw enough of that chance to make them spare their boats to us! See yonder. They're coming now."

A small crowd of villagers was heading down the coomb. Some of the men carried weapons, hastily snatched up, but word must have gone round that the fighting was done, for the women were with them, and even some children, skirmishing and crying out shrilly on the outskirts of the crowd.

They came to a halt a few yards away, and after some muttering and shuffling one man, presumably the headman of the village, was pushed forward towards the prince.

He cleared his throat, but before he could speak Baudouin said quickly: "Rhu, isn't it? Well, Rhu, the danger is past, and I—the king and I—have to thank you for giving us the fire and the tinder." His teeth showed in a brief grin of satisfaction. "As you see, it sufficed. There were five Saxon longships, fully armed, and God knows what they had planned to do, had they once landed, but you may be sure that by this, not even your children would have been left alive."

There were murmurs at that, and it could be seen that some of the women gathered their children closer to their skirts, while eyes went to the sea's edge, where a couple of bodies bobbed and wallowed in the shallows. A woman called out suddenly, shrill with anger. Two small boys, excited and curious for a closer view of the corpses, had crept from the back of the crowd and started down the shingle. They were caught and dragged back, to smacks and scolding from their mothers, and looks of amused indulgence from the men. In the brief flurry of action, the tension slackened, and Baudouin, seizing the moment, laughed and said, easily: "I'm sorry about your boats, but this should help you build new and better ones, and keep you and your families meantime."

At this there was a growl of approval from the villagers, and at a word from Rhu two of the men started to gather up the spoils. "To share fairly, later, for everyone," said Rhu gruffly, and Baudouin nodded.

"And no doubt the tides will bring you more. There's wreckage coming ashore already. The king makes no claim on it. It's yours."

This, too, brought approval and even some rough words of gratitude. Wood was scarce enough in that rocky and windswept land, and the Saxon ships had been well built. There would be rich pickings along this shore for some tides to come.

A trooper brought Baudouin's horse, and, rein in hand, the prince paused to exchange a final word with the headman. But some of the villagers still crowded close, and among the crowd there were ugly looks directed at the prisoners, and harsh mutterings. "What about those? To let them live? When they would have murdered us all, and burned our houses and taken our women, aye, and killed and eaten our little ones! Everyone knows what these Saxon wolves are like! Give them to us, prince!" And a couple of the women, armed with what looked like skinning-knives, took it up in a shrill shouting. "Give them to us! Give them to us!"

"Keep back!" said Baudouin sharply, as the troopers closed round the prisoners. "If you know what might have come to you, then we'll hear no more from you! For you, this is the end of it! The rest is for the king. As for these three men, for all we know there may be other threats coming to this land of ours, and King March must know of them. So we keep these men alive to tell him what he needs to know. They are not your meat, my friends; they are the king's!"

"Then pity help them," said someone, almost inaudibly, adding, to be heard: "The king your brother should reward you nobly for what you have done this day, prince!"

Baudouin, riding homewards, found himself wondering, almost with apprehension, what his brother would in fact say to him. There would certainly be no noble reward. March was a good enough ruler for this wild and remote kingdom; he was harsh, as were his people and their ways, but he was also subtle, and enjoyed plotting and guile, and the besting of other men by secret means. Not for nothing was he known to his peers as King Fox. But cruelty and cunning are not traits that make a man beloved of his people, and the Cornish people had no love for their king. Baudouin, the young man of action, who understood their ways and spoke to high and low alike, he had their love.

And King March saw, and burned, and said nothing.

2

The king came home three days later, and before he was
well within the courtyard of his stronghold he heard
about the attempted Saxon landing and his brother's success in repulsing it. From the captain of the troop that
Baudouin had led, to the groom who took March's bridle
and the servant who drew off his boots, all were eager to
tell the king what had happened, and to praise the
prince's resourcefulness.

"So where is my brother now?" asked March.

"I saw him come in barely an hour before you, sir,"
said the servant. "He went to his own chambers. The
little boy was ailing earlier this week, and your brother's
lady wife was anxious."

"Hm." The king betrayed no anxiety about his
brother's child. This was a boy just over two years old,
and so far the only child of Baudouin and his young wife
Anna. A lively, and normally a sturdy child, he served as
another spur to the elder brother's jealousy: March had
no son, and though he was attentive—some said too
attentive—to his Irish queen, she bore him no children,
and he was too jealous of her youth and beauty to put her
aside. The thought that his brother's son Alexander
seemed likely to be the sole heir to the kingdom only

served to add to the bitterness that thinned his blood and put rancour in all his days.

As was customary on the king's return after an absence from court, March held a council that evening. It was an informal affair, merely a meeting of the Cornish nobles and officers held before supper in the great hall. The queen was not present. Baudouin sat, as usual, on the king's right, and Drustan, his nephew and the king's, on March's left. While the men were still waiting for the king to enter the hall and open the proceedings, Drustan leaned across the empty chair to speak with Baudouin.

"A word with you, cousin." The two men were much of an age, so that between them the title of 'uncle' would have come absurdly. Drustan was a big man, brown-haired and fresh-skinned, with the look of a fighter. Which, indeed, he was. He was the son of King March's sister by the lord of Benoic, and had the open nature and gallant bearing learned at the court of that splendid ruler. Of him, too, March was jealous, and in fact had good reason for being so; but suspicion was not evidence, and of that there was none. So Drustan was still, perforce, made welcome at the Cornish court.

He had been with King March on his Welsh journey, so was eager, now, to hear Baudouin's account of the adventure with the Saxon ships. He, too, had heard the rumours of a Saxon attempt to make landfall in the remoter parts of the west, and praised the other man's action. "As," he added with a grin, "you won't hear yourself overmuch commended by our gracious lord. But never mind that. Less said the better till we see how the wind blows. So . . . They tell me that young Alexander was ailing while we were abroad? I trust he's better now?"

Baudouin, thanking him, assured him that all was well

in the nursery, and then the king came into the hall, and took his place.

"Ha, brother." It was the first time March had seen Baudouin since his return. The greeting was loud, for all to hear, and hearty enough, if brief. "They tell me that you have been busy defending our shores. It was well done, and we thank you. Later, after we have examined the prisoners, and know perhaps a little more about the purpose of this raid, we will talk again. But for the present our business must concern what was said and agreed between myself and the Welsh king—and then, by the gods, to supper! Our lodging in Dyfed was well enough, but we fared thinly on the road home!" He gave his great laugh, and clapped Baudouin on the shoulder, but he was looking the other way, at Drustan, and there was no mirth in the pale eyes. "And there are other things a man is hungry for, after so many days and nights away!"

At that council, no more was said to Baudouin, and once supper was over the king did not stay to speak with anyone, going straight to the queen's rooms, but next afternoon a servant sought Baudouin to tell him that his brother would see him privately that evening, for supper.

When he told Anna, his wife, she said nothing, watching with careful calm as her maids drew fresh clothes for him from the cedar chests and laid them ready on the bed. Only after the girls had gone, their soft steps dying away down the stone stair of the tower where Baudouin's family was housed, did she turn swiftly, her eyes anxious.

"Take care. You will take care?"

He did not need to ask what she meant. "Oh, I will. But what can you fear for me? From all accounts his councils went well, and he was in a good enough temper at supper last night. Indeed, he spoke well of my fight down by the bay."

"What else could he do?" The anxiety in her voice robbed it of sharpness. "He knows, who better, what the people think of you. But you and I know—"

"Anna!" He said it warningly, though they were alone in the tower room, and the walls were thick; but most people at March's court were used to caution, and who more so than the king's heirs?

"I'm sorry, love. No more. But take care." She said it softly this time, then put a hand up to caress his cheek, and smiled. "The barber, my dear, before you go to this royal supper, and look, I finished the shirt while you were out on your adventures. Do you like it?"

He fingered the fine embroidery that she was holding, then pulled her to him and kissed her. "It's beautiful. Like you, my love. Am I allowed to wear it, or is it to be laid away with herbs and cedar-wood for Alexander to inherit?"

She nestled closer, and her lips sought the hollow of his throat. "It is for you, every stitch of it, as well you know. But tonight? You would wear it tonight? Why trouble yourself just for—I mean, just for an ordinary talk and a supper?" Then, suddenly fierce, as if in spite of herself: "And doesn't he hate you enough already, with everyone in the place dinning into his ears what a great fighter you are, and how the men love you and follow you, and now you want to go to him looking like a prince of the High Kingdom—as fine and as handsome as King Arthur himself?"

He laid a gentle hand to her lips. "Hush now, let that be enough. These things don't need words. And we had best hurry. So, my love, help me put on my best for my brother the king. Yes, this beautiful shirt; why not? My thanks. And the collar of citrines. And now the dagger for my meat . . . No, nothing more. Can I go armed to sup with my brother?" He kissed her again. "Now, enough of your fretting, Anna. Get the boy to bed, and I'll see you soon enough. I doubt if I'll be late—you can be sure I won't stay any longer than I have to!"

"As long as you stay sober," she said, and they parted with laughter.

It was late. The chamber where Anna and Baudouin slept was on the west side of the castle, in the corner tower. Though the sea was half a mile or so away, the sound of waves could be heard all night, as they washed and boomed among the hollows of the rocky coast. Through the narrow, unglazed windows the night wind eddied, gently at this time of year, and full of the scents of the cliff-top pastures and the salt of the sea.

In a corner of the room, out of the draught from the windows, the child Alexander lay fast asleep under the soft blankets woven by the princess's women from the wool of the local sheep. His mother, sleepless in the great bed on the other side of the room, turned her head sharply on the pillow, and put a hand up to push her long hair out of the way. If only she could sleep! If only Baudouin would come to his bed, then they could laugh together at her fears, and perhaps make love, and be at peace. But lying here, wondering what that fox of a brother was saying, was planning, was doing . . . In spite of herself, her mind went back over the past, the times when March's jealousy and genuine dislike of his younger brother had shown itself in petty, and sometimes not so petty, actions. And lately, how that bitterness had seemed to be directed also at the child. Little Alexander, who, for all his boldness and gay spirits, was only a baby still, and helpless against such power as March could wield. Might, in one of his sudden rages, see fit to use.

At last! Someone was coming rapidly up the tower's curving stairway. Her long breath of relief checked in her throat, and she sat up, rigid against the pillows. Those were not Baudouin's footsteps, and whoever was coming, was coming clumsily, heavy-footed and noisy, with no care for the sleepers upstairs. And he was armed. She could hear the chink and clang of a scabbarded sword against the curving sides of the tower stair.

He was almost at the door. Before the heavy steps halted, she was out of her bed and over beside her son's, with a coverlet dragged from her bed to hold round her shoulders, and Baudouin's sword naked in her hand.

When the knocking came at the door, it was, horrifyingly, not a knock, but a kick with a booted foot.

"Anna! Princess? Are you awake?"

The sword point wavered and sank, but the fierce tautness still locked her bones. She recognised Drustan's voice, but the kick at the door, the breathless syllables and the faltering steps, could only be heralds of disaster. She flew to the door and opened it.

It was Drustan, his foot raised for another kick. He was very pale, and seemed, under his voluminously muffling cloak, to be only half dressed. His shirt gaped open at the throat, and his cuffs were undone. There was sweat on his skin, and his breathing laboured. As she swung the door open he staggered, and lurched against the jamb, and she saw that he was heavy with some burden carried under the cloak. "Anna—" he said, on a gasp, and, as he came forward into the candle-light, she could see what he carried.

In the sudden silence the rustle of his cloak as he let it slip back from Baudouin's body sounded as loud as the sea-waves beyond the window. Wordless, he waited, while she stood there in her shift, staring and dumb, with the bedcover held tight to her breast while breath stopped, life stopped.

Then came back, with pain like blood after frostbite. Drustan trod, softly now, towards the bed, and laid the young prince's body down. As he did so the child in the corner stirred under his blankets, murmuring something, then slept again. But when Anna, with a cry, flung herself down by her husband's body, Drustan gripped her by the arm, and pulled her to her feet again.

"Listen to me, lady! There's no time now for mourning! The king—yes, of course it was the king, who else?—he was half mad and swearing to wipe out all his brother's brood as well, and that means you, Anna, and the boy. Do you understand? You are both in danger. You must go, leave the castle, leave Cornwall, even. You must have some place to go to? For pity's sake, lady, listen to me! There's no time! Wake the boy—"

"How did it happen? And why?" She hardly seemed to have heard him. She was fixed, white-faced, oblivious of everything but the gashed corpse lying in its spreading stains on the bed.

"Oh, March's way," said Drustan harshly. "A quarrel forced, then high words, and out comes the sword. Did he ever need a reason? Or do you need to ask for one?"

"He was unarmed," she said stonily.

Drustan leaned forward and took the sword gently from her grasp. "So I see."

"So must March have done. Surely, even he would not be so ignoble as to draw his sword on an unarmed man?"

"He was drunk. So men will say—"

"So they will." Her voice was bitter with contempt. "And they will hold him excused therefor. But I," said the Princess Anna, "will not!"

"Nor should you," said Drustan quickly. "Look, there will be time later on to think what you must do. But now you must go, and the child with you. Listen. This happened after they had supped. They were private; wine was left and the servants had been sent away. The king drank too much, and then this crime befell. But Baudouin, armed as he was only with the knife with which he had been eating, defended himself nobly, so that there was commotion, with tables and benches overturned, and the king, far gone in drink and passion, setting up such a shouting that the servants in the outer rooms were roused, and went running in. They were too late to save Baudouin, but one of them came running for me, and when I got to the supper chamber I found your lord as you see, and the king bleeding—"

"Ah," was all she said, but he answered her.

"A couple of flesh wounds, no more than cuts, but the servants called for salves and bandages, and the leech came, and between them they have held him there. But he is raving still, and now it is treachery that he is shouting, and your life and that baby's yonder that he is swearing must now be forfeit."

"For what?"

"For the treason your husband committed in defending himself with a knife against his king." Then, violently, "What does it matter? It has happened! I have brought him to you, but you cannot stay to bury him, nor even to mourn him. For the child's sake, Anna, go, and quickly!"

A sound at the door brought them both round, Drustan's sword whipping from its scabbard, but it was only the princess's woman, apprehensive and curious. "Madam? I heard something—*ahh!*"

The sound was a half-shriek as she caught sight of the blood-stained body on the bed. It roused the child, who began a whimpered protest at being wakened, and it shook Anna out of her nightmare trance of shock. Time enough, later, for the bereaved wife to weep; now she was a princess, and the mother of a prince, and this was a situation that she and Baudouin had spoken of and even, reluctantly, planned for. Baudouin was dead. His son must be saved. And they had, unforeseen, the valuable help of Drustan, who might even now be risking his own life for them. He had already—he told her this as she and the woman began hastily to pack their things—sent his servant for horses, and the man would accompany them for the first part of their way. There was no need to discuss where they would go. That, too, had been spoken of many times. Anna's cousin had owned a castle a few weeks' journey to the north, well out of Cornwall, and in gentler country; far enough for safety. This, since the cousin's death, had been kept by his widow, who had promised, if need arose, to give Anna and her son shelter. Even King March could not molest them there.

So it was that, some twenty minutes later, Drustan, with his sword ready in his right hand, and the little boy held in his other arm, kicked the door wide and prepared to lead the way down the tower steps. Anna and Sara, her woman, had crammed as much as they dared carry into bundles ready to be stuffed into saddle-bags, and the princess went armed still with her husband's sword.

"Quickly, now," said Drustan.

But Anna, on the threshold, turned suddenly back into the chamber. She ran to the bed. The other two waited for the sad farewell, the kiss on the corpse's forehead. The child, on the man's shoulder, watched silently with wide eyes still full of sleep.

She stooped over the bed, and for a grotesque few moments seemed to be wrestling with her husband's body. Then as she stood back they could see that she had stripped from him the embroidered shirt that, so short a time ago, he had put on with affectionate laughter. Across the breast, where the fine silks made the pattern, the bloodstains were already stiffening and growing darker.

It seemed she had done with kisses. She stood for a moment with the bloody shirt clutched to her, and spoke to the man on the bed.

"My lord," said Baudouin's wife, "your son shall wear your shirt and carry your sword, and when he is grown he will pay the beast of Cornwall for this night's work. I promise you this, and these three are my witnesses."

Then she turned and followed Drustan down to where the servant waited with the horses.

3

There was a half-moon, hazed over, but giving a little light. They went carefully, but when they reached the shore track the sea seemed to reflect light back to the sky, and their way showed more clearly. They kept by the shore for some miles, splashing through fords and going as fast as they dared over the rough ground, until at last the track turned steeply uphill towards the crest of the moor where the old Roman road bridged the Tamarus River, and the way lay clear towards the east.

Here, even without the sea-light, going was easier. The road ran straight, and though broken here and there and weedy, it was in reasonable repair. After a while the sky cleared, and a few stars showed.

Goren, the man Drustan had sent with them, knew the road, and the horses he had provided were good ones, and fresh. They made fair speed. Anna, straining past her bay's shoulder to watch the road for pitfalls, still had no time for grief. All her being, now, was set on escape, on securing her son's safety. Baudouin's sword was sheathed at her horse's pommel, his bloodied shirt, hastily rolled up, had been thrust into her saddle-bag, and the big bay she rode was Baudouin's own horse. For the moment, that was enough; Baudouin was with her, and

Baudouin's son slept soundly in Sara's arms. She fixed her eyes on the dim roadway, her thoughts on the journey ahead, and rode for her life and his.

Even so, they had gone barely ten miles when Goren turned in his saddle, pointing urgently to the rear. In a moment Anna could hear it, too. The beat of hoofs, coming fast along the road behind them.

She slashed the reins down on her horse's neck, and the bay quickened his already headlong pace. Behind her she heard the child start a sleepy whimpering, and Sara's frightened voice trying to quieten him.

"It's no use, lady," said Goren, breathlessly. "We'll not keep this up for long. Yon Sara's no great rider, and going like this, if she should let her nag stumble—"

"How many horses? Can you tell?"

"Two at least. Maybe no more. But two's enough," said the man grimly.

"Then what do we do? Stop and face them? I'm armed, and so are you, and by the time they come up with us we will be breathed, and they will not. If we pull aside on to the moor—"

"Aye, but not yet. There's a place a little way from here, an old road-metal quarry. There's trees there, growing thick, in out of the winds. Plenty of cover. It's all we can do—get in there, and hope they'll maybe pass by."

"Or that they're harmless travellers, and nothing to do with us?"

But on that desperate night, with the beat of hoofs hard behind the fugitives, it was not possible to believe it. She said no more until, in a very few minutes, Goren pointed ahead, and then she saw the thicker darkness of the quarry and its sheltering trees. They turned their horses in. Goren slid from the saddle, took the reins of the three horses, and led them deeper among the trees, then stood holding them with their heads against his body, muffling their nostrils in the folds of his cloak. The fugitives waited, still and tense. The approaching hoofbeats grew rapidly louder, then all of a sudden were upon them. No pause as they breasted the quarry; the headlong pace never slackened. The pursuit was going past.

Alexander, rousing more fully as Sara's horse halted, and finding himself uncomfortably bundled up in a strange place in the dark, thrust his shawls aside with furious fists and gave a yell of rage and fright.

The gallop checked. The horses stopped with a slither and clatter and some command in an undervoice. Then they wheeled back across the mouth of the little quarry, and a man's voice called out.

"Princess Anna?"

There was nothing for it. She cleared her throat and answered him. "Who is that? I know your voice, don't I? Sadok?"

"The same, lady."

"And your business with me?"

There was a pause as full of meaning as a shouted message. Then he said: "The king would not have you leave the court. He charges me to say that he is not your enemy. What happened tonight—"

"Sadok, do you know what happened tonight?"

Another pause, while the horses stamped and blew. She leaned over the bay's neck and whispered hurriedly to Goren: "Let my rein go. I'll go out and talk with them. Get back on your horse, and take the boy from Sara. They may not know you're here with us, and there might just be a chance for you to get away, and the boy with you—"

"There's just two of them, lady. I could hold them long enough—"

"No. No. Do as I say, but wait till I've spoken with them. Sadok was a friend of my lord's. If there's no help for it, and I'm forced to go with them, then leave Sara— they won't hurt her—and save the boy if you can. You know where we were going. Keep him safely, and God go with you."

"And with you, my lady."

He drew back into the darkness, and to cover his exchange with Sara she raised her voice again: "Who is that with you, Sadok?"

"My brother, princess. My brother Erbin. You know him."

"Yes. Very well, then. I am coming."

Behind her she could hear the creak of leather as Goren mounted. Alexander was quiet. She turned the bay's head, and rode out into the open moonlight of the road.

Neither of the waiting riders made any move towards her, and though they must certainly be armed, they had not drawn their weapons. Was it possible, then, that there really was some hope? She tried to steady her breathing as she drew rein beside Sadok's horse, and put back the hood of her cloak.

The moonlight was stronger now, and she could see both men clearly. Sadok was a young man, much of an age with the dead Baudouin; he had been at March's court since boyhood, and the two men had liked one another. Sadok and his brother had been with Baudouin in the adventure with the Saxon longships. It was possible, it was surely possibly—ran Anna's desperate thoughts—that in this night's expedition, as in so much else in his chequered and violent reign, King March had made the wrong choice?

Sadok cleared his throat. "Princess, I am sorry. God knows I loved Baudouin, and could wish no harm to you, but—"

"Or to Baudouin's son?"

Her horse was close to his, shoulder to shoulder. Her face, framed by the dark folds of her hood, looked fragile and lovely, wiped clear by the moonlight of the lines of stress and grief. Her eyes, large and dark, were on a level with Sadok's. He read fear in them, and appeal. Her hand looked small and fragile on the rein. Anna the fair, Anna the chaste, who had never looked at any man but her husband, would have used any weapon available to save her son. So now she looked at Sadok with those frightened, appealing eyes, and under the muffling folds of her cloak her right hand was steady on the hilt of Baudouin's sword.

She held her voice steady, too. "Sadok, Erbin—both of you—if you know what happened to my lord tonight, you know why it happened. And you know that there can be no good purpose in the king's wanting me and my child taken back to the castle. He may spare me, but assuredly he will kill Alexander. As he murdered his father, and for the same reason."

Sadok, who, with half the inhabitants of the castle, had been roused by March's drunken shouting as he tore himself free from the restraining hands of doctor and servants and lurched, sword in hand, through the rooms and courts of the castle in a murderous search for Anna and

her child, could do nothing but say, hoarsely:
"Princess—"

"You called me by my name in happier times."

"Anna—" Ironically it was Sadok, rather than Anna,
who sounded desperate. "What you say is true, God
knows! And God knows I wish you no harm, nor does
Erbin neither. But what can we do? King March would
never believe that we couldn't come up with you, and
even if he did, he would send others after you. And you—
on this long road, exposed as it is on the moor-top to the
very edge of the kingdom, you would surely be over-
taken before you could come clear of his borders. But if
you let us take you home now, and we go slowly, giving
due care to the child . . . then by the time we get back the
king will be sobered, and it will be daylight, and the
castle is full of folk who were friends of your lord and
you . . . Then surely, even he—" He broke off.

"Yes, even he." Her voice had an edge. "Even he, as
you are taking care not to say, would not murder me and
my child in cold blood in the sight of the whole court.
Perhaps not. But how long would you give us? How
long, eh, Sadok?"

"The people's love—"

"A fig for the people's love! What can they do, poor
rabble? If they had any power, they would have driven
the Fox out long since, and taken my husband for their
ruler. As, if he be allowed to live, some day they may try
to take Alexander. Will you tell me one thing, on your
oath?"

"If I may on my honour."

"What were your orders tonight?"

"To overtake you, and escort you and the boy back to
the king."

"No accident by the way?"

He was silent. She nodded. "Don't trouble, I understand. The Fox's way. Nothing said that you could fasten on him, but an understanding. Yes?" When he still did not speak, she said, more gently: "Sadok, don't think I am blaming you or your brother. You are the king's men, and you have dealt with me more gently than you need have done. So, if you cannot ride back and say you never found us—and it's true that the king would hardly believe it, and you would both suffer his anger—then for my lord's sake, whom you both loved, could you not let his son go now, and just take me back with you? It would appease the king, and if I could once speak with the queen, then I might be safe for a time at least, and some day, perhaps—"

"We will do better than that, my lady." He spoke suddenly, with resolution. "We will ride back and tell him that the boy is dead. We'll think of some tale that he'll believe—catching you at that ford back yonder, perhaps, snatching the baby from your maid so that she fell with him into the river and he drowned. And then we let you, who can do him no more harm, ride on to find shelter where you might. If you'll give me something, a shawl, maybe, to show as a kind of proof? And if, for your part, you will promise me one thing?"

The hand that gripped the sword relaxed. She took a long, gasping breath. "God be good to you, my friend!" was all she could say, but in a few moments she had control of herself again. "And your brother? Erbin? What of you, Erbin?" Then, as the younger man began to stammer something about some favour he owed to Baudouin, and his willingness to support his brother, she stretched her hand in thanks to one and then the other, and said, in a voice broken between relief and wonderment: "But what in God's name possessed March to send you and your brother to murder Baudouin's son?"

There was a wry amusement in Sadok's voice. "I told you he was still very drunk, and when he started shouting his orders I contrived to be near him."

"Some day," said Anna, "some day," and left it at that. Then, echoing Sadok's own words: "You spoke of a promise. Of course, if I may on my honour. What do you want of me?"

"Only that you will take your son into safety far from here, and rear him to remember his father's shameful murder, and some day to come back and avenge it."

"By God, I will!" she said.

"And we will be here, waiting," said Sadok. He made a vow of it, and Erbin growled his assent. "Meantime, have you money to keep you till you find safety? I have a little by me, and Erbin—"

"I have enough." Even now, she would not betray Drustan's generous help, nor the presence of Goren, invisible in the shadows with the still silent Alexander. She pulled open one of her saddle-bags. "Here. It's one of his night-robes. He was asleep when we—when he—" She was silent for a few moments, busying herself over the bag's fastenings, but when she spoke again, trying to find some more words of thanks, Sadok reached for her hand again, lifted it, and kissed it.

"No more, princess. Get you gone now, and make haste. We'll contrive to delay our return till well after daybreak, so God go with you and your orphaned son, and some day let us pray we may meet again in peace and safety."

He wheeled his horse, putting it to an easy trot, and soon he and his brother were lost in the dimness.

Goren rode out from under the trees. "I heard. We are safe?"

"We are safe, thanks be to God and to two honest men! So Alexander may now cry all he wants to. Come, Sara." She turned her horse's head eastward once more, adding, but not for the man to hear: "But so may not I."

4

It took them the best part of a month. Not knowing how
March would receive Sadok's story—or in fact if he
would believe it—they dared not take the direct road, but
went by the tracks used by peasants and charcoal-
burners, rough riding through forest or along secluded
river-valleys or across low-lying marshland, which,
when they reached March's borders and entered the
Summer Country, was perilous with bog and quagmire.
Anna found that she had money in plenty; besides what
she had snatched up as she packed her belongings, and
what Drustan had pressed on her, she found another
pouch of gold in her saddle-bag, put there, presumably,
by Drustan. So the travellers were able to pay their way.
Now and again they managed to put up at a reasonably
respectable tavern, where they could rest themselves and
their horses for a day or so, but usually they were
thankful to find the shelter of some wayside cottage, or a
farmer's barn, or even, at the worst, a shepherd's hut,
abandoned for the summer while the shepherd kept his
flock on the high hillsides.

One thing the rough riding and the constant care
needed for the child—and the support and encourage-
ment she had to give Sara—did for Anna: she had no

time for grief. The days were a strain of riding, finding a
safe way, looking, as the day waned, for shelter; and at
night she was so tired that she slept soundly, and without
dreams.

It took them three weeks to reach Glevum, and then
they had to take a roundabout route to the bridge, but
once across the Severn, and beyond the edges of the
Summer Country, where the High King's men kept the
roads between them and the Cornish border, they felt
safe, even though Anna feared that March would guess
where she was heading.

The castle where Anna's cousin had lived, Craig
Arian, lay towards the head of the Wye valley, a little
way back into the hills and beside one of the tributary
streams. The widow, Theodora, had recently married
again, an elderly man called Barnabas who had been an
officer in one of the High King's troops. Anna and her
cousin had never been close, but she had from time to
time exchanged greetings with Theodora. All parties, of
course, knew that, since Theodora had no children,
Anna's claim to Craig Arian and its estate took prece-
dence over that of the widow and her new husband, so
Anna had every right to seek refuge there, but there had
been no time to send a message reporting Baudouin's
death and begging for shelter for herself and her son.

So as the weary little party rode slowly up the winding
river valley on the last stage of their journey, Anna was
by no means sure what sort of welcome would await
them. She had never met Barnabas, and had no idea what
kind of man he was. A veteran of Arthur's army, married
to a widow of means and retired to a snug little property
in this rich countryside? It was possible, it was even
likely, thought Anna drearily, that he would shut the

gates against Baudouin's widow and the young son who could displace him and his own heirs from Craig Arian. And who could blame him if he hesitated to offend King March by taking in the fugitive princess? He could find the best of reasons for shutting his gates to her.

When at length they came in sight of the castle on its wooded crag, Anna halted her party, and sent Goren on ahead with the news of Baudouin's death, and the widowed princess's request for shelter.

"No more than that," she said wearily. "I cannot ask for more, and God knows I have little right, for myself. But for the child . . . Beg them to let the child stay in safety and in secrecy, until perhaps I can go to the High King at Camelot, and ask him for justice. Go now, Goren. We will wait for you here, by the water."

She need not have worried. When Goren came back he did not come alone, but with Barnabas himself, and half a dozen servants, and a mule litter containing his stout wife, who greeted Anna with kisses and tears of pleasure, then took her and the boy into the litter for the ride home.

"For your home it is, and his," she said, "and you are welcome. No, say no more. You look weary to death, and no wonder! Come now, and after a rest and a good dinner you shall tell us all that has happened."

"Anna," said Barnabas, a heavily built greybeard with kind eyes and a ready smile, who limped from a wound sustained in Arthur's wars, "if King March of Cornwall seeks you here, as well he may, we shall know how to keep him out, and drive him back into his own borders. So rest you now in peace, cousin, and trouble yourself no more, but look to your son, and we will keep this castle and these good lands for him till he is grown."

And the Princess Anna, for the first time since her husband Baudouin had been murdered, put her hands to her face and wept.

TWO

Alice
the Motherless

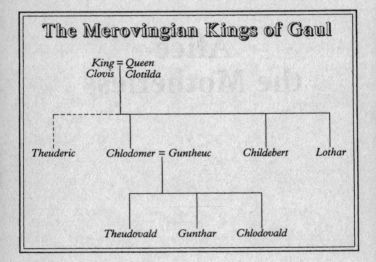

The Merovingian Kings of Gaul

King = Queen
Clovis | Clotilda

Theuderic   Chlodomer = Guntheuc   Childebert   Lothar

Theudovald   Gunthar   Chlodovald

5

The little girl lay on her stomach, flat in the dust, watching a pair of lizards. They were fighting—or mating; she did not know which. The two occupations were, she thought, much the same. The lizards writhed and wrestled, hissing with wide, melon-coloured mouths, as they darted in and out of the shade of the tamarisk tree. Then they flashed up the rough stones of the garden wall, and disappeared.

"Alice! Alice!"

It was a man's voice, high and rather toneless.

"Alice!"

The child made a face at the crevice where the lizards had vanished, and did not reply, but she rolled reluctantly over in the dust, ready to rise. From somewhere above and beyond the feathery branches of the tamarisk, a bell began a sweet, cracked chiming.

"Alice?" The voice was anxious now, and nearer.

"I'm coming, father." She got to her feet, unkilting the long gown which she had worn hitched up to the knee, and shaking the dust out of its folds. Then she picked up her sandals from among the roots of the tree where they had been thrown, and slipped them on over bare, grubby feet. The long gown, trailing, hid them. She smoothed the long, lovely mane of tawny-gold hair, folded her arms so that the loose sleeves hid her dirty hands, then, with downcast eyes, decorous, composed, beautiful, the Lady Alice followed her father the duke into the chapel of St. Jerome at Jerusalem.

Duke Ansirus was a tall man of some forty years. He had been a notable fighter in his youth, and also a notable lover, fair and handsome and discreet. This last he needed to be, since his fancy took him invariably towards married ladies who, for a variety of reasons, found a change desirable, and Ansirus very desirable indeed. He had received a bad chest wound fighting alongside the young King Arthur at the battle of Caledon, and for some time his life had been despaired of. His eventual recovery, so said the doctors (and of course the local priest agreed with them), was nothing short of miraculous, so when he had regained his strength the duke undertook a pilgrimage of thanksgiving to the Holy Land. He did not, it is true, do it the hard way; his breathing still troubled him sometimes, and the incessant fighting between the Franks and their neighbours, as King Clovis struggled to bring all Gaul under Frankish rule, made overland travelling dangerous; but he went by ship to Italy, and then to Greece, where he stayed for a month or so before undertaking the final stage to Acre and Jerusalem. And in Athens, at the house of a friend, he met a girl who—though she was unmarried and, indeed, a virgin—so captivated him that he married her out of hand and took her with him to the Holy Land. Her name was Alice, and her disposition was as discreet in its own way as his: she was a silent girl, who, having been reared as a penniless dependent, had learned very early not to let her beauty—which was undoubted—throw that of her cousins into the shade. To her, my lord Ansirus was an escape, an establishment, a fortune: if he was more, only Ansirus knew. She was a quiet and dutiful wife, who managed her domestic affairs with careful efficiency, and kneeled meekly beside her lord as he thanked God at some length daily for his restored health and now for his happiness.

She did not have long to enjoy the wealth and comfort of Ansirus' castle, back in the rich heartlands of Rheged. A year after the couple's return to Britain, Alice died in childbed, and the baby girl was handed to nurse.

It might have been supposed that the grief-stricken widower would blame the child for her mother's loss, and thrust her from him, but the past year's happiness had been intense, and his repentance of the sins of his youth was genuine. He transferred all he had of love to the baby. He had vowed himself, at his wife's deathbed, to chastity, and this vow he kept. He had vowed, too, to make another pilgrimage, and undertook this within the year. He would have taken the child with him, but the women who looked after the nursery were so horrified that he, remembering the discomforts of the journey, and the dirt and disease of the Holy Land, let himself be persuaded to go alone. But by the time the little Alice, at five years old, was growing impatient with her nurses, and running freely about the castle gardens, she was so like her mother that the bereaved father could hardly bear to let her out of his sight, and when he planned his next pilgrimage he insisted—and this time Alice insisted, too, and she had a habit of getting her own way—that his daughter should go with him. So here they were at last, kneeling side by side in front of the picture of St. Jerome with his scarlet robe and his pet lion, Ansirus with closed eyes and moving lips, his mind fixed on prayer, and the child Alice, her young face sweet as an angel's, the grey eyes lifted towards God.

I wonder, she was thinking, when the figs come ripe on that tree outside the window? Those lizards were funny, weren't they, the way they jumped and twisted together? I wonder if they have babies the ordinary way, or if they lay eggs like the newts in the pond at home? Eggs must be so much easier. Why do people have to do it the other way? Oh, and do you think we might go back in the same ship, with the captain who wore the gold earring, and used all those strange words to the sailors, and had that bird that talked, but father wouldn't buy it for me? Perhaps—if *you* spoke to him? I know you often do. And I'd love to have that bird, I really would.

Odd as it may seem, the Lady Alice, too, was talking to God.

For the more important days—saints' days and Sundays—the duke and his daughter attended the great church of the Resurrection, but for their daily prayers they used the chapel of St. Jerome, a small oratory set in one of the aisles of the church of St. Mary, which had been built two centuries before by the Roman Emperor Constantine. This church, built of vast stones, was richly decorated, being the repository of the wealth of the thousands of pilgrims who nowadays flocked to the Holy City. It was set on the Haram, the vast plateau where originally, so men said, the temple of Solomon had stood, and where Jesus Himself had listened to the rabbis, and had overthrown the money-changers. And from one of those tall towered corners the devil himself had shown Him all the kingdoms of the world.

Now all that had vanished, and the chiselled stones of the temples and law courts, evidences of the Roman rule of Herod's time, had been pillaged for use elsewhere. But at night, with the new buildings bulking tall and black, and moonlight sifting down through pines and olive-trees into the narrow streets, it was easy to imagine all those stories that were told, ceaselessly told, to the pilgrims as they followed their Lord's footsteps up the Way of the Cross, to the Pool of Bethesda under the temple gateway, to the Garden of Gethsemane, or even to the rock of the Tomb itself, hidden though this now was in the foundations of a church.

"And lucky to be there still for us to see," said Ansirus, who himself took his daughter around to show her the holy places. "If they hadn't stopped people bringing hammers in to get a piece of the sacred rock to take home with them, there'd be very little of the place left by this time. There are twice as many pilgrims now as when I last came here."

The city was, indeed, packed to its limits, and these were very busy extending each year. The whole district round the Haram abounded in inns, hospices and monasteries where the pilgrims were lodged in varying degrees of comfort or austerity. Alice and her father were more fortunate than most: Ansirus had, on his first visit to Jerusalem with his wife, stayed with friends, Romans who had had in the past some distant connection with her family. When Rome itself had fallen to the swords of the Goths a century earlier, many Romans had been forced to flee with their families, and some of these had stayed and settled in Jerusalem. Most had prospered, building or buying houses among the wooded hills at the edge of the city. It was in one of these, near the foot of the Mount of Olives, that Alice and her father were staying.

Lentulus, their host, was a banker and man of affairs; he was making, it was said, a fortune out of property, buying rubble-strewn land and clearing it to sell for building. He was involved, it was also said, in the purchase of sacred items—not, of course, to attract the faithful to the city, but, once they had come, to satisfy their souls. Splinters of the True Cross, pieces of the reed that had held the sponge of vinegar, a thorn from the Crown, a drop of the vinegar itself in a vial—these marvellous relics were still available, at a price. Alice, being shown some of these items, viewed them with simple awe, but even at five years old was moved to wonder at the ever-renewed supply of nails and thorns that were on offer. A miracle, surely? Her father put her questions aside rather uneasily, with talk of faith and symbols which, not understanding, she promptly forgot. And there was no need for him to caution her, as he did, not to ask anyone else about such matters; she had no one else to talk to. Lentulus' two sons, grown men and married, were away from home, one in business in Acre, the other back in Massilia. Lentulus' wife, Matilda, was crippled with arthritis, and kept to her own chamber, leaving the running of the house to an elderly Jewish couple who kept very much to themselves. Alice had no companion of her own age. And since she spent all day visiting the sites of pilgrimage, and making the necessary round of service and intercession, and was sent to her bed soon after supper, it did not occur to Ansirus that she might need anything else to fill her time, or, if he had considered it (which of course, since Alice was a girl, he did not), her mind. When he did think about her—and he was a devoted father—he assumed that the child was having the best possible preparation for the life she would have to live. For a girl like Alice, life held two alternatives: she must marry some suitable man of her father's choosing, and bear his children, or she must take her vows and retire to a convent, a chaste and holy Bride of Christ.

Devout though he was, the duke inclined towards the first alternative for his daughter. His beautiful little estate in Rheged, with the rose-coloured castle—*Arx Rosea* on the old maps—set in a deep curve of the Eden River, would need another master one day, and an heir; and of course a granddaughter or two would be welcome as well. Would, in fact, be delightful. So sometimes, watching that flower-like young face in church beside him lifted, rapt, towards God, he wondered if, by keeping her here with him through the whole ritual of pilgrimage, he was not driving her, headlong and far too early, into the arms of the Church.

He need not have troubled himself. With a child less intelligent, or less imaginative, it might have been true. But Alice, while of course believing all the stories, had acquired a faith that worked at the simplest—and most profound—level. She was easily able to accept the holy apostles, the saints, and the Lord Jesus Himself, as people who had walked here and done their wonders—magic or miracles, what was the difference?—and who might very well be met again one day. Of course there had been the Crucifixion, but for the pilgrims the strongest emphasis was on the Resurrection, the happy ending, as in the stories that Alice liked best.

Meanwhile life in Jerusalem surrounded her, pressed on her, excited and interested her. There was so much happening, so much to see; the carefully irrigated gardens (think of the rain at home!); the towers where storks nested and swallows darted and twittered all day; the lizards and tiny scorpions, the coloured birds (five for two farthings?); the baby camels trotting after their dams along the narrow *souks,* the goods for sale in the stalls, the streets of the coppersmiths, rug-makers, linen-sellers; the children playing in the dirt, the robed riders with their beautiful horses.

And Jesus, who had loved Jerusalem too? Some day He would be back here again, walking these streets, looking at all the new buildings, talking to the people and stopping to speak to the children; she only hoped that it would be when she and her father were here on pilgrimage. There would be plenty of chances; the duke had vowed, she knew, to make a pilgrimage every third year or so for his soul's sake . . .

And some three years later, when she was eight years old, and back in Jerusalem with her father, it happened.

He came walking along the narrow, stony lane which lay just beyond the garden wall.

Lentulus' villa was at the edge of the city, with fields beyond—what they called fields, here in the Holy Land; stretches of stony earth with sparse blades of grass in spring, and thin white and yellow flowers like daisies, and the red anemones that her father had told her were the lilies of the field. In summer there was neither grass nor flowers, and the shepherds took the flocks further and further afield to look for pasture.

And this was what this man—Jesus already in Alice's mind—seemed to be doing. He was not walking the city streets surrounded by his disciples and talking to the people; he was making his way slowly along the lane that led away from the town, and he was knee-deep in sheep. He had a crook in one hand, and across his shoulders lay a lamb, its four legs loosely gathered into his other hand.

The Good Shepherd. Alice recognised the picture she had seen of him, even though the young man himself bore very little resemblance to the paintings and tapestries in the churches. Even to an eight-year-old, who looks on thirty as elderly, and forty as decrepit, this man was young. No fair hair and neat little beard, no white robes, and certainly no halo. Just a thin young man, dark-haired and dark-eyed, his cheeks shadowed with a few days' growth of beard, and dressed in a brown kaftan girded with a knotted red cord. His feet were bare.

The sheep called and crowded close to him. He saw Alice on her perch at the top of the garden wall, in the shade of the tamarisk tree, and looking up, he smiled.

That made it certain. Alice said, a little breathlessly, though it was not possible, in the blazing sunshine, with the noise and the smell of sheep all around, to feel awe: "You did come back, then! I knew you would!"

He stopped, leaning on his crook. The lamb on his shoulder made a small sound and he slanted his head, caressing it with his cheek. "I come this way often."

Though she had spoken in Latin, he answered her in her native tongue, but that was no surprise. He would, of course.

"And you, little maid?" he said. "You are a guest here, I think, a pilgrim to my city. It must be very different from your home in Britain. How do you like it, here in the land you call holy?"

"I do like it, a lot. But I was wondering—" began Alice, then was suddenly seized with a shyness that was normally foreign to her. What in fact did one say to someone who had come back from the dead, and to a place where he had been so cruelly killed? She swallowed and was silent.

"You were wondering?" he prompted. He had very kind eyes, which were still smiling, but she found herself quite unable to go on with her questions.

"Oh, just about the sheep," she said quickly. "Those long legs, and the funny droopy ears. They're quite different from ours. And the ones we have at home in Rheged are special. They're little, with furry legs and blue fleeces, and they stay in the hills all winter. We don't have to move the flocks about like you do. Where we live there's always plenty of grass."

"I know something of your country." Of course he did. "It must be beautiful in all the seasons."

"It is. It's lovely. You will come there one day, won't you? People say that some day—"

"Lady Alice? Lady Alice?" The interruption came from Maria, her nurse, newly waking from a nap in the sunshine, and hunting the garden for her charge.

"Some day, I hope," said the shepherd, and raising the crook in a gesture of farewell, he turned away.

Alice slid down from the wall and ran to meet her nurse, whom she astounded by her good behaviour for the rest of that day.

6

"Have you noticed," said Alice, who was eleven now, and as pretty as a girl of that awkward age has any right to be, "that my father always starts talking about his soul when the wind's in the north, and the castle's full of draughts?"

She was talking to her maid Mariamne, who giggled.

"Well, it wouldn't do if the wind was from the south, would it? As it is, we'll get a good fast passage, and be in the sunshine before the end of April, God be thanked! It'll be good to be home again." For Mariamne came from a village barely two miles from Jerusalem. She had been taken into the duke's service on the previous pilgrimage.

Alice gave a little sigh. "It was lovely, wasn't it? The voyage out was best—you weren't with us then, though—such good weather as we had, and all the places we saw—Rome, and Tarentum, and then staying with my mother's family in Athens. You did see Athens on the way home. And then the pilgrimage itself . . . Of course Jerusalem's wonderful, though there's never a lot to do apart from—I mean, I know one really goes for the good of one's soul, only—" The sentence died on something very like a sigh.

Mariamne's hand paused in its task of stitching a new shift for her mistress. The needle flashed in the sunlight which, for March, was surprisingly bright, and, in Alice's chamber which faced south, reasonably warm, though to Mariamne, even after nearly three years, the chill of the British winter still struck deep.

"Only?" she prompted.

"Oh, it's just that I don't want to leave home just as spring's coming. Look what we miss, the primroses are coming out already, and my pony will drop her foal in June, and—well, but I suppose we might even be home again in time for that."

"Home again by June? Oh, no, my lady, you're forgetting. The sea trip alone took all those weeks, and I remember every one, being so sick as I was! You'll never be home by June."

Alice left her chair and crossed to the window. Sunlight slanted in over the wide stone sill, and the scents of early spring—earth and pine resin and budding trees and all the smells of growth—came sifting in on the mild breeze. She thought she could even smell the snowdrops that still lay in late drifts under the trees. She turned to smile at the other girl. For all the difference in their ages—Mariamne was some four or five years older than Alice—it was the latter, mistress of Castle Rose and its acres since the day of her birth, who often seemed the elder of the two.

She spoke gently, the adult breaking bad news and offering comfort. "I'm sorry, Mariamne. I've been wondering just how to tell you. My father doesn't plan to go to Jerusalem this year. He talked with me about it yesterday, and it seems that the journey would be too dangerous, even by sea. Even Rome would be impossible, with the Emperor backing the Burgundians, and there has been no news from Athens since my great-aunt died. I'm sorry. I'd have liked to see Jerusalem again myself, and I know how much you were looking forward to going home."

Since Mariamne had been handed into service by her family for a due consideration, and her status in consequence was, unofficially, not much better than a slave's, she knew that her expectations mattered not at all, and that in condoling with her Alice was showing a kindness that she would have met with in few other situations. With the patience which was one of the strengths of her race, she said nothing, but went back to her work in silence.

"If things change," said Alice, "I'm sure we will go again next time. And I promise to see that you go with me."

"It's no matter, my lady. You are too good to me. And indeed, I am very happy here." The needle paused again. "But you said . . . I thought you said that my lord duke was planning a journey? For his soul's sake, you said? And that you might be home by June? What is there, as near as that? Oh, yes, there's the holy man up on Table Hill, or the Chapel Perilous where the High King's sword was kept and drawn, but that's hardly a Christian shrine, and your father wouldn't want to go there. It can't just be another ride to the convent where your lady mother lies buried—that's hardly a pilgrimage, is it? Nine miles, ten? So where is there to go, besides Jerusalem?"

Alice laughed. "You sound just like me! Only one place in the world for you—Jerusalem for you, Castle Rose for me! But we're both going to Tours."

"Tours? Where's that?"

"In Gaul. It's in King Chlodomer's country, quite a

long way to the south. The king's capital is Orleans, but Father says that Tours is a nice enough town. It's set on a big river, the Loire, that runs through beautiful country, and very rich. It sounds lovely. He says that the old queen—that's the king's mother—spends a lot of time there, and she's very devout, so the accommodation for pilgrims is good. Not that that is a consideration, of course."

"Of course not," agreed Mariamne gravely. "And if it's far enough to the south, it might even be warm. So what takes the Christians to this city of Tours?"

"The shrine of St. Martin. He was a bishop, I think." Alice was vague. "Anyway, he does a lot of miracles. Father didn't tell me much, but he did say that the old king, King Clovis, that was Chlodomer's father, was baptised there. He turned Christian in gratitude for winning some battle or other. Queen Clotilda was a Christian, and she persuaded him. I don't know who he was fighting; they're always at war over there, Father says."

The duke had in fact told his daughter a good deal.

Men's fears about the turmoil on the Continent following the death of King Clovis had been more than justified. As was the custom among the Salian Franks ("And a foolish one, as we see it," said Ansirus), the lands which Clovis during a lifetime of war had conquered and brought under one central government, were divided after his death among his four sons. The eldest, Theuderic, son of one of the king's concubines, inherited large territories in the north; Chlodomer, the legitimate heir, received the fertile lands along the River Loire; Childebert, the third son, took a broad swathe of coastal land from the Loire to the Schelde, while the fourth son, Lothar, was granted territory north of the river Somme, along with part of Aquitaine. The partition was far from equal, and the consequent quarrelling among the brothers made travel through the Salian lands dangerous, even for pilgrims.

"Except for Chlodomer's kingdom of Orleans, that's safe enough," said Ansirus. "He's a Christian, at least in name, and the roads are open to pilgrims. In fact they are made welcome. Queen Clotilda, Clovis's widow, spends a lot of time at Tours. If she is there during our visit, then I shall hope to present you to her." He smiled. "No, don't look so excited, child. Remember these Franks are rough people, who live for war, and, whether Christian or not, think nothing of murder when it suits them. Be thankful that our status will protect us, but don't expect Camelot."

"I wish," said Alice wistfully, "that a bishop or someone would die and do miracles at Camelot, then we could go there."

But she did not say it aloud.

7

They came in sight of the city of Tours on the evening of a wet and windy day in April.

The Frankish city was certainly no Camelot. The citadel was grimly built of grey stone, the houses crowded near it—cowering under it, it seemed—were at best half stone, half wooden, and at worst mud brick with dripping thatch. The circling river, majestically broad, was grey too, with rushing caps of white under a low grey sky. Anything further removed from the rose-red charm of Ansirus' castle, or the sun-baked and crumbling splendours of Jerusalem, it would be hard to imagine. But the pilgrims' hostel, on the river bank across from the town, was stoutly built and dry, and welcomed them with fires, meat and a red wine better than any they had tasted before. The duke, thankful to find that no royal summons awaited him, retired straight after supper, with the rest of his party, into exhausted sleep.

Next morning the rain had gone, the sun was high, and across a dimpling blue river the little city looked, if not splendid, at any rate attractive, with blossoming fruit trees among the houses, and people streaming across the river bridge towards the morning market. There was even a gilded spire catching the sunlight, and from the citadel

a pennon flew, to announce the presence either of the
king or of the old queen, his mother.

Sure enough, the summons came as they were
breaking their fast. Queen Clotilda was in Tours, and
would receive the duke and the Lady Alice once their
first devotions had been paid at the holy shrine, and
thereafter she would be happy to make them welcome as
guests under her roof for the duration of their stay. She
was lodged, said the messenger, not in the citadel, but in
her own palace on the other side of the city. An escort
would attend them there.

Their first sight of the "palace" was as disappointing as
the rainswept introduction to Tours.

"Palace? It's just a farm!" said Alice to Mariamne,
whose mule ambled alongside her pony. She spoke
softly, in case the men sent to escort them might hear her,
and looked doubtfully down at the embroidered prim-
rose-coloured skirt of her best gown. "I wish I'd brought
my thick shoes instead of these slippers! I suppose it
must be the right place, but are you sure the messenger
this morning said 'a palace'?"

"Yes," said Mariamne, who, before her first sight of
Castle Rose, would certainly have judged this to be, if
not a palace, a very prosperous-looking place indeed.
"But it looks nice, doesn't it, like being in the country? I
didn't think much of the town! Those beggars everywhere, poor things—I'd hate to have to go anywhere
without an escort to keep them off! And didn't the streets
smell bad?"

Since at that moment they were riding up a narrow
roadway, something like a farm track at home, their
progress hindered by a herd of pigs being driven in from
the woods, Alice laughed.

"I suppose that anywhere a queen lives is a palace. It's the queen that makes it, after all. But I do hope that the floors are clean!"

Queen Clotilda, widow of the great Merwing king Clovis, would have lent royalty to a pigsty. Which may have been just as well, since the byres and sties of what was certainly a farmstead were very near the room where the duke's party was received. This was a large, long room, a hall which still had about it some of the dignity of its Roman origin; the floor was of well-made mosaic, the wall-hangings were worked in bright colours which had faded pleasantly, and the fourth wall of the hall was open, where a series of arches gave on a courtyard with some tubs of flowers and orange trees gay with both fruit and blossom, and a very pretty fountain. The sleeping-chambers and guest rooms made up two other sides of the court, and the fourth was open to a slope of pasture leading down towards the river. Beyond the guest-chambers lay the kitchens and servants' quarters, and separated only from the royal rooms by a narrow strip of garden and orchard were the stables and barns and store-houses of a large and prosperous farm.

The "palace" was indeed a farmstead, but rather more; like most of the houses of the Frankish nobles, it was a unit, a settlement in miniature, self-sufficient in times either of peace or war. On the April breezes, along with the smells of stable and sty, the lowing of cattle and the incessant cackling of poultry, came other sounds: the clink of a smith's hammer, the different clangour of an armoury, the clack of shuttles and the laughter and calling of women's voices busy over the washing down at the river's edge.

But inside the hall there was, if not ceremony, a respectful silence. At the end of the hall was a low dais, at the centre of which stood the great chair of state. Some score of men stood near, and a couple of women, the latter both in the sombre habits of nuns. Most of the men were obviously warriors, dressed in armoured leather, with jewelled belts and armlets; to a man they were tall and blue-eyed, with shoulder-length fair hair and long moustaches. Two other men waited in the background; one in priestly habit, his face hidden by his cowl, the other a young man, tall and dark-haired, in a long robe, with round his neck a silver chain that seemed to denote some sort of palace functionary.

The queen herself was standing by one of the archways, with a sword in her hand, turning the blade this way and that in the sunlight, her head bent to study its line, and her thumb trying the edge. A man, a slave by his dress, and wearing the leather apron and wrist-guards of a smith, stood by her, apparently waiting for her verdict on his work. When the chamberlain announced the newcomers she looked up and turned, in the same movement throwing the sword to the man. The blade struck him, clanging against the studs of the tough leather, then slid down, and the fellow, shifting quickly, caught the sword as it fell within an inch of his foot. He hefted it safely, grinned at Alice's shocked face, and crossed the courtyard towards a gate which must lead to the workshops.

"My lord duke." The queen had not even glanced to see where the sword fell. "And your daughter, the Lady Alice? Be welcome to our kingdom here."

There were chairs set outside one of the archways, where the spring sunlight fell warmly on the courtyard's flagstones. She led the way to these, and a servant brought a dish of some savoury pastries, and a flagon of wine, pale gold in colour, and smelling deliciously of flowers. Alice, seated on a stool beside her father's chair, sipped and listened to the exchange of courtesies, watching the white doves as they strutted and cooed on the rooftops, and wondering if this pilgrimage, like the one to Jerusalem, would do good (presumably) to her soul, but none at all to her brain or her body. If only her father's friends were not all so old!

"Old" though she naturally appeared to a child's eyes, the queen was perhaps a year or two short of fifty. When a girl she must have been handsome; one could guess at the proud and vital look, the direct blue gaze, the upright carriage. Now she was thin, and care had worn lines in the fine skin and hooded the eyes with weariness. Her hair was hidden under a veil, and the robe she wore was of a sombre colour somewhere between brown and green. It was a plain, almost nun-like garb for a queen, but her girdle had a golden buckle most beautifully worked, and at her breast hung a jewelled cross on a gold chain. The slippers showing beneath the sober gown were of soft bronze-coloured kidskin. Nun-like the dress might be, but the effect was one of subdued elegance, and the pride and vitality were still there, unimpaired by age.

But Alice saw none of this. If only, she was thinking, if only their hostess had been young, a young queen with children of Alice's age . . .

And at that moment, as if her thought had been a wish, a boy came running up through the pasture from the river bank, and into the courtyard, with a woman, red-faced and anxious, toiling after him and calling his name.

"Theudo! Prince Theudo! *Theudovald!* Come back! Your grandmother has guests, and you know you are to stay with me!"

She saw the queen, and her voice trailed away. She halted, dropping a curtsey as the boy, paying her no heed, ran laughing towards the queen, then, seeing Alice and the duke, paused and, with a composure a little breathless, made his bows.

The woman, his nurse presumably, bobbed again, muttered something, and scuttled away. Neither the queen nor the boy took any notice of her. It seemed that the Merwings were not accustomed, thought Alice, to paying much attention to their inferiors.

"My grandson." There was pride in the queen's voice, and also quite a new note; it seemed she was fond of the boy. He was younger than Alice, some six or seven years old, but well grown for his age. His hair was fair, like that of the other menfolk, but he wore it very long, hanging almost to his waist. That, with the clear skin and blue eyes, and full-lipped childish mouth, might have made him look girlish, but for a lift of the head that spoke of arrogance, and a touch of stubbornness in the set of the jaw. He went confidently to his grandmother's side. One of her hands touched his shoulder lightly, and she ran a tress of the long hair through her fingers.

"This is your son's, King Chlodomer's, eldest, I take it?" said Duke Ansirus, smiling at the boy. "He's a fine, well-grown boy. You must be proud of him. And there's a brother, I believe, a few years younger? Are they both here with you now?"

"Yes. Whenever I am here in Tours, the boys come to

me. Their father is abroad, as often as not, and Queen Guntheuc goes with him. There are three of them now; another boy was born last spring. The second boy, Gunthar, and the baby Chlodovald stay with the nursemaids, but Theudovald is of an age when he would rather be with the men"—her lips thinned in what might have been meant for a smile—"or with me. He knows that I count him already a man grown."

Duke Ansirus made some reply, and soon the queen and he were deep in talk about the recent settlements of the Frankish kingdoms, and what they might mean. The same old talk, thought Alice, sitting on her stool with hands folded in her lap and her eyes fixed rather wistfully on the sunny prospect of treetops beyond the courtyard roof, though here her father was unlikely to give his views on the subject of land-partition that inevitably brought with it quarrels and fighting, with all the dreadful consequences of war, not least the temporary ruin of the very land that was fought over . . . Ah, they were safely past that subject, and starting to talk about the holy shrine, and the plans the queen had for its embellishment. And that, too, could go on for a very long time . . .

A tug at her skirt drew her attention. Theudovald, with a jerk of the head and a question in his eyes, was silently inviting her to go with him and leave the adults to their talking. She nodded eagerly, and cleared her throat for the formal address suitable to their company.

"Madam, my lord duke—father. With your gracious permission—"

"I'm going to show Alice the horses, grandmother," said Theudovald, and, apparently in no need of permission, gracious or otherwise, he took Alice's hand and pulled her to her feet. He was nearly as tall as she was.

She threw a look, half-laughing, half-apologetic at her father, received his smiling nod, and followed the boy out into the sunlit yard. The queen glanced her way, but never faltered in something she was saying about her son King Chlodomer and the sacred trust he had inherited in the church of St. Martin, with the constant stream of pilgrims to the holiest shrine in Europe and the great basilica that had been built over the site a few hundred years before.

Alice, with a bob of a curtsey, turned and ran across the courtyard after the prince.

8

The place—palace or farmstead—was even bigger than Alice had thought, a vast, sprawling complex of cottages and farm buildings, garths and orchards where men dug and planted, and yards where maids bustled with baskets of provisions or armfuls of clothing. In the stableyards, men—the guards and fighting men, one could guess—lounged idly about or sat over dice games on the warm flagstones, while grooms and cattlemen were busy about their charges.

The prince led the way at a run between two rows of beehives and a pen crowded with white goats, and Alice, kilting up the primrose skirts, followed him, picking her way as best she could over cobbles which had certainly never been swept. They passed the forge, where the smith, at work again on the sword he had shown Queen Clotilda, gave them a nod of greeting. Behind him in the flickering firelight of the smithy Alice could see a forest of lances stacked in a corner. Queen Clotilda's palace could probably supply, mount and equip a small army.

Theudovald paused to wait for her where a narrow archway, casting an arc of deep shadow, led out of the maze of buildings into the vineyards beyond. These stretched, open to the sun, right up the sloping valley-side to a crest of woodland nearly half a mile away. The vines were just budding, small stumpy plants set in careful rows up the hillside, with no promise of the harvest to come. Even so, it could be seen that they were better than the vines so carefully tended in the sheltered half-acre at Castle Rose. The sun was hot now, blazing down on the young leaves and rosy buds, and between the ranks of vines the soil was already drying to summer dust. No wonder, thought Alice, that the wines of the Loire tasted quite different from the vintages of Rheged.

They were out of sight now of the servants and guards in the courtyards. Theudovald cast a look behind him. "Quick!" he said. "This way!" and ran in among the vines.

There was a track leading straight uphill, bisecting the vineyard. It was wide enough for a cart, and deeply rutted. It was also very dusty. Alice's slippers had already suffered more than a little, and she did not have so many grand dresses that she could afford to spoil the primrose silk. She hesitated, but the boy repeated it urgently: "Quick! Come quickly!" and went up the track at a run. She hoisted her skirts above her knees and followed him.

At the head of the slope, between the vineyard and the woodland, was a low wall of dry stone, in places over-grown with weeds and bramble-bushes. There were gaps where the stones had fallen. "This way," panted Theudovald, jumping to the top of one such gap.

Alice paused, dismayed. Her slippers were probably ruined for good, but the primrose silk was not, and was too precious to risk. Even had she been able to scramble over the wall, the wood beyond it looked tangled and thick with undergrowth.

"Where are you going?"

"Quickly! They haven't missed us yet!" As he spoke, he jumped down into the wood.

Alice, still hanging back, heard the thud as he landed, then a gasp and a cry bitten off short. She ran to the wall and looked over.

"What is it? Have you hurt yourself?"

"There was a loose stone. I'm all right, but these thorns . . . I can't get out!"

He was well and truly caught. Tripping on landing, he had gone head first into a patch of brambles, and was trying to wrench himself free of the long, whippy boughs that had fixed themselves in his clothes, and were holding him fast.

Alice, back in the sheep country at home, had many a time had to go to the aid of a ewe trapped by the fierce barbs of bramble or briar. So after all it was goodbye to the primrose gown. She set her pretty mouth, bunched her skirts higher, and prepared to climb the wall. "Stay still a moment. I'll help you. I've got scissors in my purse—"

"No, no! I'm nearly out. There's just this—" An exclamation in the Frankish tongue, which Alice, perhaps fortunately, did not understand. She saw now that the boy was caught not only by his clothes, but also by the long hair which, like the cloth, was wound tightly round the thorns.

No thought for his clothes there: with a wrench of tearing cloth he dragged himself clear and, still on his knees, pulled a sharp little dagger from his belt and hacked off the piece of thorn-twig that was still tangled with his hair and the torn strip from his tunic. Holding this gingerly, he clambered back across the wall. There was blood on his hands, but he did not seem to notice. He was trying—still with mutterings in the Frankish tongue—to unwind the tangle of cloth and hair and thorn.

"Here, let me," said Alice, reaching into her reticule for the scissors she always carried.

Theudovald snatched the tangled lock out of her reach. "No! I can do it!"

"But your hands, they're bleeding! If you'd let me look—"

"No, put those things away! I tell you, you mustn't cut it! Never that!"

"Why not?"

But even as she spoke she remembered something else her father had told her about these strange people, the Franks. "Their kings never cut their hair," he had said. "The long hair is a sign of royalty, the lion's mane. To cut it short is shame and humiliation. It could mean the loss of a kingdom."

She put the scissors away hastily. "I forgot. My father did tell me about it. He said that the long hair was a royal symbol. I'm sorry. Can you do it?"

"Yes. There, it's done." He threw the twig down, and carefully smoothed the long hair back. "What's a symbol?"

"I—I think it means that it stands for something. A sign. Like, well, like a cross."

"Or a crown?" The heir of the Merwings, wiping his scratched hands down the front of his tunic, invited Alice, with a gesture, to sit down beside him. She hesitated again, looking doubtfully at the dusty stones, but the prince was her host, and manners were manners, so she kilted the long skirt up again and, choosing the cleanest part of the wall, sat down.

"Where were we going? What was the hurry?"

He nodded downhill, and Alice saw where, coming up through the archway, were four men. The sun flashed on weapons. One of them, apparently the leader, raised a hand in salute and called something. The men came on up the track. Theudovald stayed where he was, kicking his heels against the wall. "If we'd been quicker we could have gone on into the wood and hidden. There are places where they'd never find us, but you couldn't get there in those skirts."

"I suppose not. I'm sorry. You wanted to hide?"

"Of course."

"Why?"

"Do you need to ask? Look there! It seems it's the same for you." And only then did she see that Mariamne, skirts kilted up like her own, was toiling uphill in the wake of the soldiers.

"Don't you ever want to get away, just by yourself, with no one telling you what to do?" asked the boy. "Do they ever leave you to be alone?"

"At home, yes, sometimes. But it's different when you're travelling. My maid's supposed to stay with me."

"What harm do they think you would come to here?"

"I don't suppose they think about it." Alice was not sure if the question had masked resentment. "They just follow orders. I expect it would be different if I were a boy."

"Not if you were me." The men had halted some yards away, apparently awaiting the prince's pleasure. Their weapons were still in their hands.

They were out of earshot, but Alice lowered her voice. "Well, it's different for you, you're a prince. But this is your home! Your grandmother's home, anyway. What harm do they think could come to *you* here?"

"Oh, anything. I'm always guarded, but even with the guards, you never know who to trust. My grandmother's spies keep watch, but one can't always know one's enemies."

"What enemies? You're not at war now, are you?"

"Not fighting, no. My uncles are both in Paris, so my father says that the three of us—my brothers and I—are safe enough, but when he's away my grandmother comes here from Paris with her people, and she looks after us."

"But—did you say your *uncles*?"

He nodded, obviously misunderstanding the force of the question. He was quite matter-of-fact. "My uncle Childebert, and King Lothar. Especially my uncle Lothar—these are far better lands than his. Of course they would like to seize them from my father. My uncle Theuderic is the eldest, but he's base-born." Pursed lips and another nod. "For all that, my grandmother says, if they promised him enough, he would help them. Of course, they would not keep their promises afterwards."

Brother murders brother, and father, son, Duke Ansirus had said. Alice, looking at the boy, the smooth childish brow, the royal hair now in a sad tangle, the torn tunic and dirt-stained knees and hands, was silenced by a sharp stab of compassion, mixed with unbelief. Still a child herself, she had never known distrust or betrayal, faces of evil that this boy, even younger, found familiar.

"But—" she began, then stopped as Mariamne, red-faced and breathless toiled up the last few paces to stand, panting, in front of them.

"Madam—my lady—" She paused for breath, with an uncertain look at the boy. Clothes torn, dirty and blood-stained, Theudovald was by no means Mariamne's idea of a prince. But she managed a bob of a curtsey, aimed somewhere between the two children. "I thought you were still with your father, madam. They were showing me the stillrooms, and—oh, mercy on us! Your slippers! And that dress! On that dirty wall! It'll never come clean again! What were you thinking about? You'd best come straight along with me now, and let me try—" The look of amazement on the boy's face stopped her short, and a hand went to her mouth. "I'm sorry, my lady—"

"It's all right, Mariamne. The prince was showing me the view over the valley. We were talking. Now, if you will wait with the men?"

Mariamne dropped another curtsey, this time calculated to restore her mistress's dignity, and withdrew to the waiting group of soldiers.

But Theudovald had already slid down from his perch on the wall. "It's no good. We'll have to go back. There's my grandmother's steward coming now. It must be dinner-time. And anyway, I'm hungry. Aren't you?"

"Come to think of it, yes," said Alice. She stood up and started to shake the dust from her skirts. There was a good deal of it. "If we are to wash our hands before meat—"

"What's the point of that? Wash them afterwards, when they're greasy," said the prince cheerfully, and ran off down the hill. The guards made haste to follow him, but the steward, with a word to Mariamne, came on to meet Alice.

It was the young man whom she had glimpsed at the back of the hall where the queen received them. Seen now in the sunlight, he was tall, dark-haired and dark-eyed, soberly dressed in a fawn-coloured tunic with an over-robe of dark brown. The chain of office on his breast was of silver, and from it hung the queen's badge, gilded. There was a brooch at his shoulder of worked silver, and at his belt, which was of good leather tanned and glossy as a horse-chestnut, hung a wallet and a bunch of keys. The queen's steward, Theudovald had said. A trusted servant. But, thought Alice, a foreigner, surely? He did not look like a Frank. A Roman, perhaps? One of those unfortunates, often of good or even noble family, who had been taken in war and enslaved by the Frankish conquerors?

But it seemed not. Before the man could speak, Mariamne, flushed and excited, was there at his elbow.

"Lady Alice! Just imagine! He's from my own country—the next village! And here in Tours! Isn't it like a miracle?"

The young man straightened from his bow. Alice, hands still gripping her skirts, stood stock-still, staring up at him.

"You?"

It came out as a kind of gasp.

His brows went up. "Madam?" Then his face lighted to a smile. "Why, it's the little maid! The little maid from Jerusalem! No longer a little maid, but a lady grown, and a lovely lady, too! How is it with you, and with the little blue sheep of your British hills?"

"I thought you were Jesus." The words came out with all the force of simplicity. Next moment she would have called them back, and felt herself going scarlet. She added, quickly: "I was very young then, and you were carrying a lamb, and you seemed to know who I was, and—please don't laugh! I've always remembered it, and I know it was silly, but sometimes I tried to pretend it was true."

He did not laugh. He said gravely: "You did me honour. If I had known, I would have told you that I was only a farmer's son, and a very ordinary man, but that my name was—is—in fact Jesus." He smiled at her look. "We do not think as you do about using that name, little maid. But here I am known as Jeshua. It is the same name, and you would find it easier to use, I think?"

"I—yes, of course. So—how do you come to speak my language so well?"

"Jerusalem was always full of pilgrims, many from your country. I have always found it easy to learn new tongues. A useful gift—" he smiled again—"if one is ambitious."

"I see . . ." She found that she was still clutching the skirts of the primrose gown. She settled the silk to its decorous length, smoothed it down, and with the action felt her composure returning.

"And now you are the queen's steward?" It was the Lady Alice again. "How did you come here, Master Jeshua?"

"If I may tell you on the way down? It's dinner-time, and you are waited for. Take my arm, lady, it's a rough way."

"I'm afraid my hands are dusty. I don't want to dirty your sleeve."

He only laughed, and lifted her hand to his arm, and they went down through the vineyard together, with Mariamne, smiling happily, behind them.

9

If Alice had been able to hear what Queen Clotilda was saying to the duke, she would have understood more clearly why the young prince was so closely guarded, even in his own home.

"God and His saints only know for how many years we will be able to welcome pilgrims to Tours. As you know, duke, the land north of the river is in the hands of my son Childebert, so the road you took on your way along the valley, and the monastery where you lodged last night, belong to him."

"Indeed. And we travelled in safety and comfort. What reason is there to think that he might seek to prevent the pilgrimages? And—with your leave, madam—to forgo the revenue they bring him? He is Christian, is he not? I was led to believe—"

"Oh, yes. When my lord King Clovis was received into Holy Church, my sons were baptised also, and a great number of our fighting men with them." A twist of a smile, "But our countrymen are warriors first and Christians second."

"But while you keep your state here in Tours, madam, your sons will surely maintain the shrine and the pilgrim roads as you and your husband planned?"

"While I live, yes, perhaps. But with Burgundy for ever baying on our thresholds, who knows which of the kings, my sons, will survive the next campaign? Prince Theudovald is well grown, and clever, yes, and I have seen to it that he is devout, but he is not yet seven years old, and already the Burgundians are making threatening gestures along our eastern borders."

The duke hesitated, and the queen, with another of her wry smiles, gave a sharp little nod.

"You are remembering that I myself am from Burgundy? Rest easy, duke; I had no love for my uncle Sigismund, and though I was used in my marriage as a pawn in his game of power, I did not stay a pawn—save in God's hands, and for God's holy purpose."

"Straight to the eighth square, and mate?" said the duke, smiling, and she laughed.

"Yes, crowned queen, and a Frankish queen, in name and spirit! If my lord Clovis had lived, he would have moved one day against Burgundy, whatever that time-server in Rome had to say to the matter. And I would have said no word to prevent him. But he is dead, and my sons, alas, quarrel among themselves, so Burgundy may see his chance all too soon."

"Even so, could Burgundy—alone, for I doubt very much if the emperor would risk an alliance—raise the kind of army that could stand against the full might of the Frankish kingdoms? For, surely, in face of such a threat, your sons' differences would be forgotten, and a united Frankish army would take the field?"

"That is what I pray for."

"And work for, madam?"

"And work for." This time the smile was grim. "So I move between my sons' capitals, and—I make no secret of it—I still have friends near the Burgundian court who keep me informed. For old time's sake—" the words were said mockingly, but the duke thought they were sincere—"I keep my own palace here, near St. Martin's shrine, and the monastery that he founded, the first in Gaul, and the holiest. So Childebert sits in Paris, while I watch his border here, and Chlodomer waits in Orleans for Godomar of Burgundy to move. As long as I am here . . ." She lifted her shoulders again in a shrug, and let the sentence die.

"I cannot believe," said Duke Ansirus courteously, "that such a queen will not succeed in anything she sets out to accomplish."

"Hah!" It was a disconcerting bark of laughter. No fool, the old queen, thought Ansirus. She knows as well as I do that those sons of hers, skin-deep Christians at best, will, given the least excuse, tear the country apart as surely as hungry wolves tear a carcase. Well, let us hope, for her sake and young Theudovald's—and more than that, for the sake of Britain and the fragile peace that the High King Arthur keeps there—that Chlodomer stays alive long enough to see his sons grown and his kingdom safely and peaceably bestowed.

His eyes met Clotilda's. Assuredly no fool, the old queen. She nodded, as if in answer to his thought.

"Well, we shall see," she said.

And here, to the duke's relief, dinner was announced, and a steward sent to summon the two children.

THREE

The Knight-Errant

10

Alexander's mother did not marry again, though her youth and beauty—and perhaps the snug little property that was hers now in the Wye Valley—brought a few hopeful gentlemen to her door. But all were disappointed. The Princess Anna remained there unwed, living in comfort and a slowly growing contentment. Theodora and Barnabas were unfailingly kind; the former was happy to have Anna's company, and the latter, relieved as time went on of the fear that Anna, with a new marriage, might bring in another claimant to Craig Arian, devoted himself to their welfare. With the help of this good and gentle man Anna soon learned to manage the affairs of the small estate, which she and Barnabas did together in Alexander's name.

As is the way of things, she recovered in time from the shock and grief of her husband's murder, but she never abated her hatred of King March, nor her determination that some day he should be made to pay for his foul deed. She took care, as the boy grew up, that he should learn what kind of man his father had been, and learn also to be proud and glad of that inheritance. Men called him, in pity, Alexander the Fatherless, but in fact the child did not lack the father's presence as much as he might have done, because Barnabas saw to it that he learned the skills he would need, those of a fighting man, and of the master of an estate, albeit a small one. So Alexander grew up in safety, and even in happiness, for the place was a peaceful one, and "the High King's peace" was a reality in the gentle valleys he knew.

That happiness was not marred by any knowledge of his father's death. When, childlike, he had first asked about it, Anna told him merely that he had been born in Cornwall, where Prince Baudouin had served his elder brother King March, and that Baudouin had died when his son was two years old. Since Baudouin, as a younger son, would have had no claim to land in Cornwall, Anna had (she said) decided to leave and stake her own and Alexander's claim to Craig Arian. And rightly, she would add, since King March, though he had no child of his own, was still living, so for both her son and herself there was a better life and a better future in the rich valleys of the Welsh border.

"He must be an old man now," said Alexander one day, when they were speaking of it again. He was fourteen, tall for his age, and considered himself a man grown. "And he has no son. So soon, perhaps, I should travel into Dumnonia and see Cornwall and the kingdom that may one day be mine?"

"It never will," said his mother.

"What do you mean?"

"You would be better to forget Cornwall and all it holds. It can never be yours. King March is not your friend, and even if he were, and left you the ruling of the kingdom, you would have to fight for every foot of its barren soil. Since Duke Cador died, who used to hold Tintagel, his son Constantine has ruled there. I am told that he is a hard and cruel man. March clings to what is his, but when he dies it will be a strong man and a fortunate one who keeps his stronghold after him."

"But if it is some day to be mine by right, then surely the High King will support and help me? Mother," said Alexander eagerly, "at least let me go to Camelot!"

Anna refused, but he asked again and again, and each time it was harder to find a reason, so that at length she told him the truth.

It happened one day, in the spring of Alexander's eighteenth year, that he rode out with Barnabas and two other men—they were the castle's retainers, not strictly fighting men, but ready, as men were in those days, to defend themselves and their lord—to ride the bounds of the estate. In a curve of the river, where the water ran broken and shallow over smooth stones, they saw on the far bank a group of three armed horsemen apparently preparing to cross. These were strangers, and as Alexander pressed nearer, he saw that on the breast of one man's tunic was a boar, the badge of Cornwall. Spurring forward, he hailed the man eagerly.

It so happened that the Cornishmen, who were heading for Viroconium, had missed their way and, knowing that they were straying on some lord's territory, were looking for a crossing-place which might lead to a farm cottage or the hut of a shepherd who could set them back on their road. But at Alexander's shout they thought their crossing was being disputed. They halted, then the fellow with the badge, seeing what he took for a young knight accompanied by three armed men, shouted some sort of challenge in return, and drawing his sword, set his horse at the water.

A moment of shock, a warning shout from Barnabas, and then it was too late. Alexander, young, ardent, and filled with tales of bravery and daring, had been spoiling for just such a moment as this. Almost before he had thought, Baudouin's sword was in the boy's hand, and there, in the middle of the dimpling waters of the Wye, Alexander struck the first blow of his first fight.

It was a lucky one. It met the other's blade, knocked it aside, and travelled straight and deadly fast into the man's throat. He fell without a sound. Barnabas and the servants spurred forward to the boy's side, but the fight, such as it was, was over. The dead man must have been the leader of the group, for as he fell the other two pulled their horses' heads round and galloped away.

Alexander, breathless with excitement and the shock of his first kill, sat, instinctively controlling his plunging horse, and staring down at the body sprawled in the shallow water. Barnabas, as white as he, caught at his bridle.

"Why did you do that? See the badge! That's the Boar of Cornwall! Those were March's men!"

"I know that. I—I didn't mean to kill him. But he would have killed me. He drew first. Did you not see? I called out to know his business, that was all. But then he drew, and the others with him. Did you not see, Barnabas?"

"Yes. I saw. Well, it can't be helped now. You two, take the body up. We'd best get back and tell your lady mother what's happened. This is a bad day, a bad day."

The horses splashed up out of the river, and the party rode slowly back to the castle.

11

Anna was in the orchard, watching one of the gardeners pruning an apple tree. When Alexander began to tell her his story she took him by the arm and quickly led him aside, out of the man's hearing, "Because," she said urgently, "if these were indeed March's men, there could be danger here." And she would not let him say anything more until they were in her private chamber, and she had dismissed the maid who was busy there.

"But mother," protested Alexander, "the men were trespassing on our land, and the one I killed—he attacked me. If you ask Barnabas, he'll tell you how it happened. I saw the Cornish blazon, and I called out to greet them and ask their business, and the fellow drew on me. What else was I to do?"

"Yes, yes, I know. There could be no trouble because of that. But the others—when they get back to Cornwall—you say you and Barnabas had two of our men with you? Were they close? Close enough for March's men to see their badges?"

"Certainly." The boy was impatient. "And they would surely know from them that they were on our land, but even that did not stop them."

Anna was silent for a moment, then, with a little sigh,

83

she turned and walked slowly over towards the window. A chair stood there, with her embroidery frame beside it. She pushed the work aside, and sat down to stare, chin on hand, out of the window. One of her white doves, seeing her there, flew up to strut, cooing softly, on the stone sill, hopeful of grain.

She neither saw nor heard it. She was back in that midnight room in March's castle, with all the memories she had striven to keep alive, and at the same time forget. She turned sharply away from the window, straightening in her chair. At the movement the dove, startled, rose with a clap of wings and flew away.

"Alexander—"

"What is it, mother? You look pale. Are you not well? If I've distressed you, I'm sorry, but why should you speak of danger? You said yourself there could be no trouble about the man I killed, and it's true—"

"No, no. It's not that. This is a different matter, and a heavy one. There's something I must tell you. I planned to tell you when you were turned eighteen, and ready to go to the High King to offer your service there. But this has happened, so I must tell you now. Here, take this."

She put a hand to the bosom of her gown and withdrew a small silvery key which she handed to the boy.

"Go to that press in the corner and open it. Pull harder, the hinges will be stiff. That's it. Now look, there on the floor, that leather box with the rope round it, bring it here, to the light . . . Yes. Now open it. No, don't trouble with the knots; there'll be no need to tie it up again. Cut them. Use your dagger. So."

She turned in her chair to look out of the window again. "I don't want to see what's there, Alex. Just open the box, and tell me."

Below the window the gardener was working still among the orchard trees. His children, a boy and a little girl, ran and shouted, playing with a half-grown puppy. But all that Anna heard, loud above those happy sounds, was the creak of leather hinges and then a rustle, a dry rattling sound, and Alexander's voice, so like Baudouin's, sounding puzzled.

"There's nothing much here, mother. Just some clothing ... A shirt, an old shirt, and it's—faugh—it's filthy! Stains, blackish, and gone stiff ..." A sudden sharp silence. Then in a different voice: "That's blood, isn't it?"

"Yes." She was still resolutely turned away.

"But—whose? What is this, mother? What is it?" Then, before she could speak, on a sharply drawn breath: "No, I don't need to ask. My father's? Why else would you keep such a thing? It was his?"

She nodded without speaking. He had been kneeling over the box, fingering the stained cloth fastidiously. Now he took the shirt in both hands, holding it fast against his breast. He got to his feet.

"How was he killed? You told me—you let me think he had died of some sickness! But this—why have you kept this dreadful thing all these years? He was foully killed, that's it, isn't it? Isn't it? Who killed him?"

She turned then. Alexander was standing full in the sunlight, with the embroidered shirt clutched to him. "King March," she said.

"I guessed it! I guessed it! Whenever that name has been mentioned, you've had this same look. Mother, tell me how!"

"Yes, I'll tell you. It's time you knew." She motioned him to lay the shirt down in its box, then sat back against the cushions with a kind of relief. The moment had come and gone, and it was time, more than time, to let the long-cherished ghost recede. "Sit down, here beside me, my dear, on the window-seat, and listen."

She told him from the beginning, from the day when the Saxon warships sailed into the bay below the cliffs. Her voice was dry and even, long since purged of grief, but at one point in the narrative, when she described how Baudouin had put on the shirt and laughed with her, Alexander reached a hand to lay it over hers. She went steadily on; the flight, the encounter with Sadok and his brother, the safe refuge at Craig Arian.

He began to say something, some word of comfort, but she shook her head. Drawing her hand from under his, she turned her eyes on him. They were dry and very bright.

"I don't need comfort. I need vengeance. I vowed many years ago that when you, my son, were grown, you would seek out this vicious fox of a king and kill him. Will you do that?"

It would not have occurred to the young Alexander that he might do anything else. He said so, hotly, and jumping to his feet, began at once to make plans for a journey into Cornwall, but she stopped him.

"No. Listen still. I told you that I'd planned to tell you this story when you were turned eighteen. I have done it now because your meeting with March's men this morning changes things."

"But how?"

"Didn't you take it in? Sadok was sent after us that night to murder us. He promised me that he would tell March that you were dead, and, if it seemed needful, that I was dead too. Don't you think that if the Fox had thought you were still alive, he would have sent long since to seek us out and kill you? And he would surely have sent spies up here. Where else would I take you?"

"Then these men today were spies?"

She regarded him. He was a tall youth, blue-eyed like his father, with brown hair falling thickly to his shoulders, and a slender but well-muscled body. Standing tall and aggressive-looking in the bright sunlight from the window, he was the very picture of a splendid young fighting man. No need—Anna admitted it to herself, indulgently—no need for such a man, young and handsome and lord of a snug little castle and fertile lands, with good servants and a clever mother, to have quick wits as well.

She said, without impatience: "No. I believe this encounter was an accident. But these were March's men, and if by chance they recognised you—you who are the living spit of your father—they will go back to Cornwall and tell the Fox that Baudouin's son is still alive, and well found here at Craig Arian. And by killing his man— no, my dear, I know that you had to, wait—you have given him the excuse to send now to seek you out and finish the work that Sadok was supposed to do all those years ago."

"So," said Alexander with triumph, "I will go first! If I set out straight away, and ride hard, I can be in Cornwall before they get there!"

"No. What chance would you have? This must be done differently. Times have changed, Alexander. This morning you killed because you were attacked, and you cannot be impugned for that—"

"But you said that it has given March the excuse to seek me out for it and kill me!"

"March does not work by rule of law. I am talking about law. For the killing today you have a right. But a killing purely for revenge, and the killing of a king, at that—times have changed. It must be done by process of law. You will go to the High King and take your case, and its proof there, with you. You will go to the Round Hall and tell my story, show them the bloody shirt, and ask for the High King's judgment. From all accounts, Arthur and March are not friendly, and Arthur is very likely to let you challenge March and fight him in the course of law. You are young yet, Alexander, and this will give you time and experience to make yourself a match for such as March. You are not that yet, my son, and this is an arrow that must not miss. Do you not see? There was a time—those first years—when I would have given the world for March's death, come how it might, but we grow wiser with the years. If you went now to Cornwall and managed, though God knows how, to kill him and escape the swords of his guard, you yourself would be arraigned by Arthur's law-keepers, and we would gain nothing. Go to Arthur first, and then we have right and law on our side."

"Will the High King believe me?"

"I think so. He knows March. And there must be men still at March's court who remember that night. Drustan is not in Cornwall now; he is at his castle in the north, but he will stand by us if need be, and of course there is Sadok, and he—"

She stopped on a gasp, and a hand went to her throat. "Sadok! And Erbin, too! Ah, God, I should have thought it straight away! Once those men get home to March with their report, we can guess what will happen to Sadok and his brother!"

Before she had finished speaking, Alexander was on his knees beside her chair. "I'll go today! No, Mother, hear me! You said just now that you had planned to tell me about my father's death when I was eighteen, and then send me to the High King to seek vengeance on the murderer?"

"Yes, but—"

"This is the day! What happened this morning— you could call it fate! Anyway, it has happened, and— you said so—there could be danger, so what matter a few more months? I will be eighteen within the year! So I will go now, today—"

"*Today?* Alexander—no, listen! Even if it were possible to let you go on such an errand—"

"Then the sooner the better!" He swept on, his eagerness blowing her protests aside like a high wind. This was his own ground, man's business, and himself a man after his first fight and his first kill. He did not need wit and subtlety for this; he was his father's son, brave and high of heart, but also young enough—and inexperienced enough—to see this as an adventure, like the tales of excitement and wonder he had listened to as a child. "Why not? With good horses, and two or three men, you can be sure we will overtake those two long before they reach March's border. They'll see no reason to hurry; in fact they may hang back from telling King March how their officer was killed, and even, perhaps, their news of Baudouin's son. He sounds the kind of king who would have the tongue out of a bringer of bad tidings!"

"But—if you don't manage to come up with them? If they take a different road? In any case you don't know the way."

"I'll take someone with me who does, a couple of men.

Uwain, I think, he's a good man, and another—no more. Just the three of us; we'll travel all the faster. We'll catch them, never fear."

"And when you do?"

He sprang to his feet. "Need you ask? They won't take their news to King March, to put Sadok and his brother at risk. That's what you want, isn't it?" Something in her expression checked him. "What is it, mother? You needn't fear for me, you know! They won't be expecting us. We'll have surprise on our side, and—"

"It's not that. You're forgetting. These men are not likely to be March's spies, why should they be? They must have been here by accident, on other business. I would like to know what that was."

He stared in dismay. "You mean let them live? March's men?"

"Even so. Until we know who they are, we can't know if they were also Baudouin's—your father's—friends. I would not risk your killing men who perhaps stood against your father's murder, perhaps even fought with him when he fired the Saxon longships. True, they serve March, but I would not have them killed without we know more about them."

"Ye—es, I see. And have news of Cornwall?"

"That, too. Believe me, Alex, if they do seem dangerous, we will make sure they take no news back to their master. If they were Baudouin's men, they'll not try."

"I suppose not. Well, all right, mother, of course I'll do as you say. We'll bring them back to you, all of us scatheless. And a pretty tame affair this promises to be!" He took her hand, and lifted it to kiss. His look of disappointment had gone, and the sparkle of eagerness was back. "But afterwards, have I your leave to ride to seek Drustan, and go with him to the High King?"

She smiled, and lifted a hand to touch his cheek. "How could I stop you? Of course. But one thing more, Alex; even if you have to send Uwain and the other man on, do not go yourself inside March's border. Not yet. Not until we know more. Do I have your promise?"

"Well—yes, I suppose so. Yes, mother, I promise."

So it was left. Further than this she knew she could not, should not protect him. Though his eighteenth birthday was almost a year away, she knew as well as he did that she could not have prevented him from doing as he wished. But she was satisfied. He would keep his word, and later, when, as she had planned, he went with Drustan to Camelot, he would be secure, with a strong sword and good guidance, till he could demand Arthur's sanction and support. She was conscious mainly of a deep relief and release. The burden she had carried through all these years, of knowledge and the dread of action, had been lifted from her. As he had said, this was the day.

She drew a deep breath. "Then go with my blessing," she said, "and God go with you."

12

There was no way to guess which road the Cornishmen would take, but their own way was easy enough to choose: the fastest. So they headed south-east from Craig Arian, to cross the Wye by the Roman bridge at Blestium, and then through the hills to the Severn estuary and the short crossing some way east of Venta.

Once past Blestium, a small township boasting a decent inn, the road was hilly, in places little more than a rough shepherd's track, but the weather had been fair, so the going was dry, and they made good speed. They got no glimpse of the men they followed, and the stony track did not hold hoof-marks, but there were signs—fresh horse-droppings here and there—that riders had recently passed this way. They were barely a mile short of the Severn ferry when, light failing, they halted in a clearing by a woodcutter's hut, to rest their horses and eat the food they carried. The hut itself was deserted, the wood-cutters having gone, with the good weather, deeper into the forest, but the hut stank, so, the night being fine and dry, they preferred to sleep outside. Uwain and Brand, who both knew the road, assured Alexander that the first ferry would cross soon after daybreak, so it would not advantage them to be there before that. The hut where the ferryman slept was on the far side of the river. So the three of them ate their rations, and soon, to the comfortable sound of the horses grazing nearby, Alexander, wrapped warmly in his cloak against the night dews, fell asleep.

The morning came in fine, with an early mist hanging wreath-like from the trees and veiling the hilltops. They reached the long hill that led down towards the ferry while the sun was just inching up behind the crests of the hills and sending shadows long and blue in front of them. Mist lay in long clouds along the waters of the estuary, and between its white banks the water gleamed, flat and quiet. The tide was rising, and seabirds circled and called. They could see the ferry's brown sail about a third of the way over towards them. Brand had told them of a tavern he knew, a short way beyond the southern end of the crossing, and the thought of breakfast was a good one.

"If they've been this way, we'll get news of them from the ferryman," said Uwain. "And if they haven't, why then, we'll be ahead of them, and we can wait for them on the high road from Glevum. They won't be pressing their horses, after all. They wouldn't expect to be followed."

In this last, at any rate, he was right. The Cornishmen had ridden the same way, and at their ease, not being over-anxious to get home with their news. They had not, as it happened, recognised Alexander, so their only news would be unwelcome, the loss of one of March's trusted men. And March, as Alexander had guessed, was not a master who received bad news pleasantly. So they went slowly, with the result that they missed the last ferry, and had to spend the night in the ramshackle hut at the water's edge, where the ferryman slept if chance or bad weather prevented him from making the last crossing of the day.

As Alexander's party approached, coming out from the shade of the trees and clattering down the gravel road towards the jetty, the two Cornishmen were leading their horses out from behind the hut, their eyes on the approaching sail out on the tide.

At the sound of hoofs they turned, but not in alarm; their swords were still in their sheaths. The badge of the Boar showed white on the breasts of their tunics.

Then one of them, a big fellow holding the bridle of a roan horse, gave a sudden shout, and there was a flash as his sword seemed to leap into his hand.

"That's him! That's the murdering young bastard that killed Kynon!"

And almost before Alexander's party knew what was happening, the two men were in the saddle, and were racing on them with swords drawn and at the ready.

The speed and anger of the attack left no time for words, or even thought. Swords met and clashed, and the horses circled, their hoofs sparking on the stones. There was no chance to cry halt, to manoeuvre for a parley; no way that Baudouin's son could have identified himself and tested where the Cornishmen's allegiance had lain all those years ago. What he could not have known was that the man he had killed in that fateful skirmish had been the brother of the man who now strove, with more strength and skill in combat than the young prince possessed, to kill him in his turn.

Afterwards Alexander could never remember just what happened. The big fellow on the roan beat at his guard, forcing him back, pace by pace, his horse plunging and skidding on the stones, towards the ditch and bank at the side of the road. The fight with Kynon in the river had not been like this; here there was no room for fear or exhilaration: time seemed endless, and at the same time flying. Beside him was a crash and a cry, and a loose horse blundered into his opponent's side, and in that moment he felt his sword slip past the man's guard. It was beaten aside, but came out bloodied at the tip.

Alexander was gasping for breath now, dragging air into his lungs with snorting gulps past teeth bared in the grin of extreme effort. He spurred his horse savagely, driving it forward against the roan, just as the Cornishman, recovering, knocked the prince's sword high and wide, driving in below it for the final, killing stroke.

It missed by a hair's breadth; by the breadth of the armoured strap on the prince's shoulder, which it severed. Then Brand's horse hurtled against Alexander's, and Brand's sword, metal screaming along metal, forced the Cornishman's weapon aside and sliced past the armoured gorget and into the fellow's throat. He fell with a crash to the gravel of the road, and his horse, whinnying with terror, whirled round and bolted into the woods, splashing the stones with blood as it went.

"You're hurt, sir?"

Alexander, still caught up in the aftermath of the fighting, shook his head dazedly, while with unsteady hands he tried to slide the sword back into its sheath. "It's his blood. It splashed. I owe you thanks, Brand. I believe he had me there. He's dead, is he?"

"Yes, sir. They both are. There was no time for anything else."

"I know. It can't be helped. Are you all right?"

"Yes, sir, but Uwain's hurt."

"Badly?" He wiped the sweat from his eyes with the back of a blood-smeared hand. The sun, just clear of the hilltops, blazed straight into his eyes, level and brilliant, blinding him. So few moments had passed in that desperate encounter. He swung himself out of the saddle, threw his bridle to Brand, and ran to where Uwain was lying.

The fallen man had a cut in his side across the hipbone. When they had washed the worst of the blood off—there was a trickle of spring water in the bank nearby—the wound looked clean, but it was deep and jagged, and after they had dressed and bound it as best they could, still bled sluggishly.

"The ferry," said Alexander urgently. He was kneeling at Uwain's side, holding a cup of water to the wounded man's lips. "If we can get him down to the ferry, and across as far as the tavern you spoke of—"

"Look there," said Brand, pointing.

Alexander stood up. The estuary stretched gleaming and bright, the mist clearing in the sun. The brown sail was still there, but it was almost at the farther shore.

Alexander stared. "He was called back? I don't see anyone waiting there."

"No, sir." Brand was contemptuous. "He went back. He must 'a seen the fighting, and such as he won't come near till all's done. He won't come over again till he sees us gone. So what's to do now?"

Alexander glanced down at Uwain. The latter was trying to drag himself to his feet, protesting that the wound was nothing, he had had worse at hunting, he was good for a day's hard riding . . . but the prince put out a hand to press him back.

"No, wait. Rest there a minute." Then to Brand: "We

must get rid of the bodies. If their horses are still about, turn them loose. If other travellers come this way, we don't want questions asked, not yet. At least you needn't go into Cornwall now. This one first. You take the heels. That way, I think."

Between them they dragged the dead men off the road into the woods. There was a quarry, overgrown with brambles and bushes, where road-metal had once been dug, and here they found a shallow ditch where the bodies could lie. With daggers and their hands they scrabbled loose stones and gravel to cover them. The roan horse, grazing near, they caught, stripping it of its harness, and sending it off with a thwack from the flat of a sword. The other horse had gone. Then they went back to Uwain, and helped him into the saddle.

There was still no sign of the ferry. "But all the better," said Alexander, who had had time to think. "If we crossed to find the tavern and lodge there, the news of this would run the length and breadth of Dumnonia almost before nightfall. As it is, all the ferryman saw was a skirmish at the edge of the woods, and when he does bring himself to come over, I doubt if he'll look further."

"And Uwain?"

"There was a good-looking tavern in Blestium. We'll get him back there—you can manage that far, Uwain? Good man. We'll get you there and get that leg seen to. We can lie up there for a day or two, to see how it does."

"Your lady mother won't be too pleased."

"That's true, but you can tell her how it happened. There was no chance to do otherwise. It's like the first fight—as if a sort of fate was at work. And it would have been my fate, had it not been for your sword, Brand. See that you tell my mother that, Uwain."

"I will, prince. But you? Are you not going home with us?"

"Not yet. I—my mother will know where I am going."

"Not into Cornwall?" said Brand sharply.

"No, no. I promised not to cross that border. Just tell her that I follow my fortune. She will understand."

It is possible that all three of them added, to themselves, the simple prayer *I hope*. But though the two troopers did exchange a doubtful look, they said no more. And at length, in the light of a crimson sunset, they came in sight of the Roman bridge, and the welcome lights of the tavern pricking out yellow in the dusk.

13

The tavern was comfortable, and a doctor was speedily found for Uwain. The latter's wound, once properly dressed, was declared to be clean and already on the way to healing. The three of them stayed there for two days, until the doctor gave Uwain leave to travel, then they set out on the ride home to Craig Arian.

But when they came to the fork in the road where a steep track led westward into the valley of the Lesser Wye, Alexander, halting his horse, bade the other two farewell.

"For," he said, "once embarked in this adventure, I must finish it. My mother will understand. It's not done yet." He hesitated. "There's something she told me which I may not talk about, not yet, but you may give her this message; that I have set out to do what she would have me do, only a little sooner. Tell her that I'm riding north to seek out my cousin Drustan at Caer Mord, and I'll send a message to her as soon as I can. It may be that I will ride this way with Drustan, when he goes back to Camelot, and I'll see her then."

Brand and Uwain tried to persuade him to go home first with them, and take the northward route after he had spoken again with the Princess Anna, but Alexander (who, once free of the leading-strings, had no intention of letting his mother tie them on again) refused to listen, repeating the message to his mother, and then turning his horse's head to the north, and leaving them shaking their heads and staring after him.

So he rode north alone, with a light heart. He was seventeen, he had fought in two sharp fights and emerged scatheless from both. He had a good horse, a pouch of money, a new suit of clothing, his mother's (possible) blessing and his father's sword, and it was May, with the sun high in the heavens and the early morning dew sparkling on the grass. Small wonder that his spirits were high, and that he sang as he rode. He was young and strong and on his way to seek his fortune. And it was extra fortune that he could, in that year of Our Lord five hundred and twenty-three, seek it at the hand of Drustan, one of the honoured Companions of Arthur, High King of all Britain.

As for his first purpose, revenge for his father's long-ago murder, and the justice he had been so eager, only a few days back, to seek on King March, he was no longer thinking about that. The day's promise and the day's adventure were what filled his mind. When the road he followed led downhill, and he could see, through the trees, the gleam of water which promised a ford, his thoughts and hopes immediately sprang to the tales he had heard, of fording-places guarded by outlaws lying in wait for travellers to rob. As his horse, scenting water, pricked its ears and quickened its pace, he loosened the sword in its scabbard and rode downhill as if to a happy meeting.

What he did find was exactly what he might have

expected: a shallow crossing, where the river lisped across its stony bed, and, above the flood markings on the farther bank, the workshop of a wayside smith with the anvil outside, and beside it, crumbling with age but still recognisable, the image of Myrddin the god of going, with an offering of fruit at his feet.

The smith, who was seated against the bole of a nearby oak, with the remains of his dinner wrapped away in a kerchief on the grass, cast an expert's eye over Alexander's horse as it splashed through the ford towards him, and then stayed where he was.

"Good day to you, master. You'll have no need of me today, I see. Are you going far?"

Such men are eager collectors and purveyors of news, and Alexander, even if he had seen any need for caution, was too full of his new freedom to keep it to himself.

"As far north as need be. I go to join Sir Drustan at Caer Mord in Northumbria."

"Then you've a long road ahead of you, young master, but, thanks be to Arthur's men that ride the roads, it'll be a safe one." His little black eyes, twinkling under shaggy brows, were busily taking in Alexander's clothing, his lack of blazon, the good housing of his horse. "And where are you from, young sir?"

"From Blestium." No need for more, to have every traveller knowing that the young lord of Craig Arian took such a long journey alone. "You'll know the best road, smith?"

"I should. I keep my eyes and ears open," said the smith, "and I hear all that passes. You'd best keep to the old road, the Romansway, they call it. You can strike it at Viroconium, and then it's straight north into Rheged, and the road east from Brocavum. It's a long road, master, but you've a good horse there. Take care of him and he'll take care of you."

"Of course. But—Rheged? So far north? I thought to head north-east long before that."

"As to that, there's a road setting eastward not more than four days' ride from here, but it's a bad one, that I do know, and after that there's no way through the mountains till you reach Rheged. You'd be better going by Rheged. But suit yourself, and God speed to you." A gesture towards the Myrddin image at the forge's doorway, and he turned to gather up the kerchief with the remains of his meal.

Alexander said quickly: "I'll go to Rheged. By Viroconium, you said? Is there good lodging there?"

"I've never been there," said the smith, "but I can tell you the way to take. For the most part it's good enough, but for the next two or three days, I'm afraid, you may find rough going. There's been heavy rain in the hills, a cloudburst only yesterday, you could see the storm-rain from here, and I'm told the bridge is down again a day's ride northwards, where the road crosses the river. It happens with every flood. There was a courier through here early this morning, and by what he said you must needs ride a fair way west to find a crossing. See." And reaching for a stick he got to his feet and drew a diagram in the mud at the river's edge. "Here. And once across, you can turn back to the east along the river's bank, and in half a day you'll find your road again."

"And for lodging? They told me in Blestium that there was a monastery beside the bridge. I was planning to sleep there. If I make for that now, then follow the river along the next day, the way you've marked there—"

The smith shook his head. "That colt won't run,

master. The monastery's on the far side, so you'll miss that night's lodging anyway. Best turn away here, where I've put the mark. And here"—the stick prodded into the mud again—"you'll likely find better lodging than at any monastery. The lady's not at home now, being as how she's fallen foul of her good brother, and he's had her mewed up elsewhere these two years past, but those that serve her will take you in, sure enough, and give you good lodgement. And it's a soft place to lie, they say, for all it's called the Dark Tower."

If there was something sly about the smith's grin, Alexander did not notice it. "The Dark Tower? Lady? What lady?"

"The Lady Morgan, she that's own sister to Arthur himself. Queen Morgan, I should have said; she was Urbgen's queen in Rheged till he put her aside over some tangle of a lover and a try at stealing the King's sword of state, the one they call Caliburn. It was over that she fell foul of her brother Arthur, so you'd be wiser not to talk of him, young sir, when you're a guest at the Dark Tower."

"Yes, of course. Of course I understand," said Alexander, who did not understand at all, but who was finding this, his first brush with the great world, and the mention of famous names, exhilarating. It is possible that, even had the ruined bridge not forced him to turn aside for Queen Morgan's castle, he would have ridden there rather than seek lodging in the tame purlieus of a monastery. "But you said that the lady herself—the queen—would not be there?" He was careful to keep the disappointment out of his voice.

"Well, she wasn't, last time any news came by from there," said the smith. "But there has been other news.

There's been coming and going, and a tide of urgent messages passing, between the south-west and the parts north-west of here, up into Northgalis and then further up still, to the edges of Rheged. And there's been talk of meetings . . ." Here he paused, and then spat to one side, making a sign which Alexander recognised as one his Welsh groom made against magic . . . "Midnight meetings, and spells, and witches flying through the air when the moon's down, and gathering in some spot to brew evil against their enemies."

"And you believe all that?" asked Alexander.

"As to that," said the smith gruffly, "living as I do, here by the crossway ford, I see a sight of strange things. Who am I to say what to believe and what not to believe? But if I was you I'd go carefully, young master, and if you do stay over at the castle, remember what they say about Queen Morgan! Faery they call her, and the word goes that she's readier with her spells than ever was her sister Morgause, the witch from Orkney that tangled with Merlin and was hacked to pieces in her bed by her own son." And he made the sign again.

"I'll remember," said Alexander, who had heard the story, and had no wish to hear it again. He thanked the man, gave him a coin, and rode on between the banks of forest, with his head full of castles and spells and royal names and the promise of a comfortable—or at the least an interesting—night's lodging.

14

Towards late afternoon he reached the river and found that, as the smith had said, the water was swollen and fierce, pouring seawards below a steep bank that, even as he reached it, broke under the pressure of water and sent turf and stones swirling down in the flood. The only indication that there had ever been a bridge here was a stand of heavy wooden piles jutting from the far bank, where the road climbed up through the woods again.

The trees were thick, but through them he could just glimpse what looked like the corner of a building. The monastery, no doubt. He halted his horse and let it stand for a minute or two, while he calculated the depth and strength of the water. But even to his bold and inexperienced eye the river looked unfordable, so, with a shrug, he turned the horse's head away and set it trotting upstream along the river bank. The path, steep and rough in places, was nevertheless well trodden, as if this had happened many times before. How many frustrated travellers, he wondered, halted at the grimly named Dark Tower to beg for a night's lodging and shelter? Now that this prospect seemed fixed, the young man felt, behind the quiver of excited interest, some sort of nervousness. But when dusk began to draw in, and far across the brawling river he heard the first owl calling, he felt nothing but thankfulness as, through the trees some way to the right of the river bank, he saw a light.

His horse saw it, too, and perhaps smelled stable and supper. It pricked its ears and stepped out, suddenly eager, and soon horse and rider came out of the heavy shadow of the trees into a cleared stretch where the valley lay open, and there, on a bare little tableland of rocky grass, the castle stood.

It was small, a pair of towers joined by a curtain wall which curved back to enclose a courtyard where sheds and stables housed beasts and servants, and a big barn-like structure presumably held stores. Round three sides of the castle walls ran a stream, forming a natural moat. The spring that fed it was high in the valley's side, and poured down, white in its rocky bed, to wash the front of the castle, where a narrow wooden bridge led across to a door sunk in a deep archway. The place was grim rather than grand, an old building of grey stone gone black with age and weather, designed for defence in that wild and lonely place. The valley lay high among the hills, with steep forest to either side rising to crags where ravens barked. In the open valley-foot the grass, even at that time of the year, grew thin between islands of bracken and thorn. A strange castle for a queen, thought Alexander, then remembered what the smith had said of Queen Morgan, that she had been cast off in disgrace by her husband, and had, moreover, grievously offended her brother the High King. So this castle, this well-named Dark Tower, was in effect a place of banishment, a prison? What sort of welcome would there be here for a benighted traveller? It did not occur to Alexander that a lonely and imprisoned queen might well open her gates joyfully to a young and personable prince.

In any case, there was nowhere else to go. Alexander set his horse splashing through the river which here, still rapid but spreading wide over grassland, was readily fordable, then swung down from the saddle and led the tired beast across the wooden footbridge.

The light he had seen came from a torch thrust into an iron bracket on what looked rather like a gibbet-pole. It glimmered on the iron studs of a heavy, fast-shut gate. Alexander drew his dagger, reversed it, and hammered with the hilt against the planks.

"Is anyone there?"

No reply. No sound except the rush of the stream and the harsh laughter of a raven overhead. The place seemed deserted, the raven an omen. He had raised his hand to knock again, when the door opened suddenly, and a man, the porter by his dress, swung it wide to the wall, and stood back, bowing.

Beyond the man, through the black shadow of the archway, Alexander saw a courtyard where servants bustled to and fro, girls with armfuls of linen, men carrying platters, or bowls and dishes, all apparently busy with preparations for the evening meal. The delectable smell of roasting meat met his nostrils, and he felt suddenly, ravenously hungry. Dark Tower or royal prison, the swollen river had done him a favour in bringing him to this lodging. No monastery, surely, would have been serving such a meal as he could smell here.

He was opening his mouth to identify himself to the porter, and make his plea for a night's lodging, when a woman came hastily forward past the bowing man. In the darkness of the archway he could not see her clearly, but she was slightly built, and moved like a young woman. Her dress was dark and plain, but he caught, in the torch-light, the gleam of gold at her waist, and the glint of jewels. The royal exile herself, come to the gate to greet a chance traveller? Hardly. Besides, the smith had said Queen Morgan was not in residence. This, then, must be the lady who kept the castle for the queen—and who had come herself to the gate to welcome him.

The adventure was starting to take shape. Alexander stepped forward and made his bow.

"Madam—"

The lady stopped short. The porter straightened up, took one look at Alexander, another at the bridge behind him, empty of all but the horse, then, unbelievably, laid both hands to the gate to swing it shut in the young man's face.

He was not quite quick enough. The prince jumped forward, set knee and shoulder against the oak, and with a thrust of his arm pushed it wide again, sending the man reeling. He turned to see the lady, her eyes wide with alarm, opening her mouth to summon help.

He said hurriedly: "Madam, forgive me! I mean no harm—and indeed, what harm could I do? I am alone, and crave only for a night's shelter."

She merely stared, saying nothing.

He went on quickly: "I'd been planning to seek lodging at the monastery, but the river's in flood, and there was no way to cross. I'm sorry if I handled your man a bit roughly—"

"No matter. He's not hurt." Recovering from her surprise, whatever had caused it, she came forward quickly. "I ask your pardon for the rough welcome, sir, but we were expecting other guests, and my gateman is a fool, and mistook his orders. Pray come in, and be welcome. Leave your horse, the grooms will see to it."

He followed her into the courtyard. In the light of the torches that flickered and flamed in their brackets on the walls, he could see her more clearly. She was young; so far the adventure held true; but unlike the heroines of the tales he had enjoyed, she was not beautiful. Her face was thinnish, her eyes round and light-blue, with pale brows and lashes, and her mouth was small and close-lipped.

But her smile at Alexander was a sweet one, and her voice was pleasant.

"This way, sir. I'm afraid it will be plain lodging for you tonight, but it's all we can offer."

She repeated what she had said about expected guests, and the main rooms of the place already prepared for them, but with no suggestion, which Alexander was already half waiting for, that he should join the company in the hall for supper. She finished merely: "But you will be warm and comfortable, and I will send someone to see to you. So the bridge is down again? It seems to happen whenever the river's in spate, and we get travellers, parties even, who come seeking a night's lodging. We could not have taken in a party tonight, but a single traveller, who will be content with a dry bed and a good meal—"

"Of course. I'm only sorry if I've come at a bad time."

"No, no. If you—ah, here is Grif. He'll look after you."

An elderly man, a chamberlain by his dress, came hurrying across the court towards them. The lady, still with the smile, but with her mind, obviously, elsewhere, handed Alexander over with a brief, "Be welcome, sir, and God give you a good night," and hurried away, vanishing through the main door of the castle.

"This way, sir," said Grif.

Alexander, pausing only to see his horse taken in hand by a groom, followed him towards a small door set near one of the towers. It was apparent that he could not expect the honours due to a guest of his princely standing; she had not even asked his name. But supper and a good bed were all he had a right to ask for, and after the hard day's riding they were beginning to be all he wanted.

The chamberlain led him along a chilly stone-flagged corridor to a smallish chamber. This was well enough appointed, with a bed, a cross-stool, a small table and a chest for clothing, but the man spread an apologetic hand.

"My lord, it's poor lodging for such as yourself, but the best chambers are bespoken, as my lady would tell you, and if this will serve—"

"Of course it will serve. I'm grateful for your lady's kindness. May I know her name?"

"She's the Lady Luned, who was the wife of Gerin. Since his death she lives much retired, keeping this castle here for the queen her mistress, but before that she was at court."

"This must be a lonely place, after what one hears of Camelot."

"Oh, not the High King's court," said the man. "King Urbgen's, of Rheged. My lady waited on the queen there, Queen Morgan, that was Urbgen's wife and is King Arthur's sister."

This went some way to explaining the surprising amount of service that this small and isolated place seemed to offer, even in the absence of its owner. The Lady Luned still kept her state.

"And your lady still receives guests," said Alexander.

"The road looked well travelled to me. Or are the tracks worn by strays like myself who cannot get to the monastery?"

The man laughed. "There are plenty of those, my lord. The river sends a deal of company our way. Only for a night, as a rule; the flood goes down as sharp as it rises. You needn't fear to be held back for long."

"But tonight there are guests expected for whom your lady goes to the gate herself? May one know who they are?"

"Why, Queen Morgan herself," said the old man. "She's on her way from the north to Castell Aur in Wales. It seems she petitioned the High King to let her go there to her own place. She'll come escorted—under guard, that is—but he lets her have her own people about her, so this will be like her own court again." A smile and a sigh. "Ah, well, poor lady. It's a busy time, but a lively one for the valley folk. She'll maybe rest here a few weeks, if the weather's good, and the company she's brought pleases her. She should be here soon. You'd see the place was in a rush and my lady Luned herself much occupied . . . But you're welcome, she always sees to that. And now, my lord—for 'my lord' it is, by your ways, young sir?—have you all you want? I'll send a boy to you, and I'll go myself and see what the kitchens have got ready to send you. You'll find the privy straight across the passageway."

He bowed his way out. Alexander threw his saddle-bag down on the chest and pulled a clean shirt out of it. The chance traveller, understandably enough, could not expect to be bidden to the royal table, or even to catch sight of the royal guest, but when the promised boy arrived with a bowl of hot water and a fresh towel he

made a careful toilet, wondering as he did so what sort of
figure he would cut in front of a queen. For this was not
only the former Queen of Rheged, and Arthur's own
sister, but also from all accounts a notable witch, whom
men feared, and called Queen Morgan the sorceress,
Morgan le Fay.

15

By the time Alexander had changed into clean clothes, and washed the stains of the journey away, he had realised with relief what a lucky chance had saved him from giving his name to the Lady Luned, and thereafter possibly taking his place at the royal table. After his long day on the road, with no one but his horse to talk to, he had been in danger of forgetting the purpose of his journey, and that he could hardly claim his right to royal birth and title without doing the very damage that he, with Brand and Uwain, had set out to prevent. Alexander, son of Prince Baudouin, must stay dead, and Anna the widowed princess must stay unmolested, until such time as Drustan their kinsman should put them in the way of the High King's judgment and justice.

So the Lady Luned's chance traveller was a nobody, and would dine in his own chamber. And in that case, thought Alexander cheerfully, as footsteps came hurrying along the corridor, and the delectable smells of the meal approached, he could eat straight away, and not be compelled to wait for the belated royal party.

He called "Enter!" and retired into the window embrasure as a couple of servants came in with steaming platters and a generous basket of bread still hot from the oven. The boy who had served him earlier set a jug of wine down, with a goblet and a couple of napkins. The napkins were of fair linen, and the goblet was a graceful thing of silver. It seemed that one need not be royal to be given the best that the Lady Luned had to offer.

He thanked the men, who bowed and withdrew. The boy, lifting the wine-jug, and proffering one of the napkins, was apparently ready to stay and serve him, but Alexander, with a quick word, dismissed him. Even when he had gone, and the door had shut behind him, the prince did not move straight away to the table.

The window of his room gave on the outside of the castle. The opening was narrow, but afforded a reasonable view of the road leading round the edge of the moat towards the bridge and the main gate. The noise of the waterfall had hidden the sound of hoofs, but a few moments ago two horsemen had appeared, riding towards the gate. Before they reached it they drew rein, turning, apparently, to meet and greet two others who came cantering to overtake them. Then came the sound of hammering at the gate, and the shouting that would bring the porter to open.

The first of the queen's party? Alexander turned thoughtfully from the window, more than ever thankful for the chances that had kept him in seclusion.

The flare of the gatehouse torch had shown him, on the breasts of the second pair of horsemen, the badge of King March of Cornwall.

The rest of the party—the main body of it—arrived just as he had finished eating. It was a large company, some twenty armed horsemen escorting three litters and a small drove of baggage-mules. Mounted servants carried torches, so, although the night was now quite black, Alexander, at his window once more, saw it all clearly.

The queen, of course, would be in one of the litters; the foremost, borne by sturdy white mules and with gilded paint glinting, must be hers. He looked for the royal badge of Rheged, then realised that of course a rejected queen would have no right to her husband's honours, nor to his protection. Not in fact that it was protection, except as guards would provide it for their prisoner. So—with a queer little stir of excitement he realised it—the men-at-arms would probably be the High King's own. There was no badge or pennon that he could see, but he had heard that Arthur carried a plain white shield—for God to write on, said the churchmen. Well, for whatever reason, thought Alexander, men like Arthur, duke of battles, undisputed ruler of a kingdom united and at peace, was above and beyond, far beyond, the need to flaunt identity and achievement.

So, all unconsciously, impelled by a boy's instinctive hero-worship, Alexander made the first move of the fight to combat evil, without even suspecting that the evil existed.

He began to find out next day.

He slept deeply, without dreams or disturbances, and woke early to find the servants back at his door with food and fresh water. The old chamberlain Grif was with them, sent by his hostess to ask after the traveller's comfort, and to give him good wishes for his journey. The Lady Luned had not yet risen, said the old man, and managed, with the gentlest courtesy, to make it clear that when she did, she would be much occupied with waiting on her royal guest. Alexander, who was anxious now only to be on his way, sent back messages of warm thanks and good wishes, then broke his fast, packed his good clothes into the saddle-bag, together with such food as was left over from breakfast, and made his way out into the courtyard.

All was bustle there, men eating and drinking and chaffing the giggling servant-girls who carried food and beer to them; men cleaning their weapons and seeing to their horses and harness; the castle's own grooms busy with buckets and brushes, and the coming and going by the gate of market-women and local folk bringing their wares to sell.

Alexander made for the stable where he had seen his own horse led on the previous evening. It was there, comfortably housed and sharing a manger with half a dozen others. His saddle was on a wooden rack near the door. He was lifting this down when one of the grooms came in, dumping the pail he carried and hurrying to Alexander's side.

"You give me that, sir. I'll do it." He took the saddle and lifted it to the horse's back, then stooped to pull the girth tight. " 'Tis a rare handsome beast you've got here. I did him last night myself. He was tired—come a long way, had you?—but I gave him a warm mash with a drop of beer in it, and he ate up a treat. There he is now, ready to go. You going far, young sir?"

"That depends. I see people have come in this morning, country folk. Have you heard if the river's still in flood?"

"It's well down this morning, so not to worry, young master. It'll be down to no more than knee-deep by this. The track this side never gets flooded—not so's you can't get through—and the footing's good." He gave the horse's rump a caressing slap. "You're going north, I take it?"

"Yes, for Rheged and then the north-east." Alexander, grateful to the man for his care of the horse, stayed chatting for a few more minutes, then thanked him and took the bridle, leaving the groom beaming over a couple of copper coins. Without exciting more than some curious stares and a civil "Good morning" or two from the crowd in the courtyard, he led his horse out, and across to the gate. He saw no reason to reward the porter there, merely waiting in silence while the man pushed the heavy door open for him. Once across the moat he mounted and turned his horse's head along the track north of the river, heading for the road he had glimpsed yesterday, that led up past the monastery buildings from the end of the broken bridge.

He never reached it.

Three of Queen Morgan's escort, up and about even earlier than Alexander, had ridden out hunting, to find something more substantial for the castle's table than the fat geese and capons brought in by the local peasants.

They rode up into the woods that clothed the sides of the valley. Here the going was rough, the trees close-growing, with dense underbrush, and they soon scared up a deer. That it was a young doe, heavy with fawn, did not trouble them. The chase was all. The hounds were urged on with shouts and laughter, and the party galloped helter-skelter, necks for sale through the trees as the doe made downhill for the river.

The river, though it had certainly fallen during the night, was still fairly high, and running noisily, so that Alexander, riding at a swift canter along the bank, heard nothing of the hunt. The first he knew was when the doe broke suddenly out of the trees, which here grew close down to the water, and sprang clear into the road, barely three inches in front of the horse's nose.

The chestnut was a good horse, as steady as he was swift, and did not easily take fright, but the inevitable check, with the violent swerve and plunge to one side, only narrowly avoided collision with the fleeing doe. Even so, Alexander might have stayed in the saddle and kept control, had not the beast's sharp swerve taken it off the track and right to the river's edge, where the recent flood had loosened a section of the bank.

Under the slam of hoofs the ground broke, crumbled, and slid into the water. The horse fell, pitching his rider sideways into the river. The doe, untouched, flew the broken bank like a bird and was soon lost in the trees on the far side, while the hunting party, breaking from the woods a few moments later, found their hounds circling at a loss at the water's edge, and Alexander's big chestnut floundering up the river bank.

Alexander himself lay still where he had been flung, half in the rush of water, half on the stony rubble of the broken bank.

16

Alexander woke to a headache, a sharp pain in the left foot, and a nagging soreness in the left forearm. He was in bed, and it was dark, but a candle burned beside the bed, and its little light showed him that he was back in the bedchamber in the Dark Tower where he had slept last night. Last night? He felt drowsy, and slightly sick, with a heaviness in his limbs that set him wondering how long he had slept, or indeed—as the wraiths of dream still hung about him—whether he had ever ridden out from the place at all. The candle-light swam against his eyes. He shut them, and slid into sleep again.

When he awoke it was to daylight, and the click of the door-latch. The door opened to admit a stout woman with a basket over her arm and a beaker in one hand. She was followed by the boy who had served him yesterday, carrying a steaming bowl and an armful of linen towels.

"Well, and so you're with us again!" The woman spoke with a sort of familiar, almost professional cheeriness. From this, and from her plain dress and amply aproned figure and the white wimple hiding her hair, it was a good guess that she had been nurse to a couple of generations, at least, of the owners of the castle. She dumped her basket on the table. "And in more ways than one, young master! You thought you'd got away from us, didn't you, and found it wasn't quite as easy as that! Eh, well, you were lucky they found you so soon. You'll come to no harm, but you'll have to bide a few days, and let old Brigit look after you . . . Here, drink this. Can you sit up? That's right . . . Put the bowl down here, Peter, and get the other things set out for me. Quickly now! Come along, young master, all of it . . . Done you good already, by the looks of you. If you could have seen yourself yesterday morning when they brought you in from the river, like a drowned corpse you were, as white as wax and with that black bruise on your face and the blood, and dripping with water as cold as snow-broth—"

"The river?" The word brought the beginnings of memory. He put his good hand to his head, winced at the touch, and said anxiously: "My horse? He took a toss. There was a deer . . . That's right, a doe jumped into the road. Is he hurt?"

"Don't fret yourself, he's all right. Not a scratch. So you remember it now? Well, that's a good sign, anyway! Yes, you both took a toss, and you were lucky, too. Another handspan deeper, and you'd have drowned before they got you out. You hit your head, but it's no more than a bruise to spoil your handsome face for a day or two." She laughed fatly, busying herself with cloths and hot water. The water smelled of some herb mixture, and he relaxed gratefully back on the pillow.

"I've hurt my foot, I think. Did you say there was blood?"

"That was from your arm here, and a nasty little gash it is, too. Aye, you can feel that, can't you? Bide still now, we must make sure it's clean. They reckoned you must 'a speared your arm on a bit of a broken branch when you went over the bank. Your foot's naught to worry you, a sprain that'll keep you lying up for a few days, no more. I told you, you were lucky."

"It seems I was. Who brought me in?"

"There were three of them out hunting. It was Enoch carried you in here. There, that'll do you for now. You stay where you are, and rest yourself, and Peter'll bring you something to eat in a minute. Nay, young master, I said stay there in your bed . . . It'll be a day or two before you feel right enough to go about, with that knock on the head. And don't fret yourself about your horse. It's cared for. You just do as old Brigit says, and the two of you will be out of here and on your road before the week's out."

In this, as it happened, she was wrong.

Alexander ate what the boy brought him, fully resolved to get out of bed as soon as he had finished, and see if he could relieve his reluctant hostess of what must now be a decidedly tiresome guest. But either the knock on the head had been worse even than it felt, or there had been some sort of soporific drug in the drink the nurse had given him, for when he sat up and tried to rise, the room spun dangerously round him, and the feeling of nausea returned. He lay down again and shut his eyes. A little rest, yes, and then the world would hold steady and he would be himself again . . .

But when he woke once more it was dusk, almost dark, and he felt no inclination to move from his bed. His head still ached, and the arm throbbed. Peter, coming in (for the third time that day, though Alexander did not know it) with a bowl of broth and some fresh bread wrapped in a napkin, gave him a doubtful look, then set the things down and hurried out of the room, to frighten Brigit with the news that the young lord looked to him to be none too lively, and all set for a real bout of the fever such as had taken his, Peter's, uncle off that time he had fallen drunk into the moat and lain there for the whole night before anyone found him.

He was right enough about the fever, though it was brought about by some infection of the torn arm rather than by the chill of the water. For the next day or two Alexander was back in the hot and nightmare land of feverish visions, where night and day slid past in the same aching dreamland, and where faces and voices came and went unheeded and unrecognised.

Till he awoke, it seemed all of a sudden, clear-headed and with memory restored, to find that it was night again, and he was lying in a strange room, much larger than the other, and richly, even luxuriously furnished.

He was propped on silken pillows in a big bed with costly hangings, and set about the chamber were gilded chairs with brightly embroidered cushions, and carved chests, and bronze tripods holding candles of fine wax that smelled of honey. Against the wall opposite the bed's foot stood a table furnished with a white linen cloth and various vessels such as Brigit the nurse had used, but these vessels were made of silver and silver-gilt or perhaps gold. And stooping over the table, mixing something in one of the golden goblets, was the most beautiful woman that Alexander had ever seen.

She turned her head, saw him awake and watching her, and straightened from her task, smiling.

She was tall for a woman, and slender, but with a rich fullness of breast and hips and a suppleness of waist that her amber-coloured gown did little to hide. Her hair was dark and very long, hanging in thick braids as if ready for the night, but carefully bound with amber ribbon and tiny golden knots where jewels glittered. Her eyes, too, were dark, with a charming tilt of the lids at the outer corners, a tilt followed by the narrow dark brows. Another woman would have seen straight away that brows and eyelids were carefully drawn and darkened, and that the proud curves of the mouth were expertly reddened, but Alexander, gazing up weakly from his pillows, saw only a vision of beauty that would, he thought vaguely, surely vanish in a moment, and leave him with the old nurse, or the kind but unexciting Lady Luned.

She did not vanish. She came forward into the light cast by the sweet-smelling candles, and spoke.

"So the unfortunate traveller is awake? Good evening, sir. How is it with you now? No, no—" as he struggled to lift himself—"don't try to sit up. You've had a bad fever, and you must rest a while yet." So saying she laid a hand on his brow, a cool, strong hand that pressed him gently back against the pillows. No vision, certainly, but a real woman, and a very lovely one . . . This, thought Alexander hazily, this was how the adventure should have started, but no matter; that blessed deer had, in the best traditions of the old tales, brought him back to the Dark Tower and the bedchamber—was it her own?—of the lovely lady of all those boyhood dreams . . .

"You?" he said, and was dismayed at the sound of his own voice. Like a lamb bleating, he thought, and tried again. "Who are you?"

She went swiftly to the table to pick up the gold goblet and carry it back to the bedside. Stooping, she slid that cool hand behind his head and lifted it, helping him to drink.

"I am your nurse now, Alexander. When I heard what had happened I had you carried here, into my own chambers, where I could look after you myself. There is no one in the kingdoms who could care for you better. Come, drink."

The neck of her gown was loose against the creamy throat. As she stooped lower he could see her breasts, round and full, with the deep shadow between. He tore his gaze away and lifted his eyes to see her watching him. She was smiling. Confused, he tried to speak, but she shook her head at him, still smiling, and tilted the last drops to his mouth, then carried the empty goblet back to the table.

Her voice was cool and composed. "You will sleep again, and tomorrow the fever will be quite gone, and the arm healing. I dressed your hurts while you still slept. The foot will pain you for a while longer, and you must rest it. Now I shall send Brigit to you again, but I will see you in the morning."

Alexander, who knew he could never have asked this faery goddess to help him where he now needed to go, felt nothing but thankfulness as she set the goblet down and turned away. But there was something he had to know.

He said, hoarsely: "How did you know my name?"

That subtle little smile again, over her shoulder as she laid a hand to the door. She was really very lovely. "I see and I hear, and what I do not see and hear I know, from the smoke and the crystal and the voices in the dark. So good night, Alexander."

In spite of her care, or more probably because of it, a trace of the fever returned that night, and kept his mind fretting and alert. There was one person here in the Dark

Tower, and only one, who could look like that, and speak like that, and give orders for the stranger to be brought in and housed in these royal rooms. Queen Morgan the enchantress.

And how much more did she know, this witch who could look in the smoke and the crystal and listen to the voices in the dark?

FOUR

The
Pretty Pilgrim

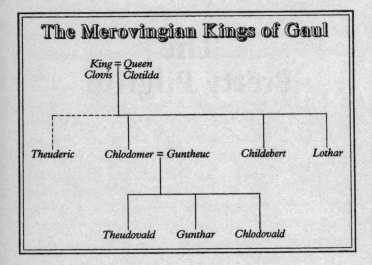

The Merovingian Kings of Gaul

King = Queen
Clovis | Clotilda

Theuderic   Chlodomer = Guntheuc   Childebert   Lothar

Theudovald   Gunthar   Chlodovald

17

Some four months earlier than this, on a cold, bright afternoon in January, Duke Ansirus sought his daughter out, and found her in her solar with Mariamne in attendance. The girls, who were supposed to be busy with their tapestry-work, were sitting together in the thin shaft of sunlight from the window, laughing at something. If Alice had been anything less than a duke's daughter, it might have been said that they were giggling. When the duke came in, the laughter stopped abruptly, and both girls rose and made their curtseys. Then Mariamne, at a glance from her mistress, bobbed another curtsey and left the solar.

Alice sat down again, and the duke pulled a chair nearer the window. In spite of the sunshine, and the warmth dealt out by a brazier, the room was chilly. He rubbed his hands together and cleared his throat, but before he could speak she said, demurely: "Yes, father."

"What do you mean, yes father? I've said nothing yet."

"No, but the wind is in the north, and the New Year is passing, and you are feeling the cold."

Her father knitted his brows and ducked his head forward, peering at her. With age he was getting short-sighted. "Well? And so?"

"So, with the castle as cold as a tomb and the draughts everywhere, it's time to go on pilgrimage again?"

He gave his dry chuckle. "Don't let Father Anselm hear you talking like that, my child! But you're right, of course. I do find myself thinking about the spring sunshine in the south, when I know I ought to think of nothing but my sins, and the hardships of the journey, and the prayers we shall offer at the other end."

"What sins?" asked his daughter affectionately. "I'm the one who does the sinning, and my thoughts just now are sin enough! I was just talking with Mariamne about the Holy Land, and how this might be the year we went again, and how I would enjoy visiting Rome again—that lovely comfortable house with the heated floors!—and the Damascus silks I'd be able to buy from that *souk* in Jerusalem. There's sin for you!"

"Don't jest about it, love."

He spoke gently, but she flushed and said quickly:

"Forgive me. But father, it's true. You're a saint, and God knows you've given me every chance to be one, too, but I'm still only a sinful girl who thinks more of—well, of this world and all the lovely things in it, than of the one to come."

"And of such things as marriage?" At her quick look he nodded, gravely. "Yes, child, that is what I came to talk about, not about journeyings and visitings and prayers."

She drew her breath in sharply, then sat back, waiting, folding her hands together in her lap, a meek gesture that did not deceive her father for a moment.

He said, carefully, as if testing her reactions: "You have passed your sixteenth birthday, Alice. It's an age when most girls are safely wedded, and looking to their own households and their families."

She said nothing, and he nodded again. "I know, my dear. We have spoken of this before, and you have been dutiful, but always begging me to wait, to wait another year . . . and then another. Now you must tell me why. You have no mother to advise you, but I will listen. Would you avoid marriage, child? Is it possible that you have begun to think about a convent?"

"No!" She spoke so sharply that he put his brows up in surprise, and she went on more gently: "No, father, it's not that. You know I could never be—I could never accept the holy life. And as for marriage, I've always known that some day I'll have to think of it, but—well, I have a household here, and a care, which is for you! May we not wait? Perhaps till I am turned seventeen? Then I promise I will obey you and let you settle my future"— she flashed him a smile, part affection, part mischief— "always providing that this young man you've chosen is handsome and brave—and landless, so he won't take me away, but will come here to live at Castle Rose!"

He did not return the smile, but spoke soberly: "Alice, my dear, God knows I would keep you with me if I might. But you know this thing must be settled sooner or later, if there is to be a sure future for either of us, or for any of our people here."

"What do you mean?"

The shaft of sunlight had shifted while they talked, and it now fell clear across his chair. In the sharp, cool winter's light she saw, suddenly, how old he looked. He was thinner, and a look of worry had pared the planes of his face, sharpening the bone structure and driving fresh lines between the eyes. His hair was quite grey.

"You're ill?" Her voice was curt with sudden fear, making the question sound like an accusation.

He shook his head. "No, no. I'm well enough. But some news has just come in, grave news. Did you not see the courier?"

"No. Mariamne said she had heard something, but—what news, father? Trouble?"

"Not for us, not directly. You were jesting just now about my choice of a husband for you . . . I think you know, from what we have said before, where the first choice might lie."

"With Drian? Yes. Has something happened to him?"

She spoke with a concern which was little more than formal. Neither she nor the duke had ever met with Drian. He was the younger brother of one of the High King's Companions, Lamorak. The latter had served recently with Drustan at the court of March of Cornwall. He and his brother were reputed to be good men and loyal servants of the High King.

The duke shook his head. "Again, not directly. But there have been sad doings in the south. There are matters of which I have never spoken to you, but no doubt you'll have heard the tales the local women tell about the High King's sister . . . ?"

He hesitated, and Alice said quickly: "Queen Morgan, that was put aside by the King of Rheged, and shut in some convent in Caer Eidyn? Yes, of course I knew that, everyone was talking about it. It was ages ago." She did not add that of course everyone had also talked, in detail, about the queen's adulterous liaison that had compounded her treachery and forced her husband to put her aside and hand her over to the King's justice.

"No, no," said the duke. "Not Morgan. Her sister Morgause, who was widow of King Lot of Orkney, and lived in the northern islands until the High King called her south to bring her sons to his court at Camelot. He has kept them in his service, but, for some trespass in the past, Queen Morgause was confined, like her sister, in a convent."

Alice was silent for a moment. Here again, she knew the story, such versions of it as had originally been allowed to come to a child's ears, and since then some further embellishments to a tale fast becoming folk-lore. It was said that, many years ago, when they were young, Morgause had lain with her half-brother Arthur, and had borne him a son, Mordred, who, known as the High King's "nephew," was now high in Arthur's trust, and close to both King and Queen at court. This in spite of the fact (it was also whispered) that Morgause had hated her half-brother, and had only let the boy live because of Merlin's prophecy that one day he would be Arthur's bane. Merlin, too, she hated, and had finally overstepped herself by trying to poison him. The old enchanter's magic had defeated her, and he had escaped with his life, but King Arthur had punished her by locking her away in the convent of Amesbury, on the edge of the Great Plain.

Alice, wondering what, if anything, the old tales of sorcery and plotting could have to do with her father, asked: "I knew of Queen Morgause's imprisonment at Amesbury, yes. You said she 'was confined'? Do you mean she has been freed? Or what has happened?"

"She has been killed there, and by her own son Gaheris." As Alice stared, shocked, the duke moved suddenly in his chair, slapping his hands down on the arms. "Here we are, discussing your marriage, and I am still dealing with you as if you were a child. Forgive me, my dear! Listen now, and I will tell you the whole. It's a shocking affair. Queen Morgause, even in a convent, and with her past sins to repent, contrived to take lovers. I do not know how, nor whom, but the latest of them was Lamorak. He was stationed nearby on the Plain, and he met the woman first when he was sent to Amesbury on King's business. It seems that he was honourable enough; he would have married her, and so it might be said that he had some right to her bed. Be that as it may, he was with her when Gaheris, one of her sons, visiting the convent privily at night to see his mother, found her with her lover, and, in a wild moment of rage, drew his sword and killed her. I am not clear about what happened then, but somehow he was restrained from attacking Lamorak, who later surrendered his sword to the High King and himself to the High King's mercy. He has been sent abroad. This for his own safety. The Orkney clan—Gaheris and his brothers—are wild folk, and the King is trying to prevent trouble among his knights. Gaheris has been banished, too." He drew a breath. "You see what this means."

"That Drian has gone abroad with his brother?"

"Not that, no. Not yet. He was at Drustan's place in Northumbria—he may be there still. But I am told that Gaheris has sworn, in spite of anything the High King can do, to hunt Lamorak down and kill him. And then in turn Lamorak's kin may look for vengeance. And so it will go on, blood crying for blood . . ." He sounded suddenly weary. "So there it is—and there is an end to our plans for the marriage with young Drian. I will not see my daughter or my house caught into a blood feud. We can only thank God that the news came in time. I had already written a letter, which would have gone north when the courier rides out again tomorrow. Now it must not go. So after all you have your respite, and we think again."

She bent her head, clasping her hands together in her lap. "I shall pray for them. For Lamorak, who meant no sin that we know of, and for Drian, who committed none."

There was a silence, while the duke stretched his hands to the warmth of the brazier, and Alice sat with bowed head.

She stirred at length, and looked about her. The quiet solar, with the brazier's glow and the thick curtains hiding the stone walls; the tapestry-frames, the baskets full of coloured wools, the spinning wheel, the harp in the corner. Her room, her everyday room, with the stair beyond the curtain, and her bedchamber opening from the landing above. The view beyond the window, of a terrace with its strip of garden, pretty even in winter, with the tubs of evergreen bushes and the herb beds. Beyond that the river, smooth-running and wide, which served as a moat, for pleasure rather than for defence, for who, in these peaceful days of Arthur's reign, need fear his neighbour? Not Duke Ansirus the Pilgrim, that devout and gentle man, who was loved by the local folk, and whose daughter, the Lady Alice, could ride anywhere within the bounds of the duchy in safety. Whose neighbours, in fact, would rally to their aid if the unthinkable happened, and an enemy threatened their peace.

But for the news the courier had brought, that peace might well have been broken. It was a chilling thought. The marriage with Drian had seemed a good one, both for herself ("a young man, landless, who will not take me away from home") and for the future of Castle Rose.

But even if the tragedy at Amesbury had not happened, what then? If Lamorak had married Queen Morgause, and Alice had been Drian's wife, what shadows of evil magic and past sins (the folk-tales had been specific enough) would have crept north to smear the edges of this loved land?

The sun had left the window. She turned to look out at the prospect that had always been so lovely in her eyes, and now, with shadow both real and imaginary veiling it, showed a thousand times more beautiful. Not to be lost, please, dear God. I will do anything to keep it, and ease my father's mind. Anything.

Looking again at her father sitting silent, an ageing grey man, in grey shadow, she thrust aside her own feeling of relief, and set out to comfort him.

"Nothing may come of this, father, no danger to Drian, or his family. Will you wait to hear what happens, or do you want to write now to Bannog Dun to see what Madoc has to say?"

The Madoc she referred to was keeper of a stronghold—too small to be called a castle—near the northern borders of Rheged. He was a distant cousin of Duke Ansirus, and related also to King Ban of Benoic. He was, in fact, the heir to Castle Rose in default of a male heir— a son born to Alice. His was a somewhat sideways claim—that is, legitimate, but through a younger son two generations back; however, it was a claim that might well stand, failing a better one. And in the direct line there was only Alice.

The duke stirred and straightened, looking, she was glad to see, relieved. "That is one of the things I came to ask you. It seems the best."

She smiled, saying, as lightly as she could: "Do I have a choice?"

"Of course."

"I remember a bit about Madoc, from when we were children. A strong boy, and bold. You've met him since then, father. What's he like?"

"Still strong and bold. A fighting man, but one, I think, to grow impatient with serving Benoic, and eager to claim land of his own." He looked at her gravely, and nodded. "Very well. I'll write. It could be a good choice, Alice. I'll show you the letter before the man rides north in the morning. But leave this now, shall we? I know I spoke of haste, and I would like this matter settled soon—but by that I mean within months rather than days. By winter will be soon enough."

This was genuine relief. She tried not to show it. "By winter? And this winter still with nearly three months to run?"

He smiled. "Yes, by next winter. You were right in your first guess, Alice. We go on pilgrimage in April. My last, before I go to my long—and longed-for—home at our own monastery of St. Martin here in Rheged ... Leaving you settled here, and wed, please God, with a strong sword to keep you." He turned a hand over in his lap. "You knew this was soon to come, my retirement. I don't ail, except that my bones creak a little, but I find I tire more easily, and more and more in the winter months do I find it tedious to ride out and care for our lands and people. I'll be glad to hand my cares over to a younger man, and retire to the peace of the monastic life. We've talked these things over many times."

"I know. But it's like my marriage; it had to come, but never soon." She straightened in her chair and smiled

back at him. "So that's settled! You write to Count
Madoc, and meantime we set sail for Jerusalem. And at
least if I'm to be a bride, you will see the real necessity of
my buying those Damascus silks!"

He laughed. "You may buy all you like, my dear, but
not in the *souks*! We are not going to Jerusalem. It's
Tours again. Will you mind?"

"Not a bit. I like Tours. But why?"

"I would like to pay a last visit to the shrine of St.
Martin before taking my vows in his monastery here.
I've had this in mind for some time, and have been wondering what the situation was over there, but now, *deo
gratias*, we can make our plans. The courier has brought
a letter from Queen Clotilda. Here it is." He handed her
the scroll.

It was a brief letter. The old queen hoped that, as Duke
Ansirus had said on their last meeting, he still wished to
make pilgrimage in this year to the holy shrine of the
blessed Bishop Martin. If so, in spite of the very real
threat of war, he could rest assured that his party would
travel in safety, and that the duke himself, "and the Lady
Alice, if she is with you," would be lodged with the
queen, whose pleasure it would be, and so on . . .

Alice handed the letter back. "It was good of her to
remember and to write. Yes, I'd like to see Tours again. I
wonder if the boys will be there? Theudovald must be—
what?—ten or eleven by now, I suppose. Probably
training for war already. This war! What must it be like
to live always with the 'very real threat' of it?"

The duke smiled. He was looking better already. Alice
thought: the prospect of travel always pleased him, but it
was not only that. Her marriage, the settlement of the
estate; yes, that, too. But most of all—and she accepted it

with sadness—the knowledge that soon, now, the time would come for his final dedication to God's service.

He tucked the scroll back into his sleeve. "Not many years ago, and that was the case here in Britain, too. I suppose one gets used to anything, and I doubt if the Franks would be grateful for peace even if it were offered! I gather from the courier—and these King's men hear everything—that it's true that the Burgundian war looks imminent. When did it not? But it's also true that the roads are still open, and pilgrims safe enough. And with Queen Clotilda's protection . . . Yes, I will certainly go, but if you would rather not—?"

"Of course I would like to go! It may be my last journey, too, and in any case my last chance to go with you."

This time next spring, she was thinking, this time next spring . . . My father still alive, please God, and happy in your service, and myself still here in Castle Rose, and sitting with Mariamne making baby-clothes for Madoc's child?

She looked into her father's anxious eyes and smiled brilliantly, reassuringly.

"Then let's get those letters off to Count Madoc, and to the queen, and start thinking about summer silks! And our souls, too, of course!"

Her father laughed, kissed her, and went to set his scribe to writing the fateful letters.

18

Arrangements for the "last pilgrimage" were soon under way. One precaution was taken; the party would not this time risk the long overland journey through Frankish territory, but would take ship right to the mouth of the Loire, and, changing vessels there, sail clear up the river to Tours itself.

Nothing more had been heard from Queen Clotilda. Nor from Madoc, who, it appeared, was abroad somewhere, but who—said the message from his man of affairs—"would of a certainty be more than happy to discuss the duke's proposal; the alliance was one which had, it was well known, been for a long time near to his heart."

"I'm sure it has," said Ansirus, a little drily, and left it at that.

They embarked in mid-April. The voyage was uneventful, the weather calm, turning steadily from spring to early summer as they sailed south. They dropped anchor briefly at Kerrec, in Less Britain, and stayed there for some days, resting at the house of a kinsman. From there Duke Ansirus sent a message to Queen Clotilda, letting her know of his party's progress. This as a mere matter of courtesy, but when at length their ship docked safely at Nantes, the busy estuary port of the Loire, they were surprised and flattered to find an escort waiting for them, a strong troop of armed men bearing the old queen's colours, and sent by her, their officer said, to help the British party re-embark on the smaller ship that would take them to Tours, and to accompany them there in safety.

"Safety?" Ansirus' question came a little sharply. "What danger could there be to us on the river?"

"None, sir." The officer's voice was smooth, like his neat, well-barbered person. No Frank this, but a Roman by his accent and bearing; and his troop bore, unmistakably, the Roman marks of discipline and order. Following his upward glance they saw that the standard at the masthead, like the troop's colours, sported the queen's emblem.

"Then this is Queen Clotilda's own ship?"

"Indeed, sir. The river-boats that normally ply here make half a dozen calls between here and Tours—a tedious end to your long voyage." His eyes slid to Alice in a kind of hesitating, sideways look, then away again. She had the impression that he changed what he had been about to say, and added instead: "When the queen had news of your coming she wished to make the journey easier for you. The *Merwing* will carry you swiftly and in comfort, and once in Tours, my lord, you are to be lodged in the castle itself. The queen is not—that is, she does not stay in her own palace at present."

"We are indebted to your mistress for her care and courtesy. She is well, I take it?" The duke spoke calmly, adding polite enquiries after the health of the other members of the royal family, but through it all, and through the briefly formal replies of the officer, Alice could sense anxiety on the one hand, and on the other, a growing and even grim reserve. As soon as the British party was safely embarked on the trim little royal ship, Ansirus and the officer, who gave his name as Marius, went below together, leaving Alice with Mariamne on deck. They stood together at the rail, watching the sunlit countryside slip by.

After the sea voyage, this promised to be a journey of sheer delight. The river, smooth and majestically wide, flowed in vast curves through country rich in forest and vineyard and pastureland. From time to time they passed villages—settlements, rather, with some important-looking stone-built house or grange surrounded by orchards and well-tended gardens, supporting and supported by a cluster of wooden or turf-built huts which presumably housed the servants and slaves who worked the estate. It all looked very peaceful, the blossoming orchards and lush gardens, the rows of bee-hives with their straw skeps showing golden in the sun, a flock of white geese grazing by the river's edge, a boy with clappers scaring away birds from the vineyards where the young growth showed green. Here and there a church could be seen, a small structure of wood or wattle crouching well within the protective walls of a settlement. A rich and lovely country, but where one had to go chin on shoulder for fear of one's neighbour; a country (thought Alice) which had had no Arthur, duke of battles, to bring its warring kings together, and seal its beauty and wealth with peace.

They passed a wharf, and then in a short while another, small ports each with a single jetty serving some settlement that crowded at the water's edge, where river-boats were moored, and where ferries plied. Here there was bustle. Waggons were drawn up at the wharfs, or moved slowly along the roads, pulled by their yokes of white oxen. The fact that all the waggons were heading the same way—westward—or that most of them seemed to be piled high with what looked like household goods and furnishings, did not mean anything to Alice, as she stood dreaming in the sunshine by the ship's rail, but she did wonder what her father and the queen's officer were taking so long to talk over below decks, and—a fleeting thought this—wished that, marriage or no marriage, they were all safely home again.

It must have been a full hour later, and the *Merwing* was steering carefully between islands shaded with gilt-green willows and alive with nesting birds, when Duke Ansirus came on deck again to his daughter's side, motioning Mariamne out of hearing. One look at his face set Alice asking anxiously: "Father? Is there bad news? What is it?"

"Bad enough." He laid a reassuring hand over hers on the ship's rail. "No, not for us, child, I hope; we are still pilgrims, and this is a Christian country, may the good St. Martin bear witness! But it will be a brief pilgrimage. This time the talk of war was no mere cry of 'Wolf!' There has been fighting already, and we cannot guess what more is still to come."

"Fighting? With Burgundy?"

"Yes."

"But—oh, father, this is terrible! And poor Queen Clotilda—"

"No poor about it," said the duke, curtly, for him. "She herself planned it. She persuaded her sons—no, drove them to it. I believe she is still fighting King Clovis' long battle to bring all Gaul under Salian rule, but that is not the lure she used to bring the Frankish kings, her own three sons and Theuderic, together against Burgundy."

"Then what?"

"What would appeal to these wolves? A crusade for Christ?" Ansirus spoke with a kind of sad and bitter contempt. "Hardly! No, she called for revenge."

"Revenge against Burgundy?" exclaimed Alice. "For what? I thought she herself was born a princess of Burgundy."

"Indeed. And Sigismund of Burgundy—he and his brother Godomar—murdered her mother and father. And would have killed her, too, doubtless, if Clovis had not seen her and demanded her hand."

"But surely—all those years ago—"

"The stories are still told, and they are tales not easily forgotten. And how could Clotilda, Christian or not, forget?"

Below the ship's rail a flight of small wading-birds flew with glinting wings and a chorus of sweet calling. They were flying westwards. Alice watched them almost wistfully; her instinct had been true.

"So what has happened?" she asked. "You say there has already been fighting?"

"There has. Marius—the officer—told me of it. It's a long tale and a sad one, but I'll be brief. The Frankish kings joined to attack Sigismund and Godomar, and defeated them. Godomar fled, but King Sigismund was taken prisoner. It was Chlodomer who took him."

"Prince Theudovald's father?"

"The same. He held Sigismund for a while, with his wife and family, somewhere near Orleans."

" 'For a while'?"

At her quick look he nodded. His look was grim. "Yes.

You might guess at it. He had them all murdered, horribly, the children too. Marius told me the whole. I shall not burden you with it, but with its consequences I must, and they are evil enough."

She listened in silence as he told her the rest. It seemed that as soon as the victorious Frankish kings had left the field of battle and gone home each to his own kingdom, the surviving Burgundian ruler, Godomar, had rallied what troops he had left, and marched to reclaim his lands, and to take, in his turn, revenge for his brother's murder. It was not yet clear what had happened; there were tales of treachery, and it was even rumoured that the eldest of the Frankish kings, the bastard Theuderic, had allied himself with Godomar against his brothers. Whatever the truth, in the ensuing battle Chlodomer was killed, and his head stuck up on a spear's point for all to see. In spite of this, or possibly because of it, the Franks rallied, and after fierce fighting put Godomar utterly to rout, and drove him once again to flight.

"So it is to be hoped that things will soon be settled," finished the duke. "According to Marius all is well in Tours, though of course since the news of King Chlodomer's death the folk in Orleans have been anxious, and some have travelled to Tours for refuge, and the town is crowded and full of rumour."

"Theudovald?" asked Alice, who had hardly heard the last part of this. "What about Theudovald? He'll be king now, I suppose? Or is he—was he in the fighting?"

"No, he's safe. He's in Paris. Queen Clotilda took the three boys north as soon as the news came of Chlodomer's death. King Childebert will support his nephews. He is planning to declare Theudovald king."

The islands had sunk out of sight in the ship's wake.

The river had widened again. To either side was the same rich, calm prospect of trees in their spring green, of orderly vines, of water-meadows with their grazing cattle. But this time Alice, leaning with elbows on the ship's rail, saw none of it. She was remembering the child Theudovald, who was heir to all this, and with it the legacy of violence and treachery that was the inheritance of the long-haired kings.

"So if Queen Clotilda is to stay in Paris till the crowning, we won't see her or the boys?"

"It seems so. Eventually, of course, she must bring Theudovald south, and there will be more ceremonial, but she will be much occupied, and will hardly look for us to stay for it. We can plead her affairs and our own, and leave as soon as we can arrange it. Unless—would you want to stay to see the boy crowned in Orleans?"

"No. No, let's go home!" She straightened up and turned to face him. "It's a dreadful story. I liked it when we were here before, but—father, how can one understand these people? The queen—she seemed so clever and so—so elegant—to start such a war, for such a reason! Is she out of her mind? Or sick?"

"I asked the same question, but rather more tactfully. It seems she has not been well, but nothing serious, some disorder of the stomach, brought on, says Marius, by the queen's new habits of austerity. It appears she has taken to fasting and very plain living, a sort of penance, it's said, in honour of the saint. And she wears rough home-spun and gives her wealth away to beggars. A changed lady—but quite sane, as far as anyone with such a driving purpose can be judged sane." The duke's hand closed once more, reassuringly, over his daughter's. "Be easy, child. These evil things will not touch us, and please God the boy will win free of them. For ourselves you may be sure that this will be a brief pilgrimage! Once we have prayed at the saint's tomb, and spoken with the bishop, we will write our excuses to the queen, and set our faces for home."

19

The royal castle at Tours was an imposing stronghold. It was stone-built, its walls grafted into the rock at the very edge of the river, which here flowed deep and wide to make a forbidding natural boundary between the kingdoms of Orleans and Paris. The castle was encircled by a moat, the water being let in by sluices from the river. The main gate was approached by a wooden bridge only wide enough for two horsemen riding abreast.

But once inside, the rather threatening approach could be forgotten. Alice and her father were housed in pleasant chambers facing south, and the furnishings were comfortable, even, in Alice's room, pretty. The sun was warm on the stone of the window-sill, and the place was full of light. Swallows, here already from the south, skimmed and twittered outside in the bright air.

From this height the little town, clustered beyond the moat, looked clean and peaceful and toylike, with its red clay roofs and its melon-patches and flowering trees crowding right up to the walls of the great basilica which had been built a hundred years or so ago to shelter the shrine of the saint. It seemed a peaceful scene, no hint of threats to come, no sense that this was a border town of a suddenly weakened kingdom. The gates in the town

walls were open, and people, beasts, carts bound for
market, tiny in the distance, were moving through them.

But Alice, sitting by the window as Mariamne brushed
out her hair, thought without regret that what should have
been a pleasant and comfortable pilgrimage must be cut
short. A day or two of rest, and her father's devotions
paid, and they would begin the long journey home. They
had been assured by Marius that the *Merwing* would be
at their disposal whenever they needed her.

She sighed. "Thank you, Mariamne. My gown now.
No, not the blue, I mayn't get the chance to wear that, but
see to the skirt, will you? I knew that stuff would crush.
Get me the fawn with the russet overdress, and the brown
cloak with the hood. I think my father wants to go
straight to the shrine now. We'd better hurry."

"Yes, madam. The fawn and the brown cloak. Here
they are, and they've travelled well. Don't worry about
the blue dress; I'll get the creases out easily enough.
Such a pity the queen's not here, isn't it? I was looking
forward to seeing you in the blue."

"It hardly matters, all things considered." Alice,
watching the maid as she smoothed the clothes laid out
on the bed, saw that her eyes looked red, as if she had
been crying. "What is it, Mariamne? It's all very
dreadful, but there's nothing for us to be afraid of—"

"I'm not afraid. It's not that."

"What, then?"

"It's nothing, madam."

Alice suddenly understood. When she had told Mariamne that their place of pilgrimage would be Tours
rather than Jerusalem, she had been surprised at the girl's
apparent pleasure, but the answer had been simple.

"Of course!" she said. "You were looking forward to

meeting your fellow-countryman Jeshua again, weren't you? Well, you couldn't expect him to be here in the king's castle, but I'll see that we make time to go to the queen's palace, never fear! Do you know if he's still in her service?"

"Yes, madam, he is. I asked. But he's not in Tours. He's gone to Paris with the queen. He's *domesticus* now, manages the whole household, a grand job, very important, they say. He would have to go with her. I suppose he'll be in charge of all the fine doings when the young prince is crowned, but we won't still be here then, will we?"

"I'm afraid not. I'm sorry."

"It can't be helped." Mariamne, with a little shrug, turned to her work again. "And if all tales be true, the sooner we're back home the better! If you'll just sit for a moment, my lady, and let me fix your veil for you ... There, that's it. How long do you think my lord your father will want to stay here?"

"Not long, I think. Is that Berin at the door? I mustn't keep my father waiting."

Mariamne knelt to smooth the russet folds and settle the girdle at her mistress's waist.

"Do you want me with you?"

Alice shook her head. She knew that Mariamne, whom she had always allowed to wait outside the Christian places of worship her mistress attended, had found the courts of St. Martin's basilica distressing, with their throngs of beggars, diseased, crippled and starving, fighting one another for the alms thrown to them by the godly, and crowding with threats and curses round anyone obliged to go there unattended. "No need. We're to be escorted. There. Do I look sober and chaste, Mariamne?"

Mariamne privately thought that her mistress looked pretty enough to turn a thousand heads, even in church, but she merely smiled and curtseyed, opening the chamber door for Alice to pass through.

It was a stately little procession that set out across the narrow bridge spanning the moat. As well as the duke and his attendants and Alice's waiting-women, there were four fully armed guards, and at the rear of the party walked two robed and cowled figures, Father Anselm the duke's chaplain, and one of the queen's priests, Brother John, their heads bent and their hands folded decorously out of sight in the heavy sleeves. The streets were crowded, but the presence of the men-at-arms, and possibly of the priests, kept the beggars and touts at bay, and most people went busily about their own affairs; but at the street corners there were gatherings, heads together, and anxious looks. Tours was safe, though the tide of war had not yet withdrawn; peace was not yet here in people's minds. But nowhere did there seem to be the distress that might have been expected for the death—the hideous death—of the people's king. A few loaded waggons were heading out of the gates, this time eastwards— the fugitives from Orleans thankfully returning home. One king dead, another to come; as long as their homes were safe what did it matter? Alice reached the church with a prayer for young Theudovald already in her heart.

The beauty of the chanting, the familiar comfort of the ritual, served both to soothe and smooth away the thoughts of death and the strange and violent future awaiting the boy she had known. She lost herself, as she had always loved to do, in the effort of prayer and in her own kind of communication with a God with whom she had always been on familiar terms. At one point in the service she stole a hand out to touch her father's sleeve, and his hand came quickly over hers for a moment. The last pilgrimage together. After this—for him, his long dream of peace; for her, marriage, and whatever came with it . . .

Forget it. The future was God's; this was now, her father beside her, and a ship waiting to take them both home.

20

They stayed for eight days.

The duke would have left sooner, but Alice could see that the long journey had tired him, so she persuaded him to rest, and, for the first two or three days, to make their visits to the shrine as brief as was acceptable. He was the more easily persuaded because he found that Bishop Ommatius was away for some days in Orleans, presumably over matters connected with the coming crowning of Theudovald. Ansirus and the bishop had met several times on the previous pilgrimage, and liked one another; since that time they had once or twice exchanged letters, and before his departure for Orleans the bishop had left a message begging Ansirus not to leave Tours before he himself could return.

Though the town was humming with rumour like an overturned bee-skep, the pilgrims were obviously in no danger. The men-at-arms who had accompanied them on the *Merwing* escorted them daily to the shrine, and (as Mariamne, awed, informed her mistress) kept guard over their rooms at night. In the absence of host or hostess, no use was made of the royal apartments or the great hall of the castle; their meals were served in a pleasant gallery overlooking the town and the southern slopes of the valley, and the major domo himself, an elderly man with a permanently worried expression, oversaw the men and women who served them. Their only company, apart from the duke's own priest, Father Anselm, was Brother John, who (to his obvious regret) had been left to his duties at home when the queen and the young princes travelled to Paris. Brother John was young enough, and human enough, to find Alice's presence something of a consolation, and for her part, since he was witty and easy-mannered, she enjoyed his company at table. But she could not help thinking that this last pilgrimage, in spite of the promise—threat, even—of excitement, seemed likely to be as lonely for her as Jerusalem.

They had been in Tours for six days when Bishop Ommatius returned from Orleans, and an invitation came for the duke to visit him the next day and remain to dine. Since their stay had so far been uneventful, Ansirus was easily persuaded to let Alice spend the day as she pleased, shopping for her silks and riding out, guarded as usual, to see the countryside. The impending festivities in Orleans had made sure that the mercers' shops were piled high with rich stuffs, and Alice soon found what she wanted; then, with Mariamne and the men-at-arms in due attendance, she rode out of the town gates and along the track to the queen's palace.

It was as she remembered it, but rather smaller. The pigs still grunted in their sties; cattle lifted incurious heads from their grazing; sheep and goats crowded the riders' horses in the narrow lane, and a gipsy-looking child was herding geese across the courtyard where Alice and Theudovald had run to escape their guardians. But there were changes. Though the servants' quarters were still busy, there were no soldiers there, and in the

deserted armoury there was no stock of weapons. Nor—
what they were mainly looking for—was there any sign
of Jeshua. It was obvious, from Mariamne's downcast
expression, that she had hoped at least for news of him,
but all they got was the assurance (from one of the stew-
ards remaining there) that he was still with the queen in
Paris, and was likely to go straight to Orleans with her
when she travelled south with the new king.

Late that night Alice was wakened from sleep by a soft
touch on her shoulder and a hurried whisper.

"My lady. My lady! Wake up, please!"

"Mariamne?" Alice, fully awake in an instant, sat up in
the bed, her mind racing to the worry that these days was
constantly present. "Something's wrong? What is it? Is
my father ill?"

"No, no. It's all right, don't be alarmed. But he's just
come back from the bishop's house, and he sent me to
wake you. He wants to talk to you."

"Quickly, then, my bedgown. Yes, that one will do.
And light those candles, will you?"

Alice ran to the door and opened it. The duke was
waiting outside, still hooded and cloaked from his walk
home from the bishop's house. He had thrown the hood
back, and her anxious look at his face told her that the
news, whatever it was, was very bad indeed.

"Father? Come in . . . No, keep your cloak, it's chilly.
Mariamne, that rug from the bed, please. Sit here, father,
let me put it round you . . . You're cold. Shall Mariamne
heat a posset?"

"No, no. I had more than enough to drink at dinner.
I'm sorry to disturb you like this, Alice, but the matter is
urgent. Tell your woman to go back to bed. I must talk to

you alone. Don't look so frightened, girl—" this to Mariamne, hovering wide-eyed by the door. "None of us is in
danger. Go to bed now, and see that you wake your mistress in good time in the morning."

When Mariamne had gone he put out a hand and drew
Alice towards him. She sank down on the footstool
before his chair. In spite of his reassuring words to the
maid, she could see trouble in his face, and feel it in the
taut grip of his hand.

"What is it, father? What has happened?"

"A messenger came to Ommatius, one of his secret
couriers. All these high-ranking clergy and nobles use
spies—it's easy to see why. The man brought news from
Paris, and I'm afraid it is bad. It could not be worse. The
boys are dead."

The word fell like a blow, stunning belief. When at last
she spoke, the words could barely be heard.

"But father . . . The boys? The princes? Chlodomer's
sons? And—all of them?"

"All of them, poor children, murdered. Yes, it was
murder. Being who they were, of course it was. I'm
sorry."

Alice's head was bowed in her hands. She was remembering the sunny day not so long ago, and the two children running up through the dusty vines to sit chatting on
the wall where the lizards played in the sun, as the
queen's guards watched from below.

"Theudovald . . . He must have been only about ten, or
eleven now. Still so young, and looking forward to
Orleans, and being crowned there." She looked up. "He
might have been a good king, father. Queen Clotilda had
brought him up, and she—But where was she? I thought
she was in Paris with the boys?"

"She was, but one gathers that she was powerless to help them. Ommatius' courier had no details, just the facts, some garbled tale from a frightened servant. All he knows is that King Lothar somehow persuaded King Childebert that he must get rid of the boys; possibly with some sort of promise that the three surviving brothers would share out Chlodomer's kingdom between them. Lothar has married Chlodomer's widow, Queen Guntheuc—yes, the boys' mother—so the boys were a threat to him whatever happened. Or so these folk would see it." He sounded weary, too weary for bitterness or condemnation. "One might have expected something like this, but it's hard to credit, even here."

"But Queen Clotilda?" insisted Alice. The tale, told like this, in the silent dark lit only by the guttering pair of candles, was not believable. "She controlled the family, or seemed to? Lothar and Childebert—they obeyed her before. So why this, now?"

"When she called them to war, yes, they obeyed her then. But this . . . We cannot know how it happened, but it seems that Clotilda was tricked into letting Lothar get his hands on the boys. All that the servant—the informant—knew was that the princes were taken to the king's palace on the excuse of being prepared for the crowning, and there stabbed to death. Ommatius' courier left straight away, before the news got out and the gates were locked. That's all we know; the rest is guesswork; but it's true the boys are dead. The man saw it."

He fell silent, and Alice did not speak. What was there to say? The distress she felt was not so much for Theudovald, whom she had known so briefly, but somehow for the evil that is there in the world, so close even to the innocent and the good. Who, at ten years old, could deserve to die? And at the hands of those he trusted? And the other two were younger still . . .

She shivered, and reached again for her father's hand. "You should go to bed, father. I'll wake Berin and he can heat a bedstone for your feet. And in the morning—"

"In the morning we go," said the duke. "It would be foolish to delay longer. We must go while the *Merwing* is still at our disposal. I have sent to the master to tell him to make ready to sail tomorrow. Now, my dear, try to get some sleep, and tell your woman in the morning to pack your things and be ready to embark before noon. We will go while we may."

They embarked shortly before noon next day and, from the deck of the little ship, watched without regret as the roofs and blossoming trees and the turrets of Tours sank back and out of sight.

21

All afternoon the breeze blew, light but steady, and the *Merwing* held on her way. Alice stayed on deck with her father, watching the countryside slip by, and looking to see, in the little settlements they passed, any signs of disturbance. But all seemed peaceful. Twice they were hailed from one of the small wharves, but only, it seemed, as a gesture of greeting: someone, perhaps, who knew the ship's master; they saw the latter lift an arm in response.

Towards evening the breeze died down, and their progress slowed. The river had widened, and islands lay here and there; the ship had to pick her way carefully through the channels between them. A servant approached to ask if the evening meal should be served, and they went below.

The royal cabin was not large, but it was comfortable almost to luxury. Queen Clotilda's new austerity had not yet found its way there. Two smaller cabins lay forward of it; in one of these Alice had her bed, with a pallet nearby for Mariamne; the duke slept in the other. As on their former voyage, guards would be set on deck at the head of the companionway.

Evening drew down, and clouds, massing in the west,

brought darkness early. The *Merwing* was still making her way slowly between the islands which, with their willows and thickets of alder, showed only like darker clouds floating on the water.

Alice retired soon after supper was done. Mariamne, who had been understandably horrified, and also very frightened, at what Alice had told her of the boys' murder, seemed to have forgotten her fears in the relief of going home; she was, indeed, inclined to be merry at the difficulties of attending her mistress in such cramped quarters, as she helped Alice undress and into her night clothing, brushed the long, shining hair, and then, having tidied the cabin as best she could, retired herself to the pallet no more than arm's-length from her mistress's bed. In a very short time she was asleep.

Alice did not find sleep come so easily. She lay on her back, listening to the creaking of timber and the sounds of water lapping along the ship's side, her eyes on the small glow of the riding-light outside the square port-hole; smoky yellow light, patched with black shadows, that swayed and swung across the cabin ceiling. She moved restlessly, trying to hold her imagination back from the pictures that kept printing themselves on her brain: the three young princes, children still and surely blameless, who, thinking themselves safe and held in honour, had left their grandmother's protection and gone trustfully to their uncle's house and the foulest of murders . . .

Prayer helped, and the thought of home, and eventually she must have dozed, because when she next opened her eyes the pattern of light on the ceiling had changed. It was brighter and steadier. No sounds came now from on deck, but very near, close under where she lay, came a new sound; something bumping gently against the ship's side.

Then voices, kept low; men's voices, whispering, but echoing from the water, and carried up through the open port. Then the soft slap of rope against the ship's side, and the creak and strain of the ladder as someone climbed it.

Alice sat up and threw back the rugs. Mariamne, undisturbed, slept on. Alice took the three steps to the port-hole and stretched on tiptoe to peer out.

Her cabin, on the starboard side, looked straight out over a narrow stretch of water towards a sizeable island thick with trees. The *Merwing* hardly seemed to be moving at all; the island seemed to float, still, black on smooth water.

But directly below the port-hole there were ripples, ringing out edged with a faint apricot shimmer from the riding-light. A boat lay close under the ship's side, and, a little way to the right of the port-hole, a rope ladder hung down. A man stood in the boat, holding the ladder steady for the climber. She tried to lean out, straining upward to see, but he must already have reached the deck. The ladder, released, came snaking down, and slid into the water with hardly a splash. The boatman dragged it in, piling it anyhow in a heap, then, with no more than a wave of the arm, thrust the boat away from the ship's side and propelled it with silent oars to be lost in the dense shadow of the island trees.

Alice snatched up her bedgown, belted it quickly round her, failed to find her slippers, and ran barefoot out of the cabin to seek her father.

The door of his cabin was open. The bulkhead lantern was lit, and showed an empty bed. She ran for the companionway, where the guards ought to be awake and on station.

Someone was coming down the stairs. Not the duke; a tall man, moving carefully, his cloak wrapped round some bulky bundle carried in his arms.

He blocked the stairway. She backed, drew breath to call out, and then stopped as he spoke quietly, under his breath.

"Lady Alice? Little maid?"

As he came into the edge of the lantern's glimmer she knew him.

"Jeshua!"

He looked weary, and there was a smear of mud on his face. He smelled of sweat and horses and dank water. He was smiling.

"The same. By your leave, lady. This is your father's bedchamber?" He went past her and stooping, laid his burden, still close-wrapped, on the duke's bed.

"What are you doing here? What's happening? Where's my father? And what is that?"

The questions poured out, as if a dam had broken that had held back the tensions of the last night and day.

He answered only two of them, but they were enough.

"Your father is on deck, talking with the master. And this"—indicating the motionless bundle on the bed—"this is Chlodovald, King of Orleans, whose brothers, as you know, were killed, and who, by your leave, is going home with you."

22

She stared at Jeshua for a breathless moment, feeling the blood rushing up into her face.

"Chlodovald? Prince Chlodovald? We were told they were all dead!"

"The two eldest are. We managed to smuggle the third boy away. Now if you—"

Her hands flew to her cheeks. She swung round to look at the motionless lump in the bed. "Is he all right? Was he hurt?"

"No, no. He's asleep. It's been a long journey and a hard one, and he's very young. He's been dead to everything for the last hour or more. Now, Lady Alice, I must go and talk to your father. He's above, with the master. I'm glad you woke. If you of your goodness would stay here with the boy, in case he should wake, and wonder where he is? He's a brave little boy, but he must be very frightened."

"Of course I'll stay with him. Ah, we're under way again. The master expected this?"

"He hoped. We managed to send word ahead, so he has been watching for us. Now by your leave—?"

"Of course."

She watched him take the steps to the deck two at a

time, heard a softly spoken word, presumably to one of the guards, and he was gone. She tiptoed across to the bedside and stooped over the boy.

In the glimmer of the tiny bud of light from the lantern she could see nothing clearly. He lay half curled up, just as Jeshua had laid him down, the thick folds of the cloak covering him completely, but for the face. He was lying turned away from the light, and she leaned closer to look. A pale forehead, fair brows and closed eyes with fair, curtaining lashes. A childish mouth and determined chin. The gleam of a long strand of hair, yellow as gold, escaping from the folds of the cloak—she was looking at Theudovald again, at six years old, the Merwing arrogance and drive lost in the deep sleep of childhood. Chlodovald, who had been a baby last time she was in Tours. Whose brothers had been murdered; whose mother had married the murderer. Who must have learned, in the most brutal fashion, to trust nobody, to fear everyone. But by God's mercy, and through the loyalty of one or two servants, he was here, and safe.

She sank to her knees by the bed, and, her first instinct in this miraculous moment, sent a prayer of thankfulness in the wake of her earlier, troubled devotions. Then, the boy still sleeping, she settled herself to watch till Jeshua or her father should come.

Time passed slowly. Eager to know what had happened, what was to happen, Alice found the waiting hard. Once the sleeping child stirred, and murmured something, but sank back into sleep again. Faint sounds came from time to time from above, but only the normal sounds of the ship by night; the creak of timber, the snap of a sail, the soft murmur of water along the sides. They must be moving faster now. The air that filtered down the companionway was fresher. She wondered if the *Merwing* had won clear of the islands and into the wide waters of the estuary. The master had said that they would be in Nantes by morning, and that there should be a British ship there to carry them home to safety.

The cabin's single chair was just under the port-hole. Clutching her bedgown round her, she knelt up on the cushioned seat, and gripping the sill, pulled herself up to peer out at the darkness.

The cabin itself was so dimly lit that her eyes adjusted almost at once to the dark outside, and she could see reasonably well. They were not yet in open water; land—she could not tell if it was the shore, or just another island—was sliding past, dark on dark. No lights anywhere, and now even the few stars were gone. The breeze was freshening, and the water slapped and gurgled along the ship's side.

It drowned the sounds that might have warned her. She did not hear the soft word spoken with the guard on deck, or the padding of swift feet down the stairway. There was a quick step behind her. Before she could even turn her head, powerful hands seized her from behind. A hand jammed itself over her mouth, stifling any sound she might try to make, and she was dragged bodily from the chair, held hard against her assailant's body. Dim though the light was, it showed the thin gleam of a knife raised to strike.

He was very strong, and the folds of her bedgown hampered her, but she struggled and kicked out. She heard him give what sounded like a grunt of surprise, and his grip slackened momentarily, so that she twisted sharply in his grip, clawing up for his face with her one free hand, and lashing out as best she could with her feet. Barefooted as she was, she could hardly have hoped to hurt him, but she caught him off balance, and as the two of them lurched across the little cabin towards the bed, one wild and random kick landed squarely on the sleeping child.

There was a gasp, a jerk of movement from the bed, then a shout in a high young voice, ringing to rouse the ship, "Guard! Guard! To me!" and the quick flash of another knife as the boy flung himself at them and stabbed down, hard.

Alice found herself on the floor, breathless, tousled, and bruised, but unhurt. Above her a curse, and another cry. It might have gone hard for the child, but the guards had heard. There was an answering shout, then the crashing of armed feet as the two men hurled themselves down the stairway and into the cabin. One of them trod on her hand as he jumped to seize the attacker. The latter made no resistance. He had dropped his knife and was clutching his right arm with fingers through which blood dripped. Someone else came running with a lantern, and the place was suddenly filled with noise and light. Standing on the bed, cloak thrown off and fair hair flying, the child Chlodovald, dagger in hand and blue eyes blazing, looked ready to strike again.

Then the duke was there, on his knees beside her.

"Alice! Child! Are you hurt?"

"No. No, I'm all right. Really I am, father. What happened? Who is he?"

"One of the crew, I think. A servant." He helped her up and set her back in the chair. "That's how he got past the guards. They knew him. He told them I had sent him."

She looked up, still dizzy with the struggle and the tossing light and shadow and the noise in the crowded cabin. The boy was shouting something in the Frankish tongue, sounding alarmed and angry, and two men—it was Jeshua and the ship's master—were trying to calm him and, presumably, explain where he was and that the danger was past. The assassin, a thickset young man whom she vaguely remembered having seen somewhere about the ship, was in the grip of the two guards.

"He was going to kill the prince?"

"It would seem so. They'll soon find out when they question him. No, stay still, my dear." He pressed her gently back into the cushions of the chair, and straightened, lifting his voice above the chaos in the little cabin.

"You men. Take him up now." This to the guards holding the attacker.

"Wait!"

It was Chlodovald, still standing on the bed, and by this keeping a commanding height. Shaken and disoriented though he must have been, waking among strangers in a strange place to find murder still stalking him, that was past, and he was himself again, a Merwing prince whose first instinct was for revenge. He had no attention, now, for anyone but the prisoner.

"You were paid for this? By whom?"

The man, scared and sullen, shook his head and muttered something unintelligible, but as one of the guards raised a hand the duke spoke sharply.

"Not here! By your leave, Prince Chlodovald. Let me present myself. I am Duke Ansirus of Rheged in Britain. I and my daughter are guests of your grandmother Queen Clotilda, and we are here to escort you to safety. So if you will, put up your dagger, and we will take this man up out of here. It seems he is one of the crew, so it will be proper to let the master question him."

Even standing on the bed, the boy had to look up to the duke. He hesitated, then, with a formal little bow that almost made him lose his balance on the soft mattress, he sheathed the long knife and jumped to the floor.

"Sir," he said, and then, to Alice: "You were hurt, lady? I'm sorry. I didn't see. I didn't see there was a lady there at all. It happened so quickly, and I was asleep."

"I know. It's all right. It's nothing." There was hardly enough room in the cabin for Alice to make her curtsey, but before she could attempt it her father's hand gently held her back in the chair.

"No, my dear. Stay quiet. Why, you're trembling. It's all right now, all's well." A pat on her shoulder, a word to the ship's captain, and then again to the guards. "You men, take the fellow up. And now, Prince Chlodovald, if you will go with the master, while I look to the Lady Alice? Ah, Mariamne, there you are. Come in, girl, stop gaping, there's no danger now. See your mistress back to her bed. And see to her hand, it's bruised and needs a salve. Good night, my dear."

"Danger?" The duke, last out of the cabin, was barely on the bottom step of the stairway before Mariamne, still wide-eyed and open-mouthed, flew across the cabin to her mistress's side. "What danger? What did my lord mean? Madam, madam, Lady Alice, that was Jeshua! Wasn't it? In this light, and he never said anything, and his face was all mud, but I could have sworn—"

Alice laughed, a little shakily. "Yes, it was Jeshua. And there was danger, but it's over now, and I think we shall find that Jeshua has done something very fine and brave. And I also think he'll be going back home with us."

Back in her cabin, while the maid dressed the bruised hand, Alice told Mariamne what had happened. The girl's shocked horror at her mistress's near escape from injury or worse was soon overcome by her pleasure at the news of the young prince's escape, but it was obvious that all else was eclipsed by the knowledge that Jeshua was on the *Merwing,* apparently prepared to accompany his master with the duke's party to Britain.

Once dismissed to her pallet, the girl soon slept, but Alice, exhausted though she now was, found sleep still far away. Her hand hurt a little, but what kept her wakeful was her guess at what must be happening on deck. She could hear no sounds but the slap and suck of water along the ship's side. She moved restlessly, trying to listen, then trying not to listen, hoping not to hear . . . She forced herself to reason, attempting calm. If the man was one of the *Merwing*'s crew, and had been paid by Chlodovald's murderous uncles to finish their work and kill the child who was now his rightful king, then no doubt he would now himself be killed as a traitor and assassin. That, in the law, was right. And once the facts were known the duke would see to it that the end was just and clean. So take comfort; take what comfort had come, thank God, out of the recent tragedy and horror, that this last murder had twice been foiled, and the boy was safe. They were all safe, and soon they would be home again. Think of that. Think of home, and the summer fields and forests, and the peace of Rheged's hills and lakes. But first . . .

But first to add a final prayer to the confused messages

that had passed that night between Alice and her God. It was a simple prayer for the soul of the wretched man who had almost killed her, and had meant, for whatever reason, to kill Chlodovâld.

And in His own way, Alice's God answered her. She was fast asleep and did not hear the heavy splash, some time later, as the body was thrown overboard.

23

It was late next morning. Alice and the duke were on deck, watching the edges of the river recede as the estuary widened towards the sea. There was no sign of Chlodovald. He must, said the duke, be still sleeping.

He himself had slept on deck, leaving his cabin to the boy, with Father Anselm on watch for his waking, and guards, freshly alert and watchful, at the companionway.

"But there's no danger now," said Ansirus. "It's certain that the fellow was telling the truth. He was one of the crew, who had heard some rumour of the murders, and the loss, as he took it, of Queen Clotilda's control over her sons. He assumed that Lothar would soon be declared King of Orleans, and that the queen's property—and that would include the *Merwing*—would be seized along with the kingdom. It was ill chance that he was on watch when Jeshua came aboard. When he saw Jeshua carry the child below and then come back to speak with me and the master, leaving Chlodovald, as he thought, alone in my cabin, he seized his chance. He planned to kill the child and then claim a reward from King Lothar. He would have taken some token as proof of the killing, and then gone overboard and swum ashore—you remember we were close in then. Well, when he came off watch he went below with a flagon of warmed wine which he said had been ordered for the boy by me, and the guards, knowing him for one of the crew, let him through."

"And he attacked me thinking I was Chlodovald?"

"He said so. You were kneeling on the chair by the port-hole, wrapped in your gown and with your hair loose down your back, so he took you for the child standing there to look out. He clapped a hand over your mouth to prevent you from calling out, and dragged you back to stab you. And found you were no child, but a young woman. Then the boy woke, and shouted out. And the rest you know."

"Not quite. The man's dead, I suppose?"

"Yes."

She was silent for a moment, head bent as she smoothed a hand along the polished ship's rail. "Did Chlodovald kill him?"

"No, no. That first wild stroke was a lucky one; it cut through the sinews in the fellow's wrist, and made him drop his dagger. Then once the first scare was over, and the boy knew what had happened and where he was— and that he was safe on the queen's ship—he was content to leave things to the master and to me. Except for—"

"Yes, father?"

"Except for insisting that the man should be confessed and shriven before he died," said the duke.

"It was Chlodovald who insisted?"

"Yes."

"Ah." It was more a sigh than a sound. Then she looked up. "Well, let's hope it's over, and the man was telling the truth. If he was really acting for himself, and wasn't sent by Lothar or the other uncles—"

"We can take it as true. He made that part of his confession openly."

She sighed again, this time with relief. "So they don't know where Chlodovald is. Thank God for that! It's really over, he's safe, and we'll soon be home ... I wonder how he'll settle there, poor boy, after what's happened? Has Jeshua told you about it?"

"As much as he knows. He was with the queen's household when the boys were sent for by Childebert and Lothar, to be made ready, they said, for the coronation. The next they knew was when one of Lothar's creatures, a man called Arcadius, came to tell the queen that the boys had been seized, separated from their tutors and their own servants, and locked up separately until they would renounce their claim to their father's lands."

"How did Chlodovald escape?"

"He'd already been smuggled away into hiding. His tutor suspected what might happen, and he and another servant hustled the child away. They didn't dare take him back to Queen Clotilda, but the servant went to tell her, and she sent Jeshua to bring him south to the *Merwing*, and see him safely into my care. They came a roundabout way, but they met with no trouble, and the tutor has ridden back to tell her the child is safe."

"So she'll soon know that he's with you, and on his way to Britain?"

"Yes. And she begged me to see him established there in some house of religion. It appears—this was from Jeshua—that she has always had hopes that the youngest of the boys would turn to the holy life, and now this does seem to be his only choice."

"If he agrees."

"Indeed. He may well be filled with thoughts of

bloody revenge. That would be normal, for a Merwing. Until we've had a chance to talk with him, we can't tell. But it does look as if a monastery would be the best place for him in the meantime."

"St. Martin's?"

"Why not? It's not far from Castle Rose, and I shall soon be there myself. We can lodge there on the way home, and I'll talk to Abbot Theodore. Ah, look, there, away on the horizon, that could be Nantes. And there is Jeshua, going below to wake the prince and bid him to eat with us. We shall have to be careful with him, Alice. God alone knows what grief and fear that child has suffered."

"He's very young," said Alice, practically, "and probably very hungry. So no doubt God will see us through."

No one was in the main cabin but the servants. They finished laying the meal, then, at the duke's bidding, withdrew. As the door closed behind them the inner door opened, and Chlodovald came in, with Father Anselm behind him.

It was like seeing Theudovald again, a fair boy, slightly built but whippy and quick-moving, with the same proud carriage. There were the wide-set blue eyes and jutting nose that would, in adulthood, be aquiline, but the mouth showed a sweeter line than the elder boy's, and this child—understandably enough—displayed nothing of his brother's mischievous self-assurance.

He had washed and tidied himself as best he could, but still wore the travel-stained shirt and tunic which were presumably the only clothes that had been salvaged for him in his flight. Though the day was warm, he kept the dark cloak still hugged about him, with the hood pulled close.

The priest stooped to whisper something, then with a bow to the duke, left the cabin. The boy still hesitated in the doorway.

Alice, smiling, lifted the cover from one of the dishes. "Be welcome, prince, to your own table. I'm glad you slept so late. I hope you're recovered now, and hungry? Won't you come and eat with us?"

The duke, moving to one side, indicated the high-backed chair at the table's end, but at that the boy shook his head. He came quickly forward and, with an abrupt gesture, pushed the hood of his cloak back.

The gesture was both dramatic and startling. His hair had been cut short. The long tresses, symbol of Merwing royalty, had gone; the hair hung straight, thick and short, roughly cut just to cover the ears. The presumptive King of Orleans had, by his own act, abdicated.

He said nothing, but stood straight as a spear, his head high, with an air of defiance, of aggression almost, that must be the nearest a Merwing prince could ever get to betraying insecurity. As Alice and her father sought for the right thing—anything—to say, the boy's hand went up in the gesture Alice remembered his brother using, the sweep of the hand to push back the heavy mane of hair. It met the rough crop and slid down over the bare neck at the back.

"It feels so strange," he said uncertainly. "Cold."

"Dear boy," said the duke gently, "I think you have done well this day. Later you shall talk with us, but now be welcome, rest and eat."

Alice merely smiled again, and began to serve the food. When the duke once more would have ushered the boy into the master chair, the latter shook his head, and pulled out a stool. "I am a prince no longer, my lord. That place is for you."

He was certainly very hungry, and over an excellent meal the constraints slackened. Neither the duke nor Alice would have mentioned the tragic doings in Paris, but Chlodovald, perhaps in reaction to the recent time of fear, seemed eager to talk.

"Jeshua told me what happened. My uncles knew that the people loved my grandmother, and they needed her support, or the pretence of it, if they were to seize our lands. Of course they knew she would never give it willingly, so they sent that rat, that—that *thing* of my uncle's—Arcadius of Clermont, to trick her or force her into it. But perhaps you know this already?"

"No matter. Go on."

He set down the capon leg he had been gnawing, and wiped his fingers. "He came early in the morning. My grandmother had been at vigil all the day before, and through the night, praying for my father's soul, and she had not yet broken her fast. That was the time he chose to force his way into her presence to tell her that my brothers were prisoners, and in danger of death unless they renounced their claim to my father's lands. He showed her a dagger and a pair of shears, and told her it was the only choice. He shouted at her. At my grandmother! And no one dared lay a hand to him. His men were at the gate, and besides, she didn't know where my brothers were being held."

He reached for his goblet and drank, then pushed his platter aside. Neither Alice nor the duke spoke, but waited for the boy to finish his story.

Though the duke had heard it already from Jeshua, the tale came more movingly, told in that childish voice, with details perhaps gleaned from some other servant who had been present. They heard how the old queen, exhausted by her vigil, terrified for the boys, and furiously angry at her sons' treachery, had reacted violently and with instinctive arrogance. "I would sooner see them dead than with their hair cut short! They are of Clovis's blood! They are kings!" Beside herself, she had almost screamed her answer, but when, minutes later, after a brief but passionate burst of weeping, she would have called the words back, Arcadius was already beyond her gates, heading at full speed for his master's court.

Chlodovald told it almost without emotion, like someone still numb from the shock of disaster.

"But we did hear, when we lay one night on the road— I forget the name of the place, but the monks were kind—that my brothers had been carried to St. Peter's church in Paris, and my grandmother saw them buried there with all the honours that were due to them, and the people wept and hung the streets with mourning."

"But how was this possible?" Alice was startled into speaking. "Surely your uncles—"

"After it was done they ran away." Chlodovald sounded indifferent. "They were afraid. They will quarrel now, and kill one another. It is with God."

"Perhaps, since the people love your grandmother, and mourn for your brothers, they'll want you to go back?"

"No. My grandmother will go into the convent now. She planned it long ago. And I—" a lift of the shorn head—"I need never be king."

" 'Need'?" That was the duke.

Chlodovald met his eyes with a sort of defiance. "I cut

my hair myself. I would have you know that. And I did not cut it from fear."

"You don't need to tell me that, Prince Chlodovald. I've assumed that you're set on entering God's service. As I am myself. My daughter and I were speaking of this earlier. There's plenty of time, before we reach Britain, to make plans for the future. We'll see you safe there, and later, when you are grown to manhood, you will know what decisions to make."

"I shall come back home," said Chlodovald. He spoke with a total lack of emphasis that somehow made the words more final than a vow.

"Home? To the Frankish kingdoms?" exclaimed Alice. "To Orleans?"

"To Orleans, I think not. But to my own land, yes. Not as a king, no, but I shall return. I have something that I must bring back to my own country."

"What is that?"

"If you will excuse me?" He slipped from his stool and went quickly into the inner cabin. In a moment he came back carrying a box.

He threw a quick glance at the door. "They will not come in?"

"Not until I bid them," said the duke.

"Then I will show you. My grandmother entrusted it to me, and she bade me keep it safely and one day bring it home."

He set the box on the table, pushing the used dishes out of the way, and opened the lid. The box appeared to be full of floss silk, blond and shining.

"Your hair?" said Alice, wonderingly. The long-haired kings held this symbol so very sacred? As sacred and precious as a real crown?

But Chlodovald pulled the soft stuff aside to show what was packed in it. A goblet, more golden than the gold hair, with gems glittering crimson and green and primrose yellow in the handles. A beautiful thing, certainly very precious, but seemingly more than that. As he unveiled the thing from the enwrapping silk, the boy crossed himself, then turned, eyes shining, to Alice and the duke.

"It's the Grail!" he said, reverently. "The True Cup! The Grail itself!"

"At least," said Ansirus to his daughter, as they stood on deck while the *Merwing* picked her way into the crowded harbour of Nantes, "he has told no one else about it. Not even Jeshua. So we stand a reasonable chance of getting it—and him—safely landed at Glannaventa and across Rheged to St. Martin's."

"But father, it can't be the Grail! You know it can't!"

"I know. I suppose I have seen as many 'true cups' as any man, being traded to and fro in Jerusalem. But it's still a treasure. A treasure that will have a most practical use."

"What use?"

"The boy has been forced to leave his kingdom—renounce it—with nothing but the clothes he stands in. Now, even without my sponsorship, the monks of St. Martin's would accept him from pure charity, but if he brings with him something of such a price—for it's both rare and ancient—you may be sure of that—why then, he brings his payment with him."

"But if he tells them it's the Grail—"

"Listen, Alice. If men believe—if they need a focus for their worship, then, grail or not, this cup will be as true for them as a cross you or I could fashion out of wood from our own orchards at Rheged. Don't you see, child?"

"Ye—es. Yes, I suppose so. But—"

"So we say nothing, and Abbot Theodore will make his own decisions. What happens will be his concern. Look, we're almost in. We'll be making fast very soon. Where's your maid, my dear?"

Alice laughed. "At a guess, getting Jeshua to help her with my baggage. You know what's happening there, I suppose? Once he's seen the pr—Chlodovald safely into St. Martin's, we'll have to find a place for him at Castle Rose."

"If his duty doesn't take him back to the queen's service he'll be most welcome in mine," said the duke. "I already had it in mind to speak to him about it. Beltrane, like me, is ageing, and I think he will be glad of experienced help. When we get to St. Martin's I plan to stay there for a few days to see the boy settled in, and to talk things over with Abbot Theodore, so it might be a good idea to send Jeshua straight home from Glannaventa with our heavy baggage. Don't you think so? He can give Beltrane warning that we'll be home sooner than expected, and help him if it's needed."

"I'm sure it will be! They won't be looking for us for at least another month, and every room will be turned out for cleaning! May I tell Mariamne?"

"Of course." He smiled. "She may help persuade him to stay, at least until you are safely wed. When I'm no longer there, it will be good to know that you have a servant as brave and as faithful as he has shown himself to be."

They drew in then to the wharfside, and Alice, in the bustle of leave-taking and disembarkation, was able, though with some difficulty, to turn her mind away from what awaited her at home.

FIVE

Alexander in Love

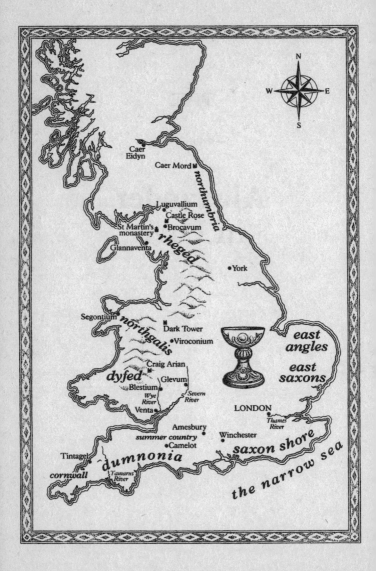

24

It would be tedious to detail the all-too-swift and inevitable process by which Alexander came to be Queen Morgan's lover. She nursed him, and if the low fever took rather a long time to leave him, why, then, the lovely queen spent all the more time in the sickroom, and all the more often brewed for him her subtle concoctions of herbs and fruits and other, secret, ingredients. The Lady Luned kept aloof; the other young men of Morgan's party might smile or sulk and talk among themselves, but the queen herself seemed to have eyes—and time—for Alexander alone.

At length the fever left him. There were some who noticed that it only left him when he was securely in the queen's toils, and then, when he was seen to think only of her, and pine for her touch, her look, her presence—why, then she withdrew herself from the sickroom, and let old Brigit do the nursing. From which time the young prince gained strength rapidly, and was soon able to leave his bed, to stand and walk about the chamber and bathe and dress himself without aid. Which he did, one evening when Brigit had left him, taking out his best clothes—which had been washed and laid carefully away in one of the chests—and set out to look for the queen.

The royal rooms where Alexander had been housed were in the central part of the castle, with doors opening on a corridor running to right and left towards the twin towers. He hesitated outside his door, wondering where the main stairway lay that would take him down to the castle's public rooms. He had no doubt that now, favoured as he apparently was by the queen, he would be received by the Lady Luned and made free of the castle's hospitality. Eager though he was to see Morgan again, he realised that courtesy required him first to seek out his hostess, tender her his respects and thanks, and wait for her invitation to join the company that evening.

A boy in Morgan's livery came running along the corridor, bent on some errand. Alexander put out a hand.

"A moment, if you please! What's your name?"

"Gregory, sir." The boy regarded him with a curiosity that Alexander found flattering. The queen's servants had no doubt been whispering about him, and he thought—hoped—that he knew what was being said.

"Well, Gregory, can you tell me where I can find the Lady Luned? Will she be free at this hour to receive me?"

"I'm not sure about that, sir. But I do know where you'll probably find her. At this time she's usually in one of the rooms where the ladies sit. Down that way." He pointed back the way he had come. "Down the staircase there, sir, and one of the servants will show you."

"The ladies? Then Queen Morgan will be there?"

"Oh, no!" The boy's amused surprise was wasted on Alexander. "She doesn't sit with the ladies! I'm on my way to find her now. They came in from riding an hour ago, and I think they'll be in the east tower."

" 'They'?"

"My mistress the queen and her knights."

"Indeed," said Alexander, conscious of an urgent wish to detach the lovely queen from such company, but still held back by courtesy, and also by another sudden thought. "No, wait a moment, please. Can you tell me— am I right in thinking—I must have heard someone say it—that there are men from Cornwall among the queen's knights?"

He knew now that Queen Morgan had not found out his name by any sort of magic art; all she had heard was some muttering in a brief bout of delirium, when some instinct had kept him discreet. To her and Brigit—and so presumably to all the castle—he was "Alexander the Fatherless," noble, apparently, but probably base-born. The thought had at first irked him, but then he saw it as another romantic touch in this adventure he had stumbled into: no doubt at some later stage there would be the discovery scene beloved of the poets when he would be revealed as a prince in his own right, and a fitting lover for a queen. Farther than this his imagination had not taken him. But he knew that now he must not risk confronting men from March's court, who might see the resemblance to his dead father, and so place his family in danger, along with Sadok and Erbin, who had shielded their escape all those years ago. So he waited anxiously for the boy's answer.

It was reassuring. "There were, sir. Two of King March's men, and two from some duchy in Dumnonia, in the south, but I forget the name. They're not here now.

They weren't the queen's knights, they just came with messages, and they left last week."

"I see. Well . . . The east tower, you said?"

"Yes, sir, but—" The boy stopped, biting his lip.

"But?"

"Forgive me, but I serve the queen, and I know what the orders are. It's no use your going now to the east tower. We all, her servants, that is, have orders to let no one in while she and her knights are in council. But later, at dinner-time, I am sure you'll be welcome."

" 'In council'? What do you mean, in council?"

He spoke sharply, and the boy, confused, began to stammer. "I only meant—they have meetings . . . I don't know what about, how should I? But she is a queen, and even if her state is small, and she is called a prisoner, she keeps her court. I'm sorry, my lord—"

"I see. It's all right. Anyway, it's the Lady Luned I'm looking for, not the queen. Thank you, you'd better go now. I'll find my own way."

The boy ran off. Alexander, watching him go, wondered briefly how long it would be before he, too, was made a member of that select and fortunate court assembled in the east tower. Not long, he thought with satisfaction; not long.

Meanwhile there was a duty to be done. He found his way easily enough to the women's rooms, where the Lady Luned and her women were busy with their needle-work. Luned received him with apparent pleasure, and the ladies exclaimed kindly over his happy restoration to looks and health. He made, and then repeated, his apologies for making so prolonged a visit at such a time, apologies she disclaimed charmingly, repeating her welcome. It was to be noticed, through all the apologies, that neither the lady nor Alexander made any attempt to bring that visit to a close; Luned because Morgan, whom she feared, had made it very clear that he must stay, and Alexander because he was fiercely determined, with all the arrogance of youth and the consuming desire that Morgan's drugs and spider-wiles had lit in him, to plunge headlong—and publicly—into this, his first real love affair. And what a love affair! Like any young man of his age, he had looked here and there, but this was not like the passing fancies of youth. This was different! The loveliest woman he had ever seen, and she a queen, and sister to the High King! And he, chosen (as he was sure) by her, and madly in love, longed only now to be taken to her bed and thereafter declared her lover in the sight of the world—or at any rate in the sight of the other young knights of her "council."

It was made satisfactorily clear that same evening, and in the sight of everybody in the castle. At dinner in the hall Alexander was led to the queen's right. To his other side was one of the queen's ladies, an elderly woman (Morgan's waiting-women were without exception elderly or plain) who gave most of her attention to her food. Luned was on the queen's left; she spoke little, and in fact was largely ignored by Morgan. The latter, in creamy white sparkling with diamonds, was robed as if for a victory feast. The dark hair was dressed high with jewels and some filmy veiling, and her face, expertly painted, looked, in the candle-light, like that of a girl of twenty.

Alexander could have wished for no more dazzling declaration of what was to come. The hall, not a large one, was crowded with the men of her party, and a scattering of Luned's and Morgan's ladies. With the High

King's guards discreetly out of sight, it could have been taken for a pleasant gathering in any lord's hall. There was talk and laughter as the food and wine went round, but it was to be seen that few people had eyes for anyone but Morgan and the handsome young man beside her.

She gave them what they were looking for. She spoke little to anyone but Alexander, leaning towards him and letting her sleeve, and sometimes her hand, brush against his. Finally she lifted her wine-cup and pledged him in sight of them all, kissing the rim of the goblet and then handing it to him to drink from. Alexander, dazzled and slightly the worse for the rich food and wine after the long abstinence enforced by his sickness, never saw the looks—one or two sullen, but mostly smiling—that went between the knights of Morgan's household, looks which could be translated, very easily, by those who knew her: "Your turn now?" the smiles said. "Then make the most of it, young cockerel! Crow while you can!"

She did not come to his chamber that night. The boy Peter came as usual to help him to bed, bearing the familiar flagon of cordial sent by the queen. Still weaker than he had supposed, and with his senses half swimming with the wine and the excitements of the feast, Alexander drained the goblet obediently, and got into bed. Peter snuffed the candle and left him.

Alexander lay for a little while, watching the door and listening—though the queen moved as lightly as the fay they called her, and he would only know of her presence in the dark by her touch and the fragrance that went with her. But the drug overtook him before even the smell of the snuffed candle had died away, and he slept.

* * *

Morgan, of course, knew what she was about. When Alexander woke next morning she was already far from the castle, out hunting with her knights, and watched as always by the King's guards. Nor did he see her that evening. She had a headache, said Peter, but she would be better tomorrow, and if the prince would meet her in the morning at about the third hour, they could perhaps ride out together . . . ?

The cordial she sent him that night tasted different, with a kind of pungency lacing the sweetness, but somehow heavy, promising sleep. The promise was a false one. When the page had seen him to bed, doused the candle and left him, Alexander spent a distressed and wakeful night full of the torments of unsatisfied love, and of wondering, even nervous, anticipation of the morning's meeting.

25

Even after the restless night, Alexander felt more normally alert next morning than for many a day. He rose early, and went down as soon as he dared, to await Morgan in the courtyard.

She kept him waiting, of course, but at length she came, alone save for the guards who accompanied her on all her ventures outside the walls. She was dressed in green, with a grass-green mantle lined with tawny silk, and a cap of the same silk with a russet plume of feathers that curled down to brush her cheek. She looked every bit as lovely as she had in the hall of feasting, or in the hushed peace of his sick-chamber. He kissed her hand, lingering over it a shade too long, then threw her up to the saddle of her pretty sorrel mare, mounted his own big chestnut, and followed her out across the wooden bridge.

She knew the country well, so he left it to her to choose which way they should go. His horse was very fresh, so she led him at a good gallop along the riverside, almost to the place where he had taken his fall, then turned uphill into a forest track which perforce they took at a gentler pace. In a while the trees thinned and they rode out into the sunshine of a sheltered upland valley where the horses could once more go side by side. Morgan slowed her mare to a walk and Alexander let his chestnut range alongside.

They were followed all the while by the four guards, and from time to time Morgan glanced over her shoulder with a rather appealing show of apprehension. They watched her constantly, she told him, and reported every move back to her brother Arthur. She was afraid of them—she confessed it prettily—afraid that soon, bored by the monotony of their task in this remote spot so far from their own people, they might send some sort of lying report to Arthur, who would give orders for her to be taken back to Caer Eidyn in the bleak north, or sent to the strictly guarded prison (so she called it) of Castell Aur in the Welsh hills. And there, it was hinted, Alexander would see her no more. Unless, of course, he would help her to escape the punishment, so unjust and harsh, that the High King had meted out to her . . . ?

But here she drew blank. However besotted Alexander was, he could not be brought to an open criticism of the High King. To him, throughout his young life, Arthur and Camelot had represented all that was good and right. Nor—with the knowledge of the state that the queen kept here in the Dark Tower, the luxury of her apartments, the food and service that was offered her, with her "court" and her "councils" and the freedom of her rides abroad, guarded though they were—nor, with all this in mind, could Alexander be brought to see the queen as a pathetic and maltreated prisoner. So he listened, sympathised, swore eternal devotion—as yet he dared not say love—but shied away from any talk of "rescue" or even of any attempt to shake off the watchers. She, in her turn, evaded any direct replies to his tentative questions about the reasons for Arthur's stern decree. He was young enough to be able, with Morgan's lovely eyes looking into his, and her hand resting on his knee as their horses paced side by side, to believe at one and the same time that Arthur had punished her rightly for a breach of faith, and that she, a sadly ill-used lady, had only been led into trouble by a lover's treachery. A lover who, praise God and thanks to Arthur, was now dead.

Morgan, of course, saw this very clearly, and saw that, however deep in love the young fool was, she had no hope of adding him to the "court" that held council in the private chamber of the east tower. These young men, some of whom had been (still were from time to time) her lovers, were all men who for one reason or another had no love for Arthur. Throughout the country, mainly among the younger outland Celts, was a growing dissatisfaction with the "King's peace," by which was meant the centralisation of government and the peaceful enforcement of law and order. Reared by custom and tradition as fighting men, they despised the "old men's talking-shop" of the Round Hall at Camelot, and longed for action, even for the "glory" of war.

For these young rebels the court that Morgan held, here and at Castell Aur, was a handy and pleasant centre for hatching plots for Arthur's discomfiture or their own advancement. They were not aware that Arthur knew all about it, and chose to allow it. In killing his sister's lover and holding his sister a captive (however silken her chains) he knew that her household could become a centre of disaffection, and herself even a focus for rebellion. But his adviser, since Merlin's latest disappearance into his tower of crystal, was a woman, wiser in the ways of women than ever Merlin could have been. "Leave Morgan her state and her lovers," Nimuë had said, "and let her plot in peace, where you can watch her doing it." Arthur had followed her advice, so Morgan kept her little train of dissidents, and occupied her time with busy—and so far harmless—plotting against her brother.

Now, balked by Alexander's stubborn loyalty, she abandoned the attempt to add him to her court. She came very near to relinquishing her plan to lead him to her bed, but she had another scheme afoot, where someone like Alexander, so patently honest, might succeed where others of her train had failed. Besides, it was time she had a new lover, and he was handsome, and young, and more than ready for it, so—

So she changed her tactics, admitted some fault with a pretty show of remorse, spoke with affectionate respect of Arthur, and begged Alexander to forget what she had said in a moment of despair, and to tell her, instead, of himself and his hopes for the future. To which end she made him help her dismount, and they sat together in a sunlit hollow sheltered by flowering gorse-bushes, while the King's men, stolidly patient, and laying quiet bets on the result of the day's outing, waited within sight but out of hearing.

They saw a charming picture: the queen, sitting on Alexander's outspread cloak with her green-and-tawny silk and velvet spread gracefully round her, and the young man lying at her feet, his gaze on her face. He talked; it is to be supposed (since he could hardly tell her the truth about himself and his journey to Drustan's castle and thence to Camelot) that his talk dealt mainly with his present hopes of love. So he talked, while she smiled and listened with a pretty air of attention, but the watchers saw, when Alexander looked away, that she yawned. Soon after that her hand went out to him, and he snatched it eagerly to his lips. She leaned forward then, smiling still, and said something that brought him swiftly to his feet with both hands held out to help her rise. She let him pull her up into his arms and kiss her, long and passionately, before he lifted her to the saddle.

There was really no need for the watchers to hear what was said. They knew. They had seen or heard it all before. The lady had whistled yet another young fool to her bed, and the fool would go, and be fooled still further, and in time, perhaps, would learn the price he would have to pay for his folly.

It was about a month later that Alexander learned the price. A wonderful month for him, the most wonderful of his young life—or so he honestly believed. At Queen Morgan's side all day, lying with her at night, seeing himself preferred above all the others of her small court, the days and nights passed like a dream of pleasure, so that reality, when it broke in, of swimming senses and headaches and, though he would not admit this even to himself, an overwhelming desire for solitude and a night or so of uninterrupted sleep, was forgotten as soon as realised. Or rather, as soon as his mistress, with some delicately drugged wine in a golden goblet, and the caresses of soft lips and practised fingers, chose to make him forget. Then he would drown again in desire, thinking it love, and vow everything to her service who wrapped him in those sweet silken strands, as a spider wraps a fly.

Then one day there was a disturbance at the castle gate, and a horseman rode in on a blown horse, asking for Queen Morgan. He was muddied and exhausted, and looked so wild that a page ran to the chamber where the queen and Alexander breakfasted together, and rapped sharply on the door.

Morgan, still abed, and languid on the pillows, did no more than raise her brows, but Alexander, who found himself irritable these days, shouted angrily: "Who is it? Don't you know better than to disturb the queen?"

"My lord, it's for the queen. It's Count Ferlas. He's back, and he must see her. My lord, is she awake?"

"How could she sleep through such a clamour? Go and tell him to wait!"

But Morgan, thrusting him aside with an urgent arm, pushed herself up in the bed, calling out: "Gregory? Send Count Ferlas here! Send him here at once!" And flinging the covers back, she leaped out of bed. "Alexander, my robe!"

"But, lady, here?"

"Where else? I must see the man! Give me my robe, unless you want me to receive him naked!"

He began to stammer something. To him the royal chamber, beautifully appointed with tapestries and silken hangings, with windows now full of the morning sunlight and overlooking river and forest—this was his bower of delight, a place sacred to their love, to memories he would, he swore, never forget.

There was a hurried trampling of feet in the corridor outside. Alexander snatched up his own bedgown and flung it on, as another knock came at the door. Queen Morgan, girding a robe round her without haste, called out a summons, and the newly arrived Count Ferlas, followed by the queen's waiting-women and a couple of pages, came into the room.

The count was a burly, powerful-looking young man, but as he went to his knee before the queen it could be seen that he was exhausted.

She gave him her hand to kiss, waved the women and boys back, and said, sharply: "What news?"

"There is none. I failed, and came back empty-handed."

"Empty-handed? You found no trace of it?"

"None. We asked everywhere, but no one seemed to know anything about it, except the usual talk about magic, and whether Merlin had—"

"Never mind that! Did you see her? Have speech?"

"No. We were told she'd gone south. So then we went, as you directed us—"

She silenced him with a hasty gesture. "Not here. Leave it. Later. You failed, so what does it matter where you went?" She was silent herself for a few moments, staring unseeingly across the room, the pretty teeth savaging her underlip. Then, as if shrugging away the disaster, whatever it was, she turned back to the kneeling man.

"So, we must try again, it seems. What of the other matter I sent Madoc to pursue? Did your brother Julian go to Bannog Dun to see him?"

"No, madam. That is what I was going to tell you. There was no need. Madoc came to see us in Luguvallium. It seems he's already in possession, and well dug in. He bade us tell you that all was well, and the business should be settled soon."

"Well, I suppose that's something to the good. I'll talk

with Julian later. I take it he came back with you? Where is he?"

"Madam, he's dead."

Alexander, hovering near, but for once ignored, glanced at her in surprise as she said, merely: "So? How?"

"By enchantment. Or so I think. As we rode away from Luguvallium he complained of sickness and pain in the side, and that night he fell into a fever, and in three days he was dead."

Alexander, stung to pity by the weary grief in the man's face, looked to see the queen signal him to rise from his knees, or at least order one of the servants to pour wine for him, but she did neither. She sat down on the bed's edge, chin on fist, brows knitted, looking at none of them, deep in thought.

The prince went to the side table, poured a goblet of the wine that stood there, and would have carried it himself to the kneeling man, but at that she roused herself, saying sharply: "No! Not that! Count Ferlas, we must talk further. In the upper chamber, you know it, in half an hour. Go now, all of you except my women, and let me dress. Go!"

The count rose, bowed and went, followed by the pages. Alexander started to speak, but she cut him off with the same curt voice and gesture. "I said all. Did you not hear? All but the women. Leave me now!" Then as he still stood, flushed and beginning to be angry, she seemed to recollect herself. She went up to him and, pulling his head down, kissed him. "There. Forgive me, my love. I must talk with the man. He was my messenger, and has news for me, grave news, I fear. I will tell you about it later."

"If I may help you—" he said, hoarsely.

"Oh, yes, you may help me," she said, and smiled.

26

He did not see her again that day, and at nightfall one of her pages came with a message—lovingly worded but firm—that the news Count Ferlas had brought had distressed the queen, and business had arisen from it which had occupied her through the day, and was still keeping her from him. She must beg his forgiveness, but she could not say when . . . and so on and so forth. She managed to make it sound no more than the headache that women pleaded at certain times, but he knew, who better? that that was not true. From her parting words to him that morning, he could not believe that this was his dismissal from her favour and her bed. However, there was nothing to be done but conceal his chagrin, and retire with what dignity he could to his own chamber in the west tower. There he passed the restless hours, pride fighting with jealousy, and setting him to pacing the chamber floor, and wondering if he would be welcome at dinner that night in the hall, or if Ferlas would be beckoned to the place of honour beside the queen.

In the event neither the queen nor Count Ferlas was present at dinner that evening. This, of course, was small comfort to Alexander, who for once ate little, and was thankful that his neighbour, the Lady Luned, seemed out of sorts, paler than ever and not inclined for talking. She rose early from the meal, and he was able to escape once more to the solitude of the west tower, there to await the hoped-for summons from his mistress.

It did not come. Instead came Peter, as usual, with another message of excuses, and the cordial which she still insisted that he take at night, "Against the recurrence of the fever, which I have known to persist for two or even three moons, if no treatment is given."

Alexander, shaken by a different fever which, had he known it, was directly induced by the queen's cordials, pointed to the table and said, with an effort at his usual friendly courtesy: "Put it down there, will you? Thank you. I'll take it later. Tell me, page, did the queen give you this message herself?"

"Yes, my lord."

"Is she ailing? She sent this morning to tell me of urgent business that kept her from riding out with me, but surely this is now dealt with? I have not seen her all day, and as you know, she was not at dinner. How is it with her?"

Peter, who had seen this happen before, and who liked Alexander, said quickly: "She's well enough, sir; nothing for you to worry over! Since this morning there have been affairs to attend to, and she confers with her council tonight. It seems they may sit late, so she asked me to beg for your understanding."

"I see. Of course. The news the count brought was so bad?" He was thinking, it could not have been the brother's death; she showed no sign of grief at that; she did not even speak of it.

"I don't know, sir. I mean, I don't know what it would mean to the queen, though one could see she was mightily put out by it. But it was bad for my lady—my own lady, that is, Lady Luned. She knew the count and his brother well, from the old days. One of her maids told me she had been weeping."

"I see," said Alexander again, remembering Luned's silence and reddened eyes. He wished he had known sooner, so that he might have spoken some sort of comfort to her. "Well, my thanks, Peter. Tell your lady that I am sorry for her friend's death. I'll speak with her myself in the morning, if she will receive me. Now leave me, will you please? I'll see myself to bed. Good night."

Afterwards he was never quite sure what combination of injured pride and jealousy and sheer frustrated curiosity drove him to do what he did that night.

After Peter left him he waited, seated in the window embrasure, watching the stars prick out into the night sky, and listening to the sounds in the castle till they dwindled and at last died into the peace of sleep. Then, not troubling to arm himself, and still in the clothes he had worn at dinner, he let himself softly out of the chamber.

Cressets, set in iron brackets on the walls, gave light enough to show his way. He hesitated at the door that opened on the courtyard. There was still movement out there. Guards—the King's men and the castle's own— were set at night, and other sounds coming from the direction of the stables suggested that some groom was wakeful with a sick horse, or maybe with a mare due for foaling. But there was a door which led through into the central part of the castle, avoiding the open court. If it was left unlocked at night . . . ?

It was. He went that way, walking softly. Past the open

door of the great hall, where some of the servants were sleeping; snores and the rustling of straw, but no one roused. Then quickly up the great stairway, and there ahead of him was the door that led to the queen's private rooms—the royal rooms that he had come to regard as his own.

He halted there, disconcerted. There were guards; King's men, with the Dragon blazon. He should have expected it, of course, though the guard must have been set each night after he and the queen had gone to bed. He hesitated, feeling suddenly foolish, but the guards showed neither surprise nor (what he had feared) amused complicity. The man nearest him drew back his spear as if expecting the prince to knock or enter, but Alexander, after another brief moment of hesitation, shook his head and turned quickly to the right, going swiftly, still soft-footed and now with quickened pulses, along the corridor towards the east tower.

He did not see the look—without surprise and certainly without amusement—that passed between the two guards, as one of them left his post to follow him.

The staircase up into the east tower was a spiral of stone, scantily lit by a single torch thrust into a bracket near the foot of the steps. Through the slit windows the night wind blew, soft with summer. An owl called. Alexander went silently up the steps. Somewhere ahead of him, muffled by door or wall, he could hear voices; a single voice, and then, from time to time, a chorus as men spoke together, or vied with one another to be heard. The sounds came from not far above him. He paused on a small triangular landing in a curve of the stairway, and listened. It was not possible to make out any words, and it seemed as if the speakers were being careful not to raise their voices. There was a pause of quiet, and through it could be heard a single voice that was, unmistakably, the queen's. Then a man speaking angrily, and others joining in, a chorus that sounded impatient, even quarrelsome. He trod swiftly up the last curve of the stairway.

There was another landing, wide this time, with a rug laid over the stone floor, and a stool against the wall to one side of a door. It was a strong door, studded with iron, and fast shut, and beside it was another guard.

Not a King's guard this time. A boy only, seated on the stool with his back against the wall. He looked half asleep, but as Alexander appeared round the curve of the stairs he jerked to wakefulness and jumped to his feet. The prince recognised him. It was the page Gregory, who had first told him about the "councils," and that the queen's servants "kept the door," and refused entry to any but the privileged.

Well, that had been a long time ago, and now everyone in the castle, not least Morgan's own page, must know him to be among the privileged. He gave the boy a smiling nod, and spoke in an undertone.

"Your mistress holds council here tonight, I think, Gregory? Will you open the door, or, if you prefer it, go in and announce me?"

The boy did not move, standing with his back to the door. "I'm sorry, sir. I can't."

"What do you mean, you can't?" Alexander let his irritation show. "Can't even go in and ask, you mean? Surely, after all this time—"

"Forgive me, sir, but we have our orders. No one to go

in, no one except the council. I did tell you before, sir. I dare not."

"Well, but that was 'before.' You must surely know that I am in the queen's confidence now!"

"But not of the council, sir. Not of her own people."

"Her own people? What people?"

"That I can't tell you, sir, but those who are always there. That came with her from Caer Eidyn and will go with her to Castell Aur when the time comes."

"I will go with her to Castell Aur," said Alexander, who, until the exasperation of the moment, had never even considered it. Had never in fact considered the future at all, nothing beyond the delights of the present. If questioned, he would no doubt have admitted knowing that the affair with the lovely queen could not last for ever, that some day he must take horse and ride away— certainly not to the alleged confinements of Castell Aur—but he might ride, as she had hinted, in her service, before ordinary life resumed and he went on with his interrupted journey to Camelot . . .

He said sharply: "She said only this morning that I could be of service to her. If that is not being in her councils—"

"I am sorry." The boy was beginning to look frightened. He was backed right up against the door, with the tall young prince looming over him, but he still kept his voice almost to a whisper, and this fact helped to bring it home to Alexander that Morgan's servants could not easily be pushed into disobeying her. "I am sorry." The boy repeated it breathlessly. "I cannot, lord, indeed I cannot! She said nothing about you to me and the others, and she—my lord, I dare not disobey! Perhaps—perhaps when you see her tomorrow you will ask her yourself?"

Alexander stood back. "I will do that. Calm yourself, I'm not angry. You're only doing your duty. The queen must have forgotten to give you instructions. I'll talk with her tomorrow. Good night."

And, saving what dignity he could, he smiled at the boy, and made his way back to his lonely room, not much the wiser for the expedition, but soothed in one respect: the tale of urgent talks was true enough, not just a pretext to banish him from their bed. And she was certainly not alone with Ferlas.

Just as certainly, he would see her on the morrow, and find out what she had meant when she hinted at some service he could render her, and at the same time he would ask—insist on—what was apparently more important to her even than her lover: to be admitted to her court and councils.

He threw his clothes off, drank down the cordial Peter had left for him and then did what Morgan had intended him to do some hours ago, sank into a dreamless sleep.

The King's guard, back at the royal bedchamber door, was whispering to his fellow.

"No. Not one of them. Young Gregory wouldn't let him in. It's my guess he has no idea."

"As we thought. A damned shame, really."

"He'll get over it, and be the wiser for it." A sly grin, that would have annoyed Alexander and amused Morgan. "And you can't deny she's a tasty dish."

"As long as he doesn't get in too deep." This was the older man. "What is he? Sixteen? Seventeen? He's my son's age, maybe less."

"He won't do that. Oh, he can't see past bedtime yet,

but she knows better than try to use him for any party stuff. You mark my words."

"I believe you. But we'll watch, just the same."

"Hush. I think she's coming. Alone, too, would you believe it?"

"Well, he was played out. He could hardly stand when he got here, and they've been talking for three hours since dinner. We'll see him here with her tomorrow, I've no doubt."

This time they were not speaking of Alexander.

27

"The Queen of the Isles?" exclaimed Alexander.

"Well, she calls herself that." In a less exalted personage than a queen, Morgan's tone might have been called spiteful. "Some petty king she married, and lucky to get him, seeing that she'd been Merlin's mistress for the gods know how many years, and he old enough to be her grandfather!"

They were sitting together in Queen Morgan's chamber—the bower of bliss. Count Ferlas, having rested for two days at the castle, had gone back to his home, taking the sad news of his brother's death to their mother, and since then the queen had been at some pains to soothe her young lover's wounded feelings, and to show him that nothing was changed between them. It had crossed Alexander's mind that, while Ferlas had remained in the castle, the interviews between the count and Queen Morgan were rather prolonged even for what they might have had to discuss. But (though he would not admit it even to himself) the respite from dancing attendance, and from ever more demanding love-making, had been rather welcome than otherwise.

For all that, when her summons came he answered it with alacrity, to find her alone in the royal apartments, sitting by the window that looked south over the river-valley. He was given her hand to kiss, no more, and rose from his knee to see a look of trouble shadowing the beautiful face.

No need to ask what irked her; she gestured him abruptly to a chair across from hers, and began to talk.

Count Ferlas and his brother, she told him, had been among the knights who had attended her even before she was banished to Caer Eidyn, and had stayed in her service through her confinement there and at Castell Aur. Though (this with a prettily rueful glance at Alexander) it could not truthfully be said that her imprisonment at her brother Arthur's hands was unduly harsh, it was still imprisonment, and her loyal knights felt, had always felt, that it was unjust. So they had banded together to offer what help they could in persuading Arthur to release her. And they knew—everyone knew—that the biggest impediment in the way of this was the King's adviser, Merlin's successor, Nimuë, wife of King Pelleas of the Isles.

It was Nimuë of whom they spoke now. Alexander had of course heard of her, the young protégée and disciple of the great Merlin, who had been placed as a girl among the ladies of the Lake shrine at Avalon, but who had left them to live with Merlin and learn all his lore.

"As once," said Queen Morgan, "he would have taught me, had he not been afraid that my power might outstrip his, so he persuaded my brother Arthur to pack me off north to marry King Urbgen of Rheged. It suited both kings to use me to tie their kingdoms to one another, so I was locked away in Urbgen's castle at Luguvallium, with an old man whose two sons were older than I, and hated me."

So the queen recounted her version of things past, where such well-known facts as must have come to Alexander's ears were carefully twisted to adorn her story. The truth was that, on her way to a splendid marriage, escorted by Merlin as Arthur's deputy, Morgan had tried to cajole the enchanter into teaching her some of his art. The cold set-down he gave her had made her his enemy, an enmity passed on to Nimuë his successor. Even the recent murder of her half-sister Morgause was somehow laid to Merlin's door, though Merlin was no longer at court, and Morgause's own son had been the murderer. But was it not known that Mordred, Arthur's son by Morgause, had stood by, on who knew what instructions from the King's adviser?

So Morgan, changing her tack to suit her lover's tiresome loyalty to the High King. Carefully watching him under down-dropped lids, she proceeded to drive the point home. Knowing all this, who could tell what might come to another queen, herself, imprisoned like Morgause on some false charge of treachery, but, unlike Morgause, with no sons or kin to protect her, other than the royal brother who listened only to Nimuë's jealous advice—advice meant to keep Morgan from her brother's side, where she might have been able to bring to his service a power even greater than Nimuë's?

Yes—at Alexander's somewhat startled look she nodded—it might have been so. There was a way, one way only, for the helpless queen to assert herself against Nimuë's magic and be reinstated at Arthur's side. There was a talisman which, could she but lay hands on it, would give her this power. It was the quest for this talisman that Ferlas and his brother had undertaken for her.

They had failed, as had another of her knights who had gone before them on the same quest.

So now how could she ask another man, however brave and gallant, to undertake so perilous a quest? Rather would she spend the rest of her days in this helpless isolation, to end, perhaps, even as Morgause had ended, by murder in the dark . . .

Whatever magic Queen Morgan undoubtedly possessed, there was one art that Merlin could not have taught her—and Alexander was not to know that most women could—the art that brought tears to the lovely eyes, a sob into the light pretty voice, and her lover back to her feet, his vague doubts forgotten, vowing by every god in the calendar that whatever she wished him to do for her, he would do, though it meant death. He was eager, burning, and very young. This was the adventure that, so long ago it seemed, he had set out from Craig Arian to seek. This was the stuff of poetry, of beauty and romance. A quest, on behalf of a queen, and so lovely and loving a queen.

Morgan, accepting his vows, his kisses, and a kerchief of fine linen to dry her tears, settled back in her chair to tell him about the quest so dear to her, a quest already attempted twice, and twice ending in failure and death.

It was the quest for the Grail.

Some of the story she began to tell him now he already knew. The secret love of King Uther and Ygraine, Duchess of Cornwall, that had resulted in Arthur's birth, had already passed into legend, along with the tale of Arthur's hidden childhood, and his sudden appearance at the dying Uther's side in battle. The subsequent scene of mystery and wonder, when, led to it by Merlin the enchanter, the young king had raised the magical sword Caliburn from the stone, to be acclaimed rightful king of all Britain, was told in song and story by every fireside.

What was not generally known, being cast into shade by the dazzling events surrounding the young King's accession, was how the sword had come originally into Merlin's keeping. Morgan knew the story, having heard it from her sister Morgause, who in her turn had had it from spies set long ago to watch all the doings of the royal household.

The sword Caliburn had once belonged to the Emperor Maximus, whom the British had called Macsen during his brief reign in their country. It had been made for him by a British smith—legend said Weland himself—at a forge in the Welsh mountains, and was possessed of magic powers. It could belong only to the king, rightwise born, of Britain.

When Macsen died abroad, some of his faithful troops, determined that the sword should not fall into alien hands, carried it back to Britain, and buried it, along with other treasures, below the altar of the temple of Mithras at Segontium, Macsen's last great stronghold on the coast of Wales. There, by his magic art, Merlin had found it, and, because he was Macsen's kin, had taken the sword as of right, to hide it and keep it for Arthur's coming.

"You know about that?" asked Morgan. Alexander nodded, and she went on: "I was too young to be there. I was with my mother Queen Ygraine in Cornwall, preparing for my marriage, but Morgause my half-sister was in the north with our father King Uther, and—" She broke off. "But never mind that. What she did then, she paid for."

She was silent for a moment, and for once her face was not beautiful at all. Alexander did not notice. For the first time apprehension mingled with the former excitement. He was recalling the other tale, told sometimes in whispers, about the true reason for Queen Morgan's disgrace and imprisonment, which went some way beyond the betrayal of her marriage-bed. It was said that she had persuaded her lover Accolon to steal the King's sword Caliburn, substituting a copy of it to allay Arthur's suspicions. What the pair had planned then could only be guessed at, since Arthur had fought and killed Accolon, and thereafter joined with King Urbgen to see that Morgan could wreak no more mischief.

She had, of course, maintained her innocence: that she only wanted the sword of power to give to her husband Urbgen, and that Accolon had persuaded her into the business, but no one believed it, and Alexander, having himself experienced Morgan's ways with a young lover, doubted if Accolon had had any power over her at all.

He said, trying to hide the hesitation in his voice: "You cannot still want the sword?"

Morgan, back in the present, saw in one swift glance that her toils of magic needed to be re-woven. She laughed, and rose to pour wine for them both, then seated herself on the cushions of the wide window-seat and gestured him to sit beside her.

"No, no. Did I not say it was the grail?"

"Yes. But I didn't understand. Grail? That is a cup, I think? What grail?"

"Don't you remember what I said, that when Merlin found Macsen's sword of power, it was with other treasures in the Mithraeum at Segontium?"

"Yes. This grail was there?"

"Indeed. A great golden cup, they say, jewelled and with wings for handles, along with other things—I forget what—but all priceless. Things saved from the emperor's treasury and brought back to this country after his death abroad. It was kept secret somehow, and the treasure stayed buried while the Mithraeum rotted and fell in over it. Merlin took nothing but the sword. He"—her voice was suddenly acid—"he thought he had no need of the grail."

"But you have?"

"Need! I like to think not, but I desire it. Alex my love, I desire it!" She set her wine aside untasted, and turning with arms held out, took his face between her hands. "More, if it were possible, than I desire you! No, no, my dear, hear me out! That grail, cup as you call it, I believe it to be more magical even than the sword! I know that whoever owns it has power, and the protection of the greater gods. I have seen this in the crystal and heard it in the whispering of the dark spirits of the air."

He would have drawn back at that, but her hands held him and her eyes compelled him. The fumes of the wine he had drunk were warm in his brain. He said, whispering in his turn: "I will get it for you, Morgan my enchantress. Of course I will! There can surely be no wrong in it, treasure buried by Macsen's troops so many years back? And you are royal, of Macsen's house; you have a right to it, as Arthur had to the sword! I will get it for you. At Segontium, you said? Only tell me where it is, this temple of Mithras!"

She let him go, and sank back among the cushions. "It's there no longer. Nimuë has it."

"Nimuë?"

"Yes, that bitch of Merlin's. He told her where it was.

She wormed it out of him as he lay sick and near death, and then she went and lifted the rest of the treasure, grail and all, from the ruins of the Mithraeum, and took it down to Arthur at Caerleon. I'm told that neither the High King nor old Merlin would touch it. So she took it back to her home in the north, and it has never been seen since that day."

He said, after a pause: "And Count Ferlas?"

"Oh, yes. He went to Luguvallium and asked here and there, but no matter of that. It's a long story, and he got nowhere. He could not come near Nimuë. He found out nothing, and his brother took ill of a fever, and died, so Ferlas came back."

"Was it a spell, the sickness?"

"Who knows? Are you afraid?"

"I'm not afraid of witches, not now," said Alexander, and laughed. She looked at him, momentarily startled by the suddenly adult and almost indulgent tone, then laughed with him.

"Nor you are, my lover. Then you will go and get this magical cup for me?"

"I said I would." He hesitated again. "If you will promise me something."

"Conditions? I have said I will love you." A smile of charming mischief that hid a secret amusement. "I will even serve your wine in the grail when you bring it here."

A half-shake of the head. He was quite serious now. "Only tell me—promise me—that when you have this magical cup in your hands with, what did you say? all the power of the greater gods, you will use it only to help yourself to freedom, and after that, in the service of the High King."

For a moment he thought he had said too much. The

sudden flash in her eyes reminded him that he was still, if not strictly a prisoner here in the Dark Tower, very much in her power. But she needed him. Her brother Arthur might move at any moment to have her transferred to stricter rule, and she had a shrewd idea that where the blunt soldier Ferlas and his predecessor had failed to come near Nimuë's secret, the innocent and patently loyal Alexander might succeed. So she only smiled, with a kind of sad sweetness, and lifted a hand to touch his cheek again.

"All I want is the power the grail will give me to win clear of my brother's mistrust, and stay free from my sister's dreadful fate. To protect me, Alex, no more, and then to serve him. I know it can. Will you grant me this?"

"Of course I will! I promise it!"

Three days later, with his horse fresh, his weapons burnished, and a new embroidered cloak over his shoulders, Alexander set out for the north, and the kingdom of Rheged, where there was a castle belonging to Pelleas, husband of Nimuë the enchantress.

28

This had happened before; the day was fine, he was well armed, astride his good horse, and adventure lay ahead of him. But Alexander had no thought for the past. Then he had been a very young man, whereas now...His thoughts still full of his mistress, and of their farewell love-making last night, he rode at an easy canter along the river's side.

His lovesick abstraction was almost his undoing. Though, warned by his former accident hereabouts, he was riding with some care for the roughness of the track, his horse shied so suddenly, and seemingly for no reason, that he was almost unseated. He came to himself with a mild curse, controlled the horse, and only then saw the ghost that had caused it to shy.

She did indeed look very ghostlike, a slight figure in a grey cloak that fluttered in the breeze, a lady whom he did not for a moment recognise. Then he saw it was the Lady Luned, alone, and apparently, from her pallor and the way she held to the stem of a young silver birch tree, frightened. The horse stood still, held hard, but rolling a white-edged eye. The lady took a step forward, still clinging to the sapling's stem as if without its support she might have fallen. But she spoke prosaically.

218

"I'm sorry if I startled your horse. I thought it must be you, but I dared not be seen, in case—" She hesitated.

"In case?"

"In case perhaps it was one of the queen's people."

"Were you waiting for me, then?" The banal question came out of embarrassment. He had looked for the lady that morning to take his leave of her and thank her for her kindness, only to be told that she had not yet left her chamber. He should, in courtesy, have waited; he knew that quite well. But in his eagerness to be gone on his new mission, and at the queen's insistence, he had left messages merely, and ridden out as soon as he had broken his fast.

He said quickly: "I looked for you earlier, but your women said you were not yet about. I wished to give you my thanks for all you did for me, and I'm very happy to have this chance to thank you. But why—I mean, how is it you've come out here alone, and so early? To speak with me? Why, lady? Surely not just to say God speed?"

"I rode out early, and left my women to say I was still abed. My horse is tied up back there, out of sight in the wood. I had to see you. While you were at the castle I was powerless to come to you in private, but now . . ."

Her voice died. Her hands plucked nervously at her cloak. He regarded her for a moment, frowningly, then slid down from the saddle and offered her his arm. "You have something to tell me? Some commission to give me? Willingly—though I don't know how long it will be before I'll be able to return. Come, lady, if it's a secret matter, then let us go into cover and talk there. Where did you leave your horse?"

Her mare was tethered in a clearing some thirty yards back into the forest. Alexander slipped the chestnut's reins over its head, and let the beast graze. He looked round for a stump, a boulder, a fallen bough for the lady to sit on, but there was nothing, and she shook her head, speaking urgently, and still with that look of fear.

"No. There's no time. I must get back before she misses me. My lord, will you hear me out? I know—who does not?—that you are Queen Morgan's man, and that she has sent you out today as she has sent others of her lovers—"

"This to me, madam? You cannot think that I will listen—"

"Oh, don't be a fool!" The outburst was so sudden, so violent, so uncharacteristic of her, that he was silenced. She swept on, a spot of colour showing now in either cheek: "You can never have thought you were the first, or even the only one! Since her lord put her aside for Accolon, she has never been long without a lover. And now that she has this—this passion for Macsen's treasure—oh, yes, everyone knows it!—why do you think Ferlas went north for her? And Julian his brother? And at least one other before that! Did she tell you that Julian died? And now it is you!"

"Do you think I'm afraid of danger? And as for Accolon, that old tale, she was trapped by him—"

"As she was trapped by you?" She took a step nearer and her hand gripped his arm. The grasp was so fragile, the hand so thin and tremulous, that paradoxically he could not wrest himself away. "Please!" she begged him. "Please listen!" And by the same paradox, because she was not young and beautiful, but a plain woman who had shown him kindness, and whose hand shook on his arm with fear, he held himself in and listened.

"I only wish you well." She spoke quickly, breathlessly. "I want you to know that. And that's the only reason why I came here today to tell you the truth before you go further on this perilous quest for the queen. If what I have to tell you is hurtful, then I am sorry. But by any god you call your own, it is the truth."

She stopped and cleared her throat. He said nothing. In some strange way he already half knew what she was going to tell him. In the brief ride from the castle in the bracingly sweet air of morning he had felt, once more, a sort of shamefaced relief at the freedom from the drowsy, honey-scented toils that held him captive.

She went on: "It's true that when King Urbgen put her aside it was for adultery, but this was a small matter beside her treachery to her brother the High King. It was Morgan who persuaded Accolon to steal the sword of power, and use it against the King. No, hear me! She said that the sword was for Urbgen, but that was afterwards, to clear herself of blame! The truth is that she gave the sword to Accolon to use in single combat against the High King, thinking that Arthur must needs be killed, and that afterwards she, with her lover, would have the royal sword of power. The plot failed, and because she is Arthur's sister, she was not put to death, as her lover was, but put aside by King Urbgen, who is Arthur's man, and placed under guard. You have seen how rigorous her imprisonment is! Comfort, luxury even, and the freedom to ride abroad when she wishes! Why do you think she wants this treasure? Did she tell you?"

"She believes there is a jewelled cup that holds some sort of power—"

"Yes, yes, this power. Why does she want that? She already has her own sort of power, as everyone knows, and as she would be the first to tell you."

He hesitated. "Her imprisonment is not severe, I grant you that, but," he quoted, remembering, " 'it is still imprisonment.' She wants the power to bring herself free and once more to her brother's side, to help him with her magic. She—you said everyone knows she has magic at her disposal."

"Magic?" Surprisingly, there was contempt in Luned's voice. "Oh yes, she has magic, skills of one kind and another. No one denies that! And least of all should you, my lord!"

"Madam—"

"Oh, no, I don't mean her woman's wiles. I mean the magic she used to make them work on you. The drugs she uses. Has used, almost daily, on you!"

"Lady Luned—"

"Wait. I am nearly done. I only came to tell you this because I am afraid of what she might do were she ever to get this extra power, a power that both Merlin and the High King held in such awe that they hid it from men's sight. My lord"—the tremulous hand was on his arm again—"I beg you, I beg you, now that you are free, stay away! Never come back! Never! Do you understand?"

"How can I? I am pledged—"

"Even so. It would be better if you never went to look for this treasure, but if you should ever find it, I want you to think hard before you bring it back to her. She told you that she would never use it for the High King's hurt?"

"Yes."

She dropped the hand from his arm, and took a step away from him; another. When she turned to face him again, she looked older, frailer, honed down by fear. "Did she tell you what these 'councils' are that she holds in that private chamber in the east tower?"

"Of course. It's all that is left to her of a court and a following."

"And of course she invited you to join them?"

"She wanted to. She would have done soon. She said so."

"Did she say what they discussed so secretly, up in the tower?"

"Since Ferlas came back she has been consulting with her knights about this quest that means so much to her."

"Did she tell you that the knight who died, Count Ferlas' brother Julian, was pledged to marry me?"

"Why, no! I didn't know that. I'm sorry—" He began to stammer something, but she cut him short.

"She knew it, so she saw to it that he went on this quest of hers. And I believe," said Luned, so calmly that against his will Alexander found himself believing it, too, "that if he did indeed die from some evil spell cast, it was she who cast it."

"But why?"

"So that he might not return. Oh, yes, she would not like one of her following casting his eyes at anyone but herself, but it was more than that. She was afraid he would tell me of those meetings in the east tower. But she was too late. I already knew."

Silence. Alexander stood like a stone, looking down at his feet, wondering what to do, what to say, what to believe. One did not give a lady the lie. Besides, he owed her much kindness, perhaps even his life. But this, from one who had been Morgan's own lady-in-waiting? She was going on, still in that calm, expressionless voice which, by its very lack of emphasis, carried some sort of conviction. Something about a faction of young dissidents, men from the outlying Celtic lands, who were dissatisfied with the King's peace and the strong central government that Arthur had imposed on the small kingdoms of Britain. Now that there were no wars to prosecute, and justice was in the hands, not of the petty kings, but of the council in the Round Hall at Camelot, many high-spirited and hot-headed young outlanders were fretting at the lack of action. The Young Celts they called themselves. Harmless enough when it had started, it now seemed as if the young adventurers were being banded together and manipulated by self-seeking men, against the interests of the High King and the united kingdom he had fought to establish. And Queen Morgan's court was one of the meeting-places of the rebellious faction.

"You must believe me!" she was saying earnestly.

He was silent, remembering his own eagerness to avenge himself on March of Cornwall, the joy of his first skirmish, the excitement of the fight by the River Severn, and even this morning's high anticipation of adventure. This much of her tale he could believe.

"And these are the councils that she holds here," said Luned. "Not often enough to alert the guards who might report to the King, but whenever there is some excuse. Once Julian was pledged to me, he was a danger. So he did not come back."

There were some things one could not believe. He still said nothing. She regarded him for another moment or two, then asked, gently: "You will still go on this quest?"

"I must. I am pledged. Besides, what you have told me—" He stopped.

"You cannot, or will not, believe? I understand that. I'll say no more. Only this I beg of you, that if you do find this grail, and you still believe that it is only to be used in the High King's service, that you do not carry it back here, or to Castell Aur, but that you go first to

Camelot and let Arthur himself judge whether or not his sister is to have it."

"How can I?"

"Without impugning her? Or is it because you know in your heart that he would not let her come near it?"

"Lady—" he said, desperately.

"And you would call yourself a loyal subject of the High King? Or would have done, a short few weeks ago?"

The only sounds in the clearing were the steady munching of the horses, and the sudden shrill song of a robin hidden somewhere in a holly-tree.

"Is that all?" he asked at length. His voice was rough.

She nodded, rather sadly. "That is all, except to thank you for listening to me. I don't even ask you to believe me; you will find out for yourself once you are away and free from—once you are away. But I have one other request of you."

"What is that?"

From under the grey robe she brought a flask, gilt-stoppered, and housed in a leathern bag. "This is wine brewed by the monks in the house beyond the river bridge, and sent to us each year as a gift. I beg that you will accept it for your journey."

He took it, and began a little awkwardly to thank her, but she smiled and shook her head.

"That is only half the request. The rest is this—that you throw away the cordial that the queen gave you last night."

This time the silence was intense. Even the horses, as if sensing something, stopped their grazing to raise their heads and stare.

He said tightly: "How do you know she gave me a cordial last night?"

"Did you not understand what I said before? That you have been drugged, enchanted, what you will, from the moment she saw you, and marked you as the next man to be sent on this ceaseless search of hers for the power and influence she once had, and lost through treachery?"

Alexander, in after years, was never to cease regretting what he did next. Luned's gilt-stoppered flask went hurtling to the ground, he jerked the chestnut's head up from the grass and swung himself to the saddle, struck the spurs home and sent the big horse plunging out of the clearing and down to the road, leaving her standing there.

29

It must not be thought that Alexander was quite so blind and foolish that he had imagined his mistress to be blameless, or himself to be irrevocably in love. Queen Morgan herself boasted of her witchcraft, and he respected and feared her powers, which, in fact, had made her interest in him the more flattering and exciting. She was, besides, very lovely, and he was young, so when she seemed bent to use her magic to entrap him to her bed for the kind of love-making that was new to his youthful and somewhat limited experience, why then he had gone to her whistle, as they say, and had enjoyed himself hugely, in spite of the recurring weakness brought about by the low fever that he had seemed unable to shake off.

It was this that now, as he rode north, occupied his mind. The fresh sweet air of morning, the steady cantering of his good horse, the sense (whether admitted or not) of freedom, all this gradually conspired to clear his mind of the anger that the Lady Luned's words had roused in him, and to calm him sufficiently to allow him to think back and weigh up what had happened in the Dark Tower. And as he did so, a sort of pattern began to emerge.

The hurt arm and the fever, the kind nursing of old Brigit, and his seeming recovery. Then the queen's coming; the subsequent banishment of the old nurse and the maids who had attended him. The medicines, carefully mixed by the queen herself. The dreaming days of weakness that followed, explained as a reaction to the fever, dreams filled with her presence, her soft touch, swimming visions of her beauty and of the promise of love. The night, even now only remembered in feverish flashes of ecstasy, when she finally took him to her bed. And after that—yes, from that time onwards he had been her willing and lovesick slave.

It was not to be thought that he regretted it; it had been something he would not forget, nor would willingly have forgone, but now, as the chestnut stallion put the miles steadily behind him, the enchanted bonds loosened with every stride, and he found himself, without wishing to, going back over what Luned had told him.

The adultery with Accolon; well, she had been young, tied by an arranged marriage to an unhappy bed. It happened all the time. But treachery to the High King? Plotting, even in the imprisonment that followed, to damage the peace of the kingdom? The Young Celts, and this quest that she had been sending them on, Ferlas and Julian and who else, the quest for the grail of power. What kind of power? He was still young enough to think that she had all the kinds of power that a woman needs. What, then? Was he to be another Accolon, another Ferlas bribed as she had bribed him, Alexander, and then rewarded for his attempted quest? Or another Julian, who had perhaps resisted the bribe and so been sent to risk death?

The road drew clear at length of the forested valley,

and stretched ahead in the open; smooth riding at last on green turf that bordered a lake. The early morning breeze had dropped, and the water lay mirror-bright and shining. There were swans in the shallows, guddling peacefully among the weeds. A sandpiper ran along the shingle with its sweet fluting call. Alexander halted his horse, and sat for a few minutes, watching the quiet scene, while his thoughts ran on.

So why was this grail worth so much to her? She would bring its power to her brother's service, she had said, and of course he had believed her. Luned had denied it, and appealed to his loyalty to submit the quest to the High King. He remembered something else. Morgan herself had told him that Nimuë, the King's enchantress, held what remained of Macsen's treasure, which the King himself had handed to her for safe keeping. Surely, if that was so, then the King could have the grail brought to his hand at any time, just for the asking?

Which effectively gave Queen Morgan the lie. And so transparent a lie that only a fool too besotted to think would have failed to see it. So, Alexander, think . . .

First: she wanted the power for herself, she had said as much, to let her displace Nimuë. Very well; he could accept that, and understand the fears she had admitted about her fate in the long banishment from Arthur's favour. Second: she had professed herself very sure that he, Alexander, young and untried as he was, could succeed where the others had failed. Why?

There was an obvious conclusion: he had not been (and, in spite of what she had said, never would be) admitted to the councils of the Young Celts, because he was known to be loyal to the High King, and whoever watched and reported what went on in the Dark Tower could confirm it. Consequently he might come near Nimuë where Morgan's other emissaries, known to be members of Morgan's court, could not.

Another conclusion sprang from this: that Luned had been right, and Queen Morgan was—wanted to be—Arthur's enemy. She could not know that Luned would tell him about the secret council meetings, but even so, how could she, Morgan, be so sure that, once Alexander was away from her, and had had time to think, he would even go on with the quest, let alone carry the grail back to her?

He sat watching the swans, a knuckle to his lip. The chestnut, finding itself unheeded, pulled the reins through his slack fingers and lowered its head to graze. The sun was well above the hilltops now, and struck a glitter from the lake.

It was as if it had struck light somehow in the prince's confused brain. Free he might be, but his mistress was a witch, so he could reckon himself to be free only as a falcon is free, at the end of a lure, to be twitched back to her service when she so willed it. And Luned had told him how it was done. He carried her magic with him, in the pretty silver flagon she had given him, with such care, and with so many kisses, as he had left her bed that morning.

He pulled it from the saddle-bag, unstoppered it, and held it to his nose. The heady fragrance, herbs, fruit, honey, all the sweet enchantments she had used came vividly back to mind. He thought of the Lady Luned and the wine brewed by the monks in the riverside monastery, and how he had flung it from him and left the poor lady to mount herself and ride back to face her unwelcome guest in the lonely castle.

The flagon's stopper was made of a carved garnet. A flick of his hand sent it spinning into the water, startling the swans, which barked at him and oared away through the rushes, hissing. The flagon went after them, the cordial making a train of spilled drops that curved like a rainbow in the sunlight, then vanished into the lake.

"Drink that," said Alexander to the swans, suddenly cheerful, "and have sweet dreams tonight!"

Five days later, at sunset-time, he came to a village set in a gently wooded valley, and asked for shelter for the night.

30

The village was no more than a huddle of peasants' huts, but it boasted an ale-house, in front of which a couple of men were sitting with horns of beer.

He halted his horse and gave them good evening. One of them, a simpleton seemingly, merely stared and mumbled, but the other, an older man, returned the greeting civilly, setting his horn aside and getting to his feet.

"Are you the landlord?" asked Alexander.

"I am, sir."

"As you see, I've come a fair way today, and my horse is weary. Can you give me food and a bed for the night?"

"As to that, sir, meaning no offence, but my house is not for such as you—"

"Let me be the judge of that." Alexander, who was tired, spoke impatiently. "If you've bread and ale, and fodder for my horse, that will do. I can pay."

He made as if to dismount, but the man came forward to his bridle. "Stay, sir. I said I meant no offence. I'll give you shelter willingly if you want it, but if your horse has another half-mile in him, there's food and lodging just a ways down the valley yonder, that's fitter for a young lord such as yourself." He pointed. "That way. You see yon big stone cross standing? Well, turn off there, and follow the track along by the oak wood and you'll come to it. It's a monastery, St. Martin's they call it. It's a good house—a great one, you might say, and all sorts of folks get lodging there. They have a grand place for travellers. I know it well, for my son works there, a gardener he is, name of John, and works with Brother Peter himself."

"I see. Well, my thanks, I'll go on there. Half a mile, you said?"

"No more than that. Hark, you can hear the bell now. That'll be for vespers, but the porter'll be at the gate, and they'll make you welcome." He stepped back. "And don't think you've missed the evening meal, neither, young master! They're used to folks coming at all hours. Why, it's only last week a great party came in not much short of midnight, noble folks they were, with a gift that's fairly set the abbot up as high as a cock on a roof-top!"

"And what was that?" asked Alexander, not because he wanted to know, but because the fellow so obviously wanted to tell him.

"Why, a great treasure, by all accounts, some sort of relic, they say, that's been brought over from foreign parts, and holy with it! Brother Peter told my John all about it. He's not seen it yet, but he says that soon, maybe at the next feast day, as soon as they've settled on a place fit to house it, which they'll be able to do, having one of the finest carvers working there in the chapel this past year or more, and him already started, so Brother Peter says, on a shrine that's to hold a statue, that'll do well enough to keep this precious cup safe, as long as it stays in St. Martin's—"

Alexander, who had already set his horse in motion, checked it again. "Cup? Did you say a precious cup?"

"Aye. A cup all gold and jewels, Brother Peter says, and came from somewhere out East, maybe even from Jerusalem! Imagine that, here in this valley of ours! Some foreign kind of name they gave it, but I couldn't rightly say what."

"A grail? Was that the word?"

"Grail? Grail? Aye, it could be that, if that's a kind of cup."

"And this grail is to be kept at the monastery down yonder?"

The man showed no surprise at Alexander's sudden interest; no doubt he took it for the fervour of a devout Christian.

"Indeed, sir. But I doubt if you'll get to see it. They've got it locked away, seemingly, till—"

"Yes, yes. But tell me, you said it was brought here last week? With a royal party?"

"As to that, I don't know about royal, but they were grand folks, nobility, John said, good horses, and a train of servants, and a lady in a litter with silk curtains, and I don't know what besides."

"A lady," said Alexander thoughtfully. "A lady brought this treasure with her?"

"That's so, but it's not really a gift, they say. It's to be housed here for a while for safe keeping, that's all. But to have such a treasure here, in our valley, why, there'll be a mort of folks coming this way for that alone, and even a house like mine'll profit from it!"

"Is the lady—is the royal party still here?"

"Aye. But there's room and to spare for travellers, young master, and you'll be made welcome, no fear of that!"

"Well, thanks. Here's for your goodwill, landlord. I'll be on my way."

"God speed, young master, and a good night's rest to you."

The monastery lay, as was usual with such places, deep in the shelter of the valley where a river curved through pasture and woodland. It was a big place, seemingly important enough to have several courtyards, and its own farm buildings set among tilled fields and orchards. A mill-wheel turned in the river, and a sluice-gate let water through to feed a stewpond within the monastery walls.

Alexander, letting his tired horse make its own pace downhill towards the gate, saw it with satisfaction. He would have a comfortable night, and—by a stroke of luck that was barely believable, but the man had been positive about it—come within sight of his quest far sooner than he would have thought possible. He would hardly be able to lay hands on the grail while it was in the monastery's safe keeping, but if Nimuë was travelling south with it, and seeking the monastery's protection only while she rested on her journey, he might at the least have speech with her, or with some of her party, and find out from one of them where they were taking the treasure. And if he could by some ruse attach himself to her train, some sort of chance might come . . .

Luned's words, and his own symbolic rejection of

Morgan along with her flask of "magic" drugs, were for the moment forgotten. Tired as he was, it did not even occur to him that Nimuë might be travelling south to carry the precious cup herself to Arthur. The landlord's words had come like a sudden stroke of fortune, a pointer, the touch of an enchanted wand. The grail, without his seeking, had crossed his path. Even had he already decided to abandon the quest, he would have been less than human to refuse even to look at it.

The chapel bell had stopped by the time he reached the gate, but the porter was there, and opened readily, pointing the way to the stableyard, beyond which, he said, lay the dormitory for male travellers. Supper? Indeed there would be supper. My lord (this with an expert, summing glance at the horse's trappings and the glint of gold at the young man's belt and sword-hilt) would be served in the refectory below the dormitory. Brother Magnus, who looked after the travellers, would show him the way. There would be supper served as soon as vespers was over. No doubt my lord would wish, later, to attend compline?

My lord wished only to eat, and to bespeak a bed, but he knew what was expected of guests in such a place, and besides, it was very probable that the grail's guardians, too, would attend the service, so he assented, and, having seen his horse into the care of a lay-brother, made his way to the quarters reserved for the monastery's guests.

As it turned out, he ate alone, but for a couple of other travellers on their way to Glannaventa to take ship for Ireland. They were foreigners, speaking only some outlandish Irish tongue, so he could not question them about the royal party, which presumably had supped earlier.

The supper was plain, but good, broth followed by a hot, thick stew with fresh-baked bread, and some sort of fish dish flavoured with herbs. After supper Alexander went to see how his horse fared, and found him comfortably housed, blanketed and busy at a full manger. Sharing the big stable-building with him were three sleek palfreys which must belong to the monastery, along with two span of sturdy working mules. No sign of the other party's beasts; they were in the other stable— the one normally used for guests—and in the charge of the party's own grooms and serving men. They had left no room for the young lord's horse, so said the lay-brother who worked as groom, but the young lord need have no fear; his horse would be as well cared for as the abbot's own.

This was plainly true. Alexander, thanking him, put a couple of hesitant queries about the other party, but met with no satisfaction. As to that, said the lay-brother, he knew nothing about them, except that one of their number—a young boy destined for noviceship—would stay after the party left. They had all, the lady and the rest, attended all the services; it seemed they were devout folks—(devout? the queen-enchantress Nimuë?)—so no doubt if the young lord meant to attend compline, he would have a chance to see them there, and maybe have speech with them afterwards. And no, he could not accept a gift for himself, but if the young lord would perhaps leave something in the offertory, God would bless the gift . . . And there was the chapel bell.

* * *

The chapel was a noble one. A high vaulted roof swallowed the light of the candles. The smell of fine wax burning mingled with the smoke of the incense that could be seen curling up into the shadowed roof. A stone screen, finely carved, cut off the rear of the building from the place where the monks worshipped. Behind this screen were the seats for the lay folk and travellers, the monastery's guests. Through the fretted carving Alexander could just glimpse the crucifix above the high altar; it seemed to be floating in the smoky candle-light. None of the monks was visible, but the singing rose strong and true into the vaulting.

And yes, the royal party was there, across the central aisle from him, a dozen or so people. Alexander, his head apparently bent in prayer, looked sideways through his fingers, studying them.

First, the lady herself, queen, enchantress, devout or devious; she was there, demurely hidden behind a heavy veil. Her dress was of a rich russet-colour, and over it she wore a brown cloak against the chill which could strike, even on a summer evening, in a stone-built chapel. He caught a glimpse of a slender wrist encircled with gold, and the glint of a sapphire on the folded hands. Cloak and veil hid the rest.

Beside her knelt an elderly man, his noble old face lifted towards the high altar, his eyes closed in prayer. He was soberly dressed, but the grey stuff of his gown was good, and the crucifix he held in the fine, thin hands was of silver crusted with some deep red stones that could be rubies. Beyond him could just be glimpsed a slight figure, no more than a child, it seemed, but robed and cloaked like a monk. That would surely be the boy destined for the novitiate. At the boy's other side knelt a priest. The other men and women, kneeling at a little distance in the rear, must be their attendants.

The office came to an end. A long pause of quiet, then the slow shuffle of feet beyond the screen as the monks filed out. The lady, rising, helped the old man to his feet. The two of them, with the boy between them, left the chapel. The rest followed, Alexander close behind them.

Outside there was a pause, before the party broke up. The lady stood for a few minutes, talking to the other two women of the party—her waiting-women, no doubt. Alexander looked to see her take leave of the old man and go with the women towards the quarters reserved for female travellers, but when at length she turned away, she went, still holding the old man's arm, towards an imposing building just beyond the chapel. The abbot's house, presumably; and of course a lady as important as Nimuë would be lodged there, not housed with the common travellers . . . One of the women followed her, the other turning aside for the guests' quarters. The priest had already vanished, with the boy, through a door into the main monastery buildings. Another boy in page's uniform ran forward to speak with the old man, then, dismissed, followed the servants who were making for the men's dormitory. But he went slowly, loitering some way behind the rest of the party, reluctant, perhaps, as one always was at that age, to be sent to bed.

Alexander went quickly after him, catching up with him some yards short of the dormitory door.

"It's too good a night to be packed off at this hour, isn't it? Tell me, do they lock the doors once they've got us in for the night?"

The boy laughed. "Yes, like hens in case the fox gets us! But at least they don't wake us at dawn—though the chapel bell does!"

"You've been here long?"

"Nearly a week."

"I just rode in today, from the south. I don't know this part of the country, at all, but this seems a good place. How long will you be lodging here?"

"I don't know. Some days, I suppose. They never tell us anything, but it wouldn't surprise me if the master wasn't aiming to stay here for a bit longer."

"And your mistress?"

"Oh, she'll be all for going home, once she's seen the prince safely settled in. Why do you ask? Who are you?"

"One who would like to have a talk with your mistress, if that could be arranged? I'm travelling alone, with no servant, but if I sent my name to her tomorrow, would she see me, do you think?"

"Well, of course!" The boy, who had been surveying Alexander in the light from the open door of the dormitory, sounded confident. "She's a sweet lady, the mistress. No ceremony, anyone can talk to her. If it's important—"

"To me it is. What's your name?"

"Berin."

"Well, Berin, can you tell me more of your lady? Is it true that—?"

"Listen," said the boy rapidly, "there's the bell. They'll be locking up in a minute. I'll tell you the easiest way to speak with my lady. She goes walking in the orchard first thing in the morning, while the master's still at prayers. It would be easy then to speak with her . . . No, no need for that, sir! Look, there's Brother Magnus now, waiting to shut the hens up! We'd better hurry! Good night to you!"

He took to his heels, and Alexander, returning the second bribe of the evening to his pouch, hastened after him.

SIX

Alice
and Alexander

31

So they met at last, Alice and Alexander, in the early morning of a beautiful summer's day, in the orchard of the monastery of St. Martin.

She was sitting under an apple tree. The tree was full of fruit, baby green apples crowding so round and glossy, among leaves and branches so symmetrically pruned, that it looked like a tree in an illuminated missal—the Tree itself, before it ripened to the Fall. Among the shorn, tawny grass at its foot, some poppies and dog-daisies had escaped the scythe, and there were butter-cups, and the little low-growing heartsease, and clover already a-flutter with small blue butterflies.

She was wearing blue, the colour of the butterflies' wings, and, intending to go to chapel later, she wore her veil. She was about to push its folds back from her face, so that she could watch the robin that had just flown down from the apple tree and was perching within a yard of her feet, on an upturned bucket that someone had left there. Then, as Alexander approached across the grass, the robin scolded and flew, and Alice paused, still veiled, and turned her head.

"Lady," he said, a little hoarsely, and made his bow.

Looking up through the veil, she saw a handsome

young man, with blue eyes bright in a tanned face, and brown hair curling thickly to his shoulders. He bore himself proudly, and his clothes, though worn and serviceable rather than fine, were good. His sword-belt gleamed bright as horse-chestnuts, and the hilt of his sword was jewelled.

"Sir?" said the Lady Alice, and waited.

And now that the moment had come, and the end of his quest for the fabled powers of Macsen was so easily, so magically in sight, Alexander found that he had forgotten all about it. There was some enchantment here that was stronger than Queen Morgan's, stronger than Macsen's, an enchantment that the first apple tree of Eden might have been able to account for. He tried to speak, cleared his throat, and said, merely: "If I might see your face? Of your courtesy, if you would put aside your veil?"

"I was just going to," said Alice. "I only ever wear it for chapel, and I think it was frightening the robin." And, pushing the fine folds back, she looked up at him, smiling.

Without knowing even that he had moved, he was down on his knees in front of her, taking breath, but only able to stammer, half stupidly: "You—you cannot be a witch! Who are you? Who are you? You are the most beautiful girl I have ever seen in my life! Tell me who you are!"

"I'm Alice, daughter of the Duke Ansirus of Castle Rose in Rheged. And I do assure you that I'm no witch, though I've sometimes wished to be! And you, sir? You have a name, too?"

She was laughing at him, but he did not notice. He answered, careless suddenly of all concealment, all pos-

sibility of danger. "I am called Alexander. My father was
Prince Baudouin of Cornwall, brother to King March.
My mother keeps Craig Arian for me, in the valley of the
Wye."

"And what brings you here, prince, to Rheged—and
expecting witches here, by the sound of it?"

"I think," said Alexander, meaning every word of it,
"that I came here only to meet you. And I think that I
love you."

In the sharp silence that followed, the robin flew down
again to the rim of the bucket, and trilled a loud, indig-
nant song that went quite unheard.

Neither of them, in later years, could ever fully
remember what happened next, what was said, or even if
anything was said at all for the first long moments while
they looked at one another, each knowing that they had
been moving steadily through their young lives towards
this meeting. To Alexander it was like coming out of
mist into sunlight, out of dark water into fresh and glittering air. The Dark Tower had never been. Some day,
somehow, its story must be told, its stupid sins confessed, but not now, please God, not yet. Now was the
moment when his life as a true prince, a knight, a man,
might really begin.

For Alice, the moment was the one where the anxious
mariner sees the lights of harbour. Or, more practically—
and Alice was always practical—the moment of recog-
nising the future master of her beloved Castle Rose, the
man to whom she could go not merely in duty, but with
joy as a lover; the young and eager sword that would
keep herself and her people safe and in peace when their
old lord had left them.

* * *

Whatever their eyes and spirits said to one another, their tongues found themselves uttering the normal civil commonplaces of strangers meeting for the first time in a place new to both. Alexander's outburst was ignored; Alice hardly knew how to reply to it, or even whether to take it seriously, and Alexander himself was not even sure that he had spoken his thoughts aloud.

So, sitting down beside her on the grass, he hurried now to say something of the beauty of the day, the welcoming comfort of the monastery; he hoped that the duke's party was well housed, wondering how long they had been on the road, and—the nub of it at last—how long they proposed to stay at St. Martin's?

"Only a few more days. We are making for home after a journey abroad, but we had to stay here awhile. My father and the abbot had business to discuss."

Business to discuss? A terrifying thought made him catch his breath. Perhaps this lovely girl was destined to become a nun? But before he could speak she smiled, and said calmly, as if answering him: "My father will one day enter this monastery, but now we came only to accompany someone who seeks refuge here. A boy from the Frankish kingdoms who was in danger there, and who also seeks the religious life."

"From Gaul? Wait—you said your father was Duke Ansirus? He whom they call the pilgrim duke?"

"The same."

"I have heard of him, of course. And of you, too. I believe our families have some connection, and I have heard my mother speak of the duke and his daughter. They call you 'the pretty pilgrim.' Did you know?"

"They mock me, I think," said Alice. She spoke quite without coquetry.

"Mock you? How could that be, when—?" began Alexander, hotly, but, partly to prevent a repetition of his first outburst, she said quickly: "Indeed yes! I believe it's thought strange for a young girl—and I've travelled with my father since I was six years old—to go on these long journeys and mingle with rough folk on the road, and sometimes meet with danger, or at any rate the risk of it. But I wouldn't have had it otherwise. I've seen wonderful things, and been to beautiful places. I don't think I shall ever forget them as long as I live."

"And now that your father plans to retire into the Order here, won't you find life dull and stale after so much adventure?"

She shook her head. "In all my travelling I've never seen a lovelier country than this, or a more beautiful place than my own home in Rheged. Even Rome, Athens, even Jerusalem, can't show anything to compare—"

"Jerusalem!" As if the word had been an arrow striking home, he remembered. The quest, so hotly undertaken for Queen Morgan; the grail; his private plan to gain the confidence of the bearers of the marvellous relic. His hope, in fact, to take it, if necessary by force.

"What is it?" asked Alice, disturbed by his look.

He turned away from her, his head bent, his hands unconsciously savaging some inoffensive weed, tough-rooted in the grass. At length he spoke, still looking away from her.

"I spoke with the tavern-keeper up yonder in the village. It was he who told me of this place, and the good lodging to be found here. He told me, too, of a party—he

called it a 'royal party'—that had recently ridden in
bearing some great treasure to be lodged here for safe
keeping. This must have been your party? Was the story
true?"

"Quite true. I told you that we came to escort a young
Frank who is to join the brothers here. He is a prince, and
he brings with him a princely treasure."

"From Jerusalem?"

"Oh, no, from Gaul. I suppose it may have come in the
first place from Jerusalem, or somewhere in the Holy
Land, but it has been in Gaul for many years. Queen
Clotilda, who was wife to Clovis, the Frankish king, first
acquired it, and kept it in her own private chapel. That's
all I know, except that now there is war, so the grail has
been sent here for safe keeping."

"Then it is the Grail?"

"They say so."

He did not appear to notice anything evasive in her
reply. He was frowning down again at the weed in his
fingers: "I was told that the Grail was here, in Britain, in
the keeping of Nimuë the enchantress, who is queen of
some castle in the north. In Rheged, she—they said."

"Macsen's treasure. Yes, everyone knows that."

"That is why—" he spoke awkwardly. "You must
have wondered when I spoke of witches. I thought that
the treasure must have been brought here by Queen
Nimuë, perhaps on her way south to the High King's
court. And you were veiled, so I, well, I—"

"Took me for the King's enchantress?" Alice laughed.
"I see. And you sought speech with her. May I ask what
your concern is with Macsen's treasure?"

"I—yes, of course I will tell you. Later I will tell you

all of it. But believe me, it doesn't concern me now. Not as it did. Do I understand that you know where it is?"

"I know that Queen Nimuë's husband, Pelleas, has a castle in the north-west near the sea, some miles beyond the borders of our land. She also has a house near Camelot, that was Merlin's house. It's called Applegarth. She spends a lot of time there, when King Pelleas is with the High King. But I don't know where she has lodged Macsen's treasure. How should I? Nobody knows. It's said that she keeps it hidden by enchantment until Arthur, or the High Kingdom, may have need of it."

He was silent, thinking back. Sitting here in the orchard, with the sunlight gilding the grasses, and the fresh sounds and scents of morning around him, it seemed impossible that he had ever fallen victim to the smoky charms of Morgan le Fay.

Alice, seeing the trouble in his face again, spoke gently: "Did you perhaps think that you yourself had need of it? I'm sorry. It seems that poor mortals such as we have no right to it, to any part of it, even if we could find where the rest of the treasure—the spear and the grail—lies hidden. Perhaps they are now beyond the reach even of Nimuë. Perhaps they are with Merlin himself, hidden in the light. You know what they say of him, that he sleeps in his own holy hill, with all his fires and travelling glories around him. So you must content your spirit, my lord, with the sight of the grail that we brought with us from Gaul."

"Yes, that—the grail you brought. This is what I don't understand. You make it sound as if there was more than one cup of the Lord's Supper!"

"Oh, there is," said Alice, a little sadly.

"What do you mean?"

"I told you that I've travelled with my father on pilgrimage—twice to Jerusalem, and twice to the shrine of St. Martin in the Frankish kingdom. In those places, especially in Jerusalem, the pilgrims are offered relics of the time when Jesus lived; relics, even, of the sacred moments of His life and death. And—but I don't want to distress you—"

"No. Go on."

"Well, there are men who make a living from this trade—for that's what it is. Relics command good prices, from poor pilgrims and also from the emissaries of the wealthy churches and courts that would own and revere such things. I'm sorry if you didn't know this."

"Only because I never thought about it! But now that you tell me . . . but do you mean that Macsen's treasure, those things of power, are false? Surely that cannot be!"

"Of course not! But from what one has heard, Macsen's grail, though like the sword they call Caliburn it's a thing of power and great beauty, is no more the cup that Jesus drank from than a dozen or so I've seen in the Holy Land."

"And the one that you brought with you?"

"It's a small cup of gold, very lovely, and beautifully made." She smiled. "But would you have thought that Jesus and his friends ate and drank off gold?"

"I—I never thought about it like that."

"I'm afraid that His cup must have been clay, a simple pot long since broken to pieces."

"But if you know this—" Alexander, she was glad to see, was not disturbed by any flaw in faith, though he still looked troubled—"if you know this, why did you—or rather why did the duke your father—let this Frank who travelled with you bring this 'grail' back to the brothers here? Already tales of its holiness are going about, and the poor folk will expect miracles!"

"Then they will probably get them," said Alice calmly.

As he stared at her, really troubled now, a bell began to ring. Alice picked up the veil that had slipped to the turf, and made to rise, but he put out a hand.

"No, please wait. Tell me what you mean. Are you—you cannot be talking of trickery?"

Not, he was thinking, while you sit there looking like a young angel.

"Not trickery. It's honest enough, a matter of faith. You see, Chlodovald—that's the prince—believes; the old queen believes; and the brothers here, too. That's the real 'grail,' that belief, even though the actual one must have been broken to fragments hundreds of years ago. It's an idea, a symbol, just as it was meant to be on that first evening. That's what my father says, anyway—and Jesus said so himself, if you remember?"

"You talk as if you'd known him."

"I think I did, when I was very little."

Another pause, while the chapel bell rang to its sweet, echoing finish, and silence came back.

"I came to find the grail," he said suddenly. His voice was rather too loud, and he lowered it. "I came on a sinful quest, to find Macsen's great cup, and take it, by guile or by force, for someone who wanted its power. Someone whom I served. Other knights have travelled abroad on the same quest. None of them have found it, and two at least have died in the seeking."

"Then," she said, very simply, "they have found some sort of truth. And you? Will you go on? This person you serve, will he require you to do so?"

"I was sent by a lady. For me, it was a quest, and an adventure. For her, it was—" He checked himself.

"For her? For its power, you said? Well," said Alice, "perhaps she thinks she has need of it. Everyone has their own grail."

"That lady?" He said it violently, then stopped, ashamed. "Forgive me," he said, very humbly. "I have been very wrong. I had no right to speak to you as I have done, or to speak about—her, as I would wish. I think I had better leave you."

This time it was she who put out a hand. "No. Please stay. Why don't you tell me about it, this quest of yours that troubles you so much?"

So he stayed. He sat down again beside her on the warm grass and told her the whole story, from its beginning at Craig Arian to its shadowed ending in the Dark Tower. There, indeed, he could not bring himself to tell her everything, but even so, when he had done, he sat in unhappy silence, not looking at her, awaiting either her censure or a silent and disgusted withdrawal.

She was, indeed, silent for some time, but when she spoke she merely asked: "And now?"

"I don't know. I can't go on with this quest, nor can I turn around and go south to deal with King March. Both quests are wrong, though I am in a sense vowed to both; I can see now that one is sinful and the other foolish. But what is left for me? What am I to do?"

Alice turned aside again to pick up the fallen veil. "It seems to me that the most important thing is what you learned from the Lady Luned about these secret meetings of men who are enemies of the High King's policies. Even if you don't know anything of their plans, you know some of their names, and one of them, certainly, will interest my father. So—ah, listen! I think they're coming out of the chapel now. Don't you think that the first thing to do, and the best, is to go and talk to him?"

32

It was some days, however, before Alexander managed to have speech with the duke. When Alice, parting from him at the door of the men's refectory, went to join Abbot Theodore and her father at breakfast, she found the place in what would have been, in less quiet and determinedly peaceful surroundings, an uproar. The abbot himself hurried to meet her with disquieting news.

Her father had been taken ill, quite suddenly, in the chapel at the end of the service. It seemed that he had felt tired that morning, and slightly giddy, but had brushed his people's concern aside, and insisted on going to the morning office. When he saw that Alice was not in chapel, he forbade anyone to give her news that might alarm her. And indeed to his servants' watching eyes all seemed well. But at the end of the service, when the duke came to get up from his knees, he half rose, then staggered suddenly as if losing strength in his right leg, and fell across his chair. Nor could he move again. When Alice had heard the chapel doors opening and the folk coming out, it was an anxious little procession bearing the duke, conscious but helpless, towards his bedchamber.

The magical moments in the orchard, Alexander himself, were forgotten. Alice did not wait to hear more, but picked up her skirts and ran upstairs to see her father.

He was in his bed in the abbot's guest-chamber, a grandly comfortable apartment, with the hospitaller, assisted by one of the nuns and by Alice's own woman Mariamne, in attendance.

Alice flew to the bedside. "Father? What is it? How are you? What happened?"

The duke, flat on his pillows, and looking grey and tired, managed a smile, but did not speak. One thin hand stirred on the coverlet, and she bent over him, taking it in both of hers.

"Father—"

The abbot, who had followed her, but more decorously, came forward to lay a kindly hand on her shoulder. "Quietly, dear child, be calm. Your father has had a slight seizure, but he will recover very soon. He's a strong man, and he's where he will have every care. Brother Luke will tell you that there is no danger. Come away now, leave him to rest."

The hospitaller, at the other side of the bed, with a hand to the duke's wrist, nodded cheerfully, and in a while he and the abbot were able to persuade Alice to leave the bedchamber. Once outside on the stair, and with the door closed, they hurried to give her what assurance they could. It was a kind of seizure, they said, they had seen such things before, and it was not easy to predict their course, but it seemed mild of its kind. Already the feeling was returning to the duke's side, and he could move the fingers of the affected hand—his right. His heart was strong, and though he was tired and a little confused in mind, he had spoken. The words were slow and blurred, but that would come right with time. Best not to let him talk yet, said the hospitaller; let him stay quietly for a few days in bed. What he needed now was sleep and a tranquil mind. If Lady Alice would speak with the messenger herself, she would be able to reassure her father later. It was important for his mind to be at peace.

"Messenger? What messenger?" asked Alice, sharply.

"You didn't know? Of course, you were out early," said the abbot. "Well, a man rode in this morning from Castle Rose. He was closeted with your father for half an hour or so before service. I myself had already gone across to the chapel, so did not see him. But I have been wondering if perhaps he brought some news to distress your father. Brother Luke thinks that might have helped cause this seizure."

Alice could almost feel the blood leaving her cheeks. Bad news from Castle Rose? Fire? A death? "I must see him. Please, straight away? He is still here?"

"Yes." They were downstairs now, at the door of the abbot's rooms. A lay-brother, busy there about some cleaning task, was sent hurrying off. "I believe he went to get something to eat. Lady Alice, would you like me to be with you when you see him?"

"Thank you. But . . . It's all right. I'm quite all right. You're very kind, but I mustn't keep you from your—" She hesitated. The word "duties" was not somehow quite right for the lord abbot.

"From my breakfast?" said the abbot, smiling. "And you should eat, too, my dear child. I'll have them bring something for you to the parlour. Take him in there, and have your talk in private. Ah, here's your man."

She had half expected Jeshua, but it was Adam, one of the menservants. His news, briefly told, was not grave, but it was easy to guess that it might have helped to strike down an elderly and worried man.

Count Madoc, instead of waiting, as he had been asked to do, for the duke's return, was already at Castle Rose. He had been in residence there already for almost a month, and had brought a troop with him; men-at-arms, said Adam, under a captain, and things were sadly at odds in the servants' quarters and the stables, and indeed, outside in parts of the estate where the count had been riding out among the duke's people. Of course they all knew that Count Madoc, being handfast to the Lady Alice, would soon be master of Castle Rose, but even so—

"He is not handfast to me," said Alice; it might even be said that she snapped it. "There hasn't yet been any talk of settlement. How could there be, till the duke gets home? Count Madoc is ahead of things, but I suppose it's understandable. Well, what's the trouble? Beltrane sent you with some complaint?" Beltrane was the head steward.

"Beltrane is ill, my lady. He's ailed for some time, and when the new man Jeshua came he was glad and thankful to pass things over to him. A very capable fellow, the Jew, and nice to get on with, and seemingly knows how to manage things, coming from a great household—"

"Yes, yes. So what's gone wrong?"

"Well, Beltrane bade us all look to Jeshua for orders, while he had to keep his bed, and we would do so willingly, but until my lord your father gets home the Jew has no authority—"

"Who says so? My father gave him letters when he left us at Glannaventa to ride to Castle Rose. You all knew he came from the duke, and if Beltrane appointed him head steward he has all the authority he needs. Does someone query it?"

"My lady, Count Madoc does. He has spoken of dismissing him. And some others of us as well."

"Indeed? Count Madoc to dismiss my father's men?"

"He made that threat, my lady. And his men are taking much upon themselves about the estate. There are . . . there are complaints, my lady."

"Such as?"

For the first time the man looked away. He mumbled something, his eye on his dusty boots.

Alice, taking breath to speak sharply, let it go again, and said quietly: "Adam, I am not a child. And with my father ailing, I am mistress of Castle Rose. Complaints? Do you mean from the women?"

"Well, there've been incidents. Bet's man got into a fight, but that's happened before. And yes, there've been others. But it's not just that. The count's men, there's some heavy drinkers there, and trouble from time to time. But nothing serious yet, my lady, nothing to knock my lord over the way it did. It was only—we all thought you'd have been home a week or more past, but with you coming here to St. Martin's first, Beltrane thought it would be best if my lord would give him a letter, a paper of some sort, showing that Jeshua and the others of us had his word to keep things right for him till he got home. That's really all the message I brought, and how was anyone to know it would overset my lord the way it did?"

Alice turned away and went quickly over towards the window. Her hands were clenched tightly at her sides, her pulse racing, quick with anger. She knew perfectly what had shocked her father into this collapse. Madoc, over-ready in his arrogance to claim Alice, and with her the rich inheritance that he was eager for, had presumed a claim before it was even discussed, and was sure enough of her, and of himself, to let his men, by all accounts, use her home like an outland camp.

Well, he had overreached himself. In its way, the news was good. There would be no need, now, to persuade the duke to call off any discussion of that marriage. Nor, surely, to sanction a different one? No need even to wait for a winter wedding to free her father for the holy life he longed for. It should be mercifully easy to set his mind at rest.

She turned back to face the man, who saw with surprise that she was smiling. "Well, Adam, it's obvious that we must stay here longer, until my father is well enough for the journey home. But I'll do what I can. I'll give you letters for Beltrane and for Jeshua. They will give Jeshua the authority to act in my and my father's name until Beltrane's well again. I doubt if Count Madoc will ignore the duke's seal." She smiled again, and Adam had the swift impression that the sun had suddenly come out through cloud. "They tell me you rode all night."

"I had to set out late, madam, when the castle was abed, and I came without stopping, except to breathe my horse."

"You've eaten, I believe?"

"Yes."

"Then after you've rested, come back to me for the letters, and tell the stable-man to saddle one of our horses for you. And Adam—"

"Yes, my lady?"

"Tell them at home not to worry too much, but just to put up with a difficult visit as best they can. And tell them that my father is recovered now, and resting, and should soon be well. Whatever it was in your news that distressed him, it will be put right the moment we get home. In fact, it's been put right already."

For the next three days Alice was constantly with her father. She sent to tell Alexander what had happened, and that his meeting with the duke must wait till the latter was fully recovered. The message came back that the prince had no plan to leave the monastery until such time as he might meet and talk with the duke, and meantime if there was any service, anything at all he could do, he was her most devoted servant.

The messenger—it was Berin, the duke's page—was sent running back with Alice's thanks, no more, but with a postscript added by Berin (now deeply interested) that he was sure his mistress meant to attend some of the chapel services, to add her prayers for her father's recovery to the fervent representations made by the monks and nuns.

So Alexander went devotedly, morning and evening, to chapel, and spent his days riding out to exercise his horse, and on the third evening was rewarded by the sight of the Lady Alice at vespers, and a smile and brief word as she hurried back afterwards to the sickroom. She looked tired, he thought, and a little pale, but her lovely serenity was unchanged. Her father was better, she told him, gaining strength almost hourly; he was fast recovering the use of his limbs, and his speech, though still slow, was clear. If Prince Alexander still wished to have speech with him—?

He did.

Well, then, very soon, she thought. In two or three days' time. Would he still be here?

He would.

Alexander went cheerfully back to the stableyard, where he spent most of his time these days in the excellent company of his horse and the lay-brother who worked as groom. It was only when the latter, hissing over the work-mules, asked him if he had been into the chapel sanctuary where Chlodovald's grail was now splendidly housed in its own carved and canopied apse, that he realised he had forgotten completely about that grail, and indeed about any other.

Except what had become his own heart's dear desire.

33

Two days later one of Ansirus' servants came to find Alexander as he sat at breakfast, to tell him of the duke's wish to see him, and to escort him to his master's bedside.

Alexander, following the man up the great stairs of the abbot's house, felt a tightening of the nerves that surprised him. Apart from his dealings with Queen Morgan, his young self-confidence had rarely been shaken, but this interview—he found himself totally unsure of what to say or how to say it, knowing only that it must somehow be said. His dealings with Queen Morgan; there lay the rub. What Alice might have told her father already of that story, and what the duke might have made of it, Alexander did not care to guess. But he was Alice's father, and the truth would have to be told.

He took a deep breath, straightened his shoulders, and went past the bowing servant into the bedchamber.

The duke was still in bed, propped on high pillows. The chamber was big and sunny, overlooking the river-meadows and the mill. Its furnishings were as good as any in a lord's house—which in fact it was, the abbot being cousin to a minor king somewhere in Wales. There was fine horn in the window-frame, and the hangings were beautifully woven and worked. Only the cushioned prie-dieu in the corner, with the crucifix hanging above it, showed that this was a room in a religious house.

Alexander made his bow and spoke his formal greetings, and the old man smiled and motioned him to a chair set between the bed and the window.

"The son of Baudouin of Cornwall, my daughter tells me? I remember him. I never met him, but he was always well spoken of. A father to be proud of. And I understand that your mother lives still?"

So Alexander repeated his story of his father's murder and their flight from King March's court and how his mother had sworn that one day he should avenge his father.

"And that was what you set out to do?"

"Not quite, sir. I would have gone, of course, but she wouldn't have it. It was not that her love and grief for my father had grown less, but that—she said—things had changed in Britain since that day. There were other ways to bring King March down to shame and perhaps death. She wouldn't let me go into Cornwall, but told me to ride to Camelot and submit the matter to the High King's law."

"Which explains why you are travelling north through Rheged?" said the duke, then smiled. "No, boy, I know why you are here. I have heard of your sojourn at the Dark Tower—what you told her of it—from my daughter. Don't think I can throw any stone of blame! Once—a very long time ago—I was young myself, and did some foolish and sinful things which I would hardly care to be reminded of now . . . But even through evil, I believe God can move us in the way we should go."

He paused, and his head went back on the pillows, as if in weariness, but when Alexander got up, ready to go, or to call in the nun who sat outside, he lifted a hand to stop him.

"No. It's all right. I'm not tired, only slow. Slow of voice, as you can hear, and even slower of thought. They tell me it will pass with time, but I am afraid that time is a luxury I do not have."

At that Alexander began some sort of protest, but the duke, smiling, shook his head. "Thank you, but I wasn't talking about death. I intend to do a great deal before that day! I am talking of now, today, what is needful to be done now, while I, alas, am not capable of doing it." He drew a long breath, and then, as if it had given him strength, he nodded, with something of vigour and decision. "Yes, there is a lot I have to say to you, Prince Alexander, and a lot to ask of you. But first, will you pour some wine? It's on that table yonder, and yes, I am allowed to have it, or I assure you that my gentle daughter would have locked it away . . . Thank you. Take some for yourself, won't you? And now sit down again, if you will, and tell me the tale that you told my daughter. Perhaps you can tell me more than you would have told to her? But I must hear it, all of it. It concerns me more nearly than you think."

So once more Alexander went through the story, this time without troubling to conceal anything. It is to be remembered that he had never known the advice or even the presence of a father, and now he found himself talking with a freedom he had not known even with Barnabas at Craig Arian. From time to time, as he talked, the duke put a question, so that when at length the prince fell silent, nothing had been held back.

The duke went straight to the same point as Alice had

done. "These 'councils' of Queen Morgan's. Have you remembered all the men who were with her?"

"I think so. I didn't know all those in her party by name, but the ones who were closest, and sat with her in the east tower, yes."

"And one of the names you heard was Madoc."

"Yes, sir. I only heard that name once, when Count Ferlas was talking with the queen."

"Then he was not there at the Dark Tower?"

"No, sir. But I understood that he had been. He had ridden north on some business of the queen's. I never knew what, only what I told you Ferlas said. But it was not this—the quest for the grail. That," Alexander finished bitterly, "was reserved for the expendable fools."

"Well," said Ansirus, smiling, "here is one fool who seems to have won clear of his folly—and you are many years younger than I was when that happened to me! No, boy, forget it. I think that things will change for you now. More wine, please, and then, of your goodness, listen to what I have to ask of you."

When Alexander had served the wine again the old man lay back for a few moments in silence, turning the goblet in hands that were slow and fragile-seeming, but quite steady. When he spoke his voice, too, seemed to come more strongly.

"I believe you told my daughter that though you were vowed to two different quests, you could not continue with either. One was foolish, you said, and the other sinful."

He paused for a sip of wine, then set the goblet aside. "For the sinful one, the quest laid on you by a witch who wants to seize power to which she has no shadow of right, that vow you can forget, and forget in honour.

Even had you not been drugged and duped into it, no one can with honour be made to sin. You understand me?"

"Yes, sir."

"And the other, the vow of revenge made all those years ago by your mother, and now laid on you, to destroy your father's murderer; that, too, you can forget."

"Sir, how can I? That, surely, must remain as a duty, even though—"

"Revenge is mine, saith the lord," quoted the duke gently.

"Sir, if you mean by that that I must leave that devil March to God's stroke—"

"God has already struck. That is what I meant. I heard it as soon as we landed. King March lies sick, and they say he will not live the year out. You need no revenge on him. Of that, too, you are free, and in honour."

Alexander merely stared, saying nothing. Later, there would be relief, joy, the bursting energy of freedom; but now the freedom came like emptiness. The question echoed again in his mind: what now? Was he to go on to find Drustan in the bleak north-east, and for what, now that March was dying? Or to turn south and find the long road to Camelot, perhaps to join the High King in the wars that were blowing up like storm-clouds on the Continent? Or what he saw now as the least attractive choice of all, to turn for home and the smallness, yes, the smallness of Craig Arian, and his mother's fond but indisputable rule?

And Alice? His hopes, that had seemed so sure and shining, had vanished like mist while the two of them were talking. The duke had been kind, but what father would accept his suit, after those weeks in the Dark

Tower? Honour had required the confession, and now honour was all he had.

The duke was speaking again.

"It seems that March's kingdom of Cornwall might be rightly yours, if you were ever to claim it. Would you?"

Alexander hesitated, then spoke the truth. "I hardly know. I don't think so. My mother told me something of it, a hard kingdom, with hard neighbours. And after all these years, a foreign land to me."

"Then you will go back to this Craig Arian and care for your lands there?"

"I suppose so. Though with Barnabas and my mother there, there's not much need of another master."

"That being so, I could use your sword, Alexander," said the duke.

His tone was casual, almost flat. It took several slow seconds for the sense of what he had said to get through to the young man's brain.

"You mean on your journey home? Or—or at Castle Rose itself? Serve you there?"

"Both. What did my daughter tell you about her home?"

"Only that it was the most beautiful place on earth, and that it, with you, my lord, had all her heart."

"And that I am soon to retire into the life I long for, of prayer and solitude. The holy life?"

"She said something about it when we first spoke, but, not knowing you then, I paid little attention."

"Then listen now. Before I can accept your service, there are things you must know. I have an heir, the younger son of a cousin who is dead. The elder brother keeps the estates in the north, and this man is landless. Before I left for Tours I sent him a letter suggesting that we meet and talk over the idea of a marriage. He was abroad at the time; I was not told where, but now I think I know. Well, I planned to proceed with the matter once I got home." A pause. "You may have heard what has happened. A few days ago I got news that this man is already at Castle Rose, with some of his fighting men, and sees himself already—according to my servants—as lord of the estate." Another pause. "And, though nothing yet has been settled, or even spoken of, counts himself as plighted and soon to be married to my daughter."

"No!" It burst out, a violent protest. Alexander would have caught it back, but the duke merely cast him a swift, amused look.

"No. No indeed. Though he is distant kin of mine, his name is not one I would want my daughter to bear. You know it, I understand. Madoc of Bannog Dun."

A gasp from Alexander. "The same?"

"The same."

"Then that was the business that took him north from the Dark Tower?"

"Presumably. You told me that Madoc had been sent north on some business of the queen's, and Count Ferlas brought word back that he 'was already in possession, and all was well.' That, I think, would be the marriage, and with it the disposition of Castle Rose."

"And the queen's interest in it? To have one of her people established there, in command of a stronghold, a central point in Rheged?"

"We can only guess at it. But I think we must suppose so."

"And he's there already, in possession! Tell me, sir, could Count Madoc hold your castle against you? Could he prevent your return?"

"That I doubt. He has only a few of his own men with him, and none of mine would help him against me. And as yet he has no idea that I know of his plans. He must still be expecting to be received as my daughter's promised husband. But if he were to refuse to go when I bid him, and if he called his allies in—well, I am an old man, and ailing a little now, and I am afraid of what may happen to my people."

"So you want my sword. Of course it's yours!" Alexander spoke with a kind of impatient violence. "But this of the Lady Alice. A marriage arranged for her, spoken of, you say, but never agreed? She said nothing of it, even though—I mean, would she—did she consent?"

"Yes, she consented. She saw it as her duty. But one," said the duke, smiling, "that she has abandoned without regret. Another marriage has been spoken of, by Alice herself. She tells me that she is going to marry you. With your consent, of course? No, don't answer, boy. Get your breath back, and have another drink."

34

They were married two days later in the monastery chapel, on the morning of another lovely summer's day. Abbot Theodore himself married them. It was the duke's first excursion from his bedchamber since his seizure, but though slower than before in his movements, he was steady enough, and the relief of the occasion, with the sight of his daughter's happiness, brought an almost youthful brightness back to his eyes. The couple were attended to the altar by a solemn child in the white robe of a novice, whom Alexander had not met before, but who, he was given to understand, was Chlodovald, the Frankish prince who had come from Tours with the duke's party, bringing the relic he called the grail for safe keeping here in St. Martin's.

After the ceremony there was a brief service of prayer and thanksgiving, then the young couple broke their fast with the abbot, the duke and Prince Chlodovald in the abbot's dining-parlour, while outside the duke's party made ready to leave that day for home. This rather against the hospitaller's advice, but the duke was anxious now to go, and had agreed to travel in the litter that Alice had used. She in her turn was happy to ride beside her new husband on the all-too-long journey home.

All-too-long, because it had been agreed, almost without saying, that the consummation of the marriage, the bride's bedding, must wait until they reached Castle Rose. A monastery was hardly the place for a wedding night, and the inns along the road were few and none of them good. The journey, for Ansirus' sake, would have to be taken slowly, with at least one night's halt on the way, and it was far from certain how many miles the party would be able to cover before the duke needed to stop and rest. To Alice, moreover, it seemed wholly right that the future lord of Castle Rose should take possession of her, and with her her beloved home, in that home itself.

A message had been sent ahead to the castle to warn of their coming. Nothing more; no word of the marriage; just enough to ensure that all the castle's retainers, with some of the folk of the estate, would, as they usually did, assemble to welcome their duke home. To them he intended immediately to announce their lady's marriage, and then publicly present their new lord.

Though this would be a severe blow to Count Madoc, Duke Ansirus did not feel himself bound by the exchange of messages made in the spring. Neither party had been committed, and the Count's arrogant pre-emption of mastership made it doubly certain that the estate people and the duke's neighbours would support him in ridding himself of the pretender. However disappointed and angry Madoc was, there was little that he, as a guest in the castle, and with only a handful of his own men, could do. Ansirus, who had never feared any man in his life, had no fear now of his young relative. Angry words there might be; talk there might even be of broken promises; but that could be countered by a more dangerous word, *treachery*, and after that, what was there for Madoc to do but accept the fact, tell Queen Morgan of his failure, then go back to his own country, there to hatch his plots against the kingdom's peace, aware that his plotting, and the queen's, were known, and might at any time be reported to the High King.

What Queen Morgan might think, when she knew that her plan for Castle Rose had been foiled by her own dupe Alexander, that young man neither knew nor cared. The lure was broken. A different magic held him. His own quest was almost accomplished, his own grail won.

So the party set out on the road north with laughter and gaiety, and with nothing in view but happiness and fulfilment.

The weather stayed fine and they went safely, with no mishaps—a true wedding journey, said Alice happily—and came at length over a gently wooded hill to see the valley of the Eden curving below.

The sun was just on setting, in a floating veil of thin, saffron-coloured cloud. No less brilliant were the trees and water-meadows of the valley, their summer richness lit to green-bronze and golden-bronze, with here and there the black glint of holly or fir, and everything, forest and hedge and dry-stone dyke, sharply outlined by the low sun with shadows of violet and deepest indigo. And glimpsed here and there as it curved through the meadow and richly billowing woodland was the cool shine of the river.

"Castle Rose is over there," said Alice, pointing. She and Alexander were riding a little ahead of the rest of the party.

"How far?"

"Another ten miles or so. We'll be there in good time tomorrow. I'm glad we managed this far today." She pointed again. "Once past that beechwood yonder, and on the valley floor, there's a small foundation that will be glad to house us for the night. They'll be expecting us, too. We told them we would come there on our way home, and I sent Berin ahead an hour ago."

"Another monastery!" This time his voice, not so carefully schooled, was very clearly that of a disappointed lover, and a dimple showed as Alice answered.

"Indeed. In a sense, our own—your own, now. My mother is buried there."

"I'm sorry."

"No need. I made my first pilgrimage there—so I am told—at the age of two. My father goes there always on special days—their wedding day, her birthday, and mine, which was the day she died. To him, I think, it's a place where they still meet."

"Then I'd have thought that he would retire there, near your mother, and nearer home, not away at St. Martin's."

"This is a place for women only." She laughed at his look. "Yes, I'm afraid it's the outer dark for you and the rest, my dear lord!"

"While you and your women sleep warm on a goose-feather bed. I will put up with this," said Alexander clearly, "for this one night only. And after that, my dear wife, if anyone, abbot, nun, or the High King himself, attempts once again to stop me sleeping in your bed—"

"No one will. And there's the convent, see? Isn't the rosy stone beautiful, set like that among the trees? That's how Castle Rose is built, too. Shall we ride back and see how my father does? Oh, and Alexander—"

"My love?"

"When we do get to Castle Rose, I promise the bed is goosefeathers."

He wheeled his horse beside hers to ride back to the duke's litter. "No more than I expect," he said, laughing, and added, but not aloud, "But I don't expect to sleep very soundly, Alice my darling."

35

When at length they came in sight of Castle Rose, they found that Count Madoc, in some state as kinsman of the duke, was awaiting them at the gate. With him was a group of his own men who, it was to be seen, went armed. But behind him, in the courtyard near the steps that led to the great door, was the castle's own keeper, Beltrane, recovered from his ailment, and standing, keys in hand, with a crowd of the castle's people near him. A rather larger crowd even than usual; there were farm tenants with their labourers, and estate workers and stablemen as well as house servants, as if Beltrane, feeling somehow threatened, had gathered as many of the duke's own people as he could. And close behind him stood Jeshua, in a robe of office (somehow conjured up, it could be assumed, by the castle's women) like the one he had worn as *domesticus* to Queen Clotilda.

The duke's litter was carried at the head of his company, with Alice and Alexander riding to either side of it. After they had stopped to eat at midday, Ansirus had tried to insist on riding for the final stage; to avoid alarming his people, he said, though Alice suspected that he did not want to show any sign of weakness to Madoc. But in the end, for the journey had really tired him, he had let her persuade him to finish it as he had begun, though making the litter into a carriage of state rather than of sickness. He rode sitting straight against the cushions, with the litter's curtains drawn back to show him fully, even grandly dressed, with a jewelled collar sparkling against the breast of his gown, and the great ducal ring, a rose of rubies, on his hand.

Madoc came forward as the litter approached the gate. He threw a quick glance of curiosity at the prince, with no sign of apprehension or even interest (so no rumour's got through yet about the marriage, thought Alice), then with the barest of salutes to Alice, he hurried to the side of the litter.

"Cousin! Be welcome!" It was the greeting of a kinsman and of an equal, rather than that of a guest to his returning host. The duke, with some formally courteous reply, held out his ringed hand, and Madoc, after the briefest of pauses, bent his head and kissed it, then asked with a look of keen anxiety, and a voice raised to reach into the farthest corner of the courtyard: "But you are ill? Injured in some way? Your messenger gave us no news of this. By the gods, dear cousin, it's as well I have been here to see to things for you—"

"Neither ill nor hurt in any way, I thank you." The cool tones carried just as far. "Only older, and more easily tired than I was used to be. If you will lend me your hand?"

So it was that the duke, showing no sign of his recent weakness, walked steadily and in stately fashion into the courtyard on the arm of his kinsman, closely followed by his own party. Count Madoc's men had perforce to bring up the rear. And when the duke came to the great steps and freed himself to receive the smiling greetings and enquiries of his people, Madoc could only fall back as the welcoming crowd pressed forward, and watch while the duke, with Alice and the young stranger, mounted to the head of the steps and turned to face the thronged courtyard.

There was no need to ask for silence. Not a man there but was eager to know who this young stranger was, with the travel-stained clothes and the bearing of a prince, and the sword of a prince glittering at his hip. And not a woman there but had already seen the ring on Alice's hand, and noted the brightness of her eyes, and had come to the correct conclusion.

The duke spoke easily, as one would to friends. "Forgive me for being brief, but it's true I have ailed a little recently, and a journey is tiring for a man of my years. But now that I am here, in my home, and with you all, I need fear no evil. The more so as I have great news for you." He took Alexander lightly by the hand and brought him forward a pace, with Alice, to stand beside him. "Let me present to you the man who, after me, will rule here at Castle Rose. He is the husband of your lady, my daughter Alice, and his name is Alexander. He is Prince Alexander, only son of Prince Baudouin of Cornwall and of the Lady Anna of Craig Arian in the valley of the Wye . . . No, a moment more, good people! A moment more! The first to kiss my daughter's cheek and to welcome the bridegroom must be my dear kinsman, Count Madoc, who has ruled in my place while I was gone. Madoc?"

It was as skilfully done as his homecoming had been. But Alice, receiving the ritual kiss and watching Madoc greet Alexander, felt a tiny thread of fear crawl up her spine, as if the hairs had brushed up like the fur on a wary cat.

Then all was laughter, and calling out, and greeting,

and joy. Alice managed, through the kisses and happy tears of her women, to come near enough to her father to urge him to go to his bed and rest, but the duke had one more thing to say, and in time a hush was called and he could say it.

"Thank you, thank you, my friends! I think it's time now for us all to go about our business. Count Madoc, let me bid you once more welcome. If you had hoped for a different outcome to your journey, I am sorry. I hardly expected to find you here before me; I would have written to you with this news, and so spared you some trouble, but now"—a smiling gesture—"I'm afraid that the arrows of love, striking at random as they do, have left us nothing to discuss, and me nothing more to say except to thank you for your care of my people during my absence, and to hope that you and your men will join us in our celebration of this happy homecoming."

Madoc, pale with anger, but holding himself firmly in, began to say something, but the duke, still smiling, lifted a hand.

"Later, my dear cousin, we'll talk later, but now, by your leave, I must rest." He turned back to the throng in the courtyard. "Listen, my friends! When my daughter and Prince Alexander were wedded at the monastery of St. Martin they vowed, both of them, that their real wedding must be here at Castle Rose. So tonight, so please you, we will hold the wedding feast, which you will all share, and after that the bride will go to her bedding here in her own home, with God's blessing and the love of us all."

At this the noise broke out again, but briefly, as the duke turned to go indoors, and Alice, blushing now and laughing, led Alexander in after him, while cooks and house-servants bethought themselves suddenly of how few hours were left in which to prepare the bridal chamber and a wedding feast that would do honour to their lady and to themselves.

And through it all Count Madoc smiled and smiled and watched with cold eyes, and his men stood like soldiers with no battle to fight, until he spoke with their captain and they withdrew from the cheerful bustle into their own quarters by the tower where they had been lodged.

36

As if nothing of beauty and joy were to be omitted that night, there was a full moon, which rose late, the colour of apricots, into a sky full of bright stars. Nor moon nor stars were even noticed by Alice or Alexander, though their bedchamber window was open to the sky. Not even when, in the dead hours towards dawn when the lovers, like the rest of the castle, slept, a beam, fading to silver, slanted across the bed to touch Alexander's eyes.

For that alone he might not have wakened fully. He stirred, murmured something, and the arm that circled Alice drew her closer, but then a sound, faint but persistent, broke through his sex-drugged sleep and brought his eyes, protestingly, open.

The sound was there still. There was someone at the door. And now a voice, soft but urgent, was added to the tapping.

"My lord! My lord Alexander!"

Anyone who interrupted this night, thought Alexander dimly, ought to be hanged. But then anyone who did so—his mind cleared very quickly as he slid from the warmth of the bed, and the chill air of dawn struck his naked body like a cold shower—must do so for some very urgent reason. And that could only mean (as he snatched up a bedgown and flung it round him) that could only mean some sort of serious trouble.

It was Jeshua outside the door. In the smoky light from the cresset by the doorway his face showed pale and tense.

"What is it? The duke?"

Jeshua shot a glance past Alexander to where Alice lay sleeping, then said in an urgent undervoice: "It may be. No, he's not ill, but I think there's danger to him, or to you. I ask your pardon for disturbing you now, but I think we must talk."

"Danger? To the duke?" Alexander had, naturally, looked with curiosity and speculation at Count Madoc in the courtyard, and afterwards in the hall of feasting, but he only saw that the count, though not at first quite able to avoid showing an understandable chagrin and anger at the failure of his marriage plans, had appeared to control himself reasonably soon; and at the wedding feast, where he was seated at the duke's left hand, he had behaved with reserve, but with smiling and careful courtesy. Alexander had seen no more than that; with eyes only for Alice, and thoughts only for the coming night, he had noticed nothing else. Nor had he given a thought to what might have passed between Madoc and the duke in their private interview after the feasting.

Now he said softly: "No, wait. Over here." Shutting the bedchamber door softly behind him, he took the other man by the arm and led him across the passageway into an embrasure where a window let in the chill air of dawn.

"Now. Tell me. You're talking about Count Madoc?"

"Who else? My lord, not for anything less would I have disturbed you tonight, and I left it as long as I dared—"

"Never mind that. Get on. What do you know?"

"Only that the count would do anything, dare any-thing, to get possession of these lands. Beltrane told me other things that have happened, but no matter of that now. I do know one thing that was to pass tonight between him and the duke, because I shall have to make the arrangements. The count is to leave, though not for a day or so. This for form's sake only. But he is to dismiss his men-at-arms tomorrow, to wait for him beyond the castle's boundary."

"Yes? Can the duke enforce this?"

"Oh, yes. But you see what it means? If the count is to move, it must be tonight."

"Move? To do what?"

But he knew, even before Jeshua said: "Have you ever heard of the Young Celts?"

"Ah," said Alexander softly. "Yes, indeed. And they—she—whoever it is—really are depending on him somehow to take possession of Castle Rose?"

"I think so. He was the obvious choice, the heir, with an easy way in by marriage. I don't know much about your country, my lord, but I understand that this would be a good place to hold, perhaps commanding the road north, or the port to the west where we landed?"

"I don't know that either, but—surely it's not very likely that he'll try anything now? Even if I were out of the way, the duke must have made it clear when they talked, that he knew of the count's links with the faction, and that he'd have no hope of the Lady Alice? What better reason could he give the man for passing over his claim, such as it was, to her hand, and bestowing it on me? What are you afraid of? What else have you heard?"

"Nothing definite. But I was there when the message

came in that the duke was on his way back from St. Martin's, and I was watching the count when the duke presented you as the Lady Alice's husband. Afterwards—when everyone was busy preparing for the feast—I followed Count Madoc to see what he would do. I know murder when I see it, my lord. He went to talk with his captain, and though I heard nothing of what was said, I saw their looks. Then I tried to warn Beltrane, but he was full of the marriage, and too cumbered with the coming feast—and besides, he would not believe me. He's a simple man, and to him this place, after a lifetime of peace, is peace itself. There may have been difficulties recently, but now that the duke is home, he cannot see that anyone can make trouble. More, he would not believe that a kinsman would harm the duke or the Lady Alice. Nor"—there was no change in the even, faintly accented voice—"would he readily believe anything that I, a foreigner and a Jew, would say about his master's kin. So I came to you."

"And what would you have me do?"

"Sir—" the voice did change now; relief and urgency. "Sir, if you would go to the duke's room. He and Count Madoc have not long finished their talk, and gone to their beds. I waited to see my lord safely to his chamber, and at present all is well, but there's only one man there to attend him, a servant who usually sleeps within call in the antechamber. I thought there would be guards set, but there has never been any need, and no one has thought of it. So, sir, if you would go there now, just for the time it takes for me to rouse some of the duke's men and set them on watch? I need your authority for that, too. I've already been down to the east tower and turned the key on the count's men. If it turns out that there's nothing planned, they'll never know. I'll open it when it's daylight."

"Good man. You've done right. I'll go. Just give me a moment to put something on, and get my sword. And perhaps—if my lady wakes to find me gone—and thinks her father is in danger—"

"I wakened Mariamne. She's here with me. She'll stay with your lady in case she wakes. Let us pray to the God we share that we need not alarm her, and that all this has been for nothing."

"Except to ruin my wedding night!"

"Let's hope you'll be back beside your lady long before she wakes," said Jeshua, and turned to call softly: "Mariamne? Come now."

She had been waiting in the shadows some way along the corridor. As Alexander went for clothes and weapon she came quickly, stopped beside Jeshua for whispered question and answer, reached up to kiss him, then slipped silently into the bedchamber and over to her mistress's side. Alice did not stir. Alexander, dressed and sword in hand, lifted a hand in salute and, as silently, left the chamber.

Jeshua had gone. Alexander, his doeskin slippers making no sound, ran along the corridor towards the duke's room.

37

The duke's rooms were on the south front of the castle, and to get to them Alexander had to reach the corner tower, feel his way (for there was no light on the tower stair) down a dozen steps of the spiral, and then find the door of Ansirus' bedchamber. From the quick directions that Jeshua had managed to give him, he knew this to be the third door along, plain to see, as it was normally lighted by two cressets, one to either side of the archway.

What was also plain to see, as Alexander ran towards the pool of light thrown by the torches, was that the door of the duke's chamber stood open.

And as he gained the doorway with a rush he saw three things. A man, presumably the duke's servant, lying on his face with a dagger's hilt standing in his back; the duke himself, asleep in the great bed and apparently undisturbed; and Count Madoc stooping over the sleeping form with a pillow in his hands.

A still, startled pause, then Alexander gave a breathless shout. "To me!" and flung himself forward. In the same moment he saw that the count was unarmed: on this secret mission he had come without his sword, and his dagger was lodged in the body of the man he had killed.

Alexander checked momentarily, and the moment was all that Madoc needed. He flung the pillow straight at Alexander's face, and as the young man dodged aside he leaped back from the bedside and tore the duke's sword and dagger down from where they hung on the wall. Then, with fury in his eyes, but showing all the terrifying control of the seasoned fighting man, he sprang to the attack.

Alexander, meeting that first rush, had all he could do to hold his assailant off. This was a very different matter from those other fights of his—so very long ago, it now seemed. The count was a big man, both angry and desperate, with more even than his life at stake, and how the fight would have gone in those first minutes if the odds had not been on Alexander's side, it is hard to tell. But fate—or justice—worked against the older man. When he had stooped over his victim, ready with the smothering pillow, his eyes had been near the night-candle that burned beside the duke's bed, and its little plume of flame still burned ghostly but blinding on his sight. And the sword he wielded was not his own: Ansirus' weapon, being a sword for state rather than for killing, was both longer and lighter than his own accustomed blade. There had been no fighting in Duke Ansirus' life for a great many years.

Alexander, on the other hand, had his eyes adjusted to the dimness, and was using his own sword—his father's sword, a fighting weapon that had already been blooded by him in the skirmishes with the Cornishmen, and since then in practice had grown used to his hand, and fought now as an extension of it.

And whatever of ambition or fear Madoc had at stake, Alexander already knew that, if he lost this fight, the duke would die also, and Alice, his sweet Alice, would be seized by the murderer and used without mercy to help him possess and control Castle Rose and its people for his own base ends.

The swords met, clashed, slithered, hacked and clashed again. Madoc, beating forward with both sword and dagger in murderous attack, managed to force the young man back and give himself a few precious seconds in which to pull away. He whirled the whistling metal round and over his head, testing the unfamiliar weight, and cursing as the jewels of the hilt grazed his hand, then brought it down to meet Alexander's blade again as the prince lunged after him. Madoc's dagger cut down at the stretched sword-arm, caught in the seam of the sleeve, and came away bloodied. He laughed, a brief breathless grunt of pleasure, and then, hand and eye adjusted, pressed forward again, urgent to finish the fight before the noise should rouse the sleeping castle.

One sleeper, indeed, could surely not fail to be disturbed. The duke was waking. He stirred, half turned, said something in a blurred undervoice, then subsided again on his pillows.

Neither man took any notice. Slashing, thrusting, dodging and leaping, first to one side of the bed and then the other, they fought, while the duke, sinking back into drugged slumber, lay without further sound or movement.

Alexander, forced back towards the doorway by the

double attack of sword and dagger, and desperately conscious of being outweaponed, and so outfought, was also sharply aware of the servant's body lying somewhere in the dim doorway behind him. To trip over it would mean his almost certain death, and he dared not, as he fought to parry both sword and dagger, take even one precious second to look aside. His left hand was out to feel for the jamb of the door, flailing behind him as he tried desperately to remember just where the body lay.

Another step back, as short as he dared make it, while Madoc's face, suffused with rage and triumph, was thrust forward towards him into the light cast by the cressets in the corridor. It was the sudden change in those gloating eyes that warned Alexander that something new had happened. In the same moment, cool and infinitely comforting, he felt the hilt of a dagger pressed into his left hand.

Alice's voice, as cool as the metal, was speaking. "Now, Mariamne! Help me pull poor Barty's body out of the way. My lord needs room. Never mind the blood, woman! It's only where I pulled the dagger out! Good. Now, quickly! Run, tell the guards to hurry, and rouse anyone else you see! Run!"

If she said more, Alexander did not hear it. Armed now equally with his opponent, and sensing the doubt overtaking the man's rage, he felt nothing but a kind of exhilaration. His cut arm he felt not at all. He laughed, brought the dagger round into play alongside his sword, and leaped forward as if this were the first attack, rather than a desperate saving from defeat.

Twelve seconds later he killed Madoc with a blow from the murderer's own dagger. Standing over the body, his breathing ragged, his tunic splashed with the count's blood, and a trickle of his own dripping down from one hand, he dropped both weapons to the floor, and turned to hold out his arms to Alice. She flew into them, and he took her in an embrace as close as any other of that stormy wedding night.

"Alice. Alice."

"I thought he was going to kill you."

"He would have done, I think, but for you."

"No, no. My brave lord, my love."

She reached up, and his head went down in a kiss that seemed to be given by his whole body. "Alice, Alice—" It was all he could say.

"Alice?"

The voice from the bed brought them both back to earth and to the present. The duke, still dazed with sleep, and the fading fumes of the drug, was trying to push himself up on the pillows.

"What is it? What do you do here, child? Alexander?"

She pulled herself from her husband's arms and ran to him. "Nothing, nothing, father. All's well, truly. It's over. And Madoc is dead."

So few minutes had passed, though to Alexander, busy twisting Alice's kerchief round the shallow cut in his forearm, the fight had seemed to take an eternity of time. The guards, sent by Jeshua, came running, and hard behind them the castle servants, sobered now and eager to rid their master's home of the threat that all had feared, but been powerless to prevent.

Now by the count's own action that threat was removed. It emerged that when he and Ansirus had been

closeted together for a private talk after the wedding feast
Madoc had spoken frankly of his disappointment, but
had agreed that no binding contract had been made. He
had even laughed, accepting the inevitable change of his
plans with a kind of wry humour ("When children fall in
love, what are grown men to say to it? Well, what's done
is done, so let us pledge them once more, cousin, and
then get to our beds."). If the duke had been less
exhausted by the events of that long day, he might, even
in his relief at the outcome of the talk, have been wary of
accepting wine poured by his kinsman. But courtesy and
trust demanded it, so he had taken the cup, and in a short
while succumbed to that heavily drugged slumber.

Jeshua had been right about the count's desperation. It
had forced him in haste into a rash and very risky plan.
By smothering Ansirus in his sleep he must have hoped
that the duke's death would be attributed to another
seizure. What he planned after that could only be guessed
at. The discovery of the body would of course have
thrown the castle into an uproar, in which it might have
been easy for the count—the duke's nearest kinsman,
who had already established some sort of right there—to
assert his authority above that of the two he had called
"children"; the authority of a regent, perhaps, for which
he could quote Ansirus' own sanction, claiming that it
had been given last night in that private talk, a statement
that no one could contradict.

And after that? Defiance by Alexander, a quarrel
easily picked, that would let him fight the young man and
kill him? Then, as kinsman and heir, Madoc's way would
be clear to invoke the duke's first proposal, and take possession of Alice, hoping that in her grief and confusion

she would accept his claim as her father's first choice of husband and ruler of Castle Rose? Knowing nothing of Alice, he might have expected that she, being young, alone, and in distress, would not try to deny his claim, but would accept his "protection" for herself and her people. And even if, in her grief, she threatened to ask for the High King's judgment over Alexander's death, she would hardly pursue the matter once she was with child by Madoc of an undoubted heir.

About the murdered servant Count Madoc, being what he was, probably did not think at all. A body carried out and flung into the river, to be found and wondered over perhaps days after that tragic night . . . ? By the time questions were asked—if indeed anyone troubled to investigate a servant's death—he himself would, with luck, be lord of Castle Rose and above questioning.

The count's men, not knowing that they had been prisoners through the night, emerged at daybreak to be told—with an irony they could not appreciate—that their master had suffered a seizure during the night and had died of it. Their captain, escorted by Jeshua to the count's room, looked at the blood-stained body on the bed and, after a due pause for reflection on his and his men's situation, agreed that it had been a seizure. His men would leave that day, and take their master's body home for burial. Meanwhile the dead servant's body was carried to the duke's own chapel, and the duke, shaking off the mists of the sleeping-potion, went there himself to add his prayers to those of the man's sister, a kitchen-girl, who knelt there weeping.

And eventually, as it usually does, morning came.

* * *

Neither Alexander nor Alice took any part in all these complicated matters. They stole out of the duke's crowded bedchamber, picking their way over Madoc's body, and went back to bed.

Epilogue

So ended the adventure of Alexander the Fatherless and
Alice the Pretty Pilgrim. They found their home and, as
the chronicler relates, "They lived there in great joy."

But first there were a few things to be settled. Count
Madoc's body was taken home by his men, there to be
given honourable burial. It is on record that the captain,
who knew something of his late master's plans, and who
certainly knew the manner of his master's death, said
nothing about either. Between the duke and his distant
kinsmen there was, as before, indifference and courtesy.

Or rather, between them and Castle Rose. The duke
did not remain there for much longer. With Alexander
confirmed as the castle's master, Ansirus made his final
preparations for retiring to St. Martin's monastery. Meanwhile a messenger, a trusted servant, was sent to Camelot.
He carried an account of all that had happened, Queen
Morgan's connection with the dissident faction, her
attempts to get hold of the grail of power, her plan,
through Count Madoc, to acquire Castle Rose for some
purpose of those same would-be rebels, and Madoc's
attack on the duke and the murder of his servant. Finally,
a kind of confession that asked for merciful judgment on
Alexander's killing of Count Madoc.

Another letter—perhaps slightly overdue—was sent at the same time by Alexander to Craig Arian to tell his mother the news of his marriage and his accession by it to the lordship of Castle Rose. With it he gave her the news of King March's imminent death, which had ended his own quest for vengeance. He had not thought it necessary, he told her, to take the matter further in his letter to the High King, nor had he any wish to pursue a possible claim to what was to him a foreign kingdom; there must surely be some other heir, whom Arthur could approve, waiting anxiously for King March's demise? As for Craig Arian, he would of course, if she wished, come south to talk with her about the settlement of the estate there, but . . .

He could have saved himself the doubts. The Princess Anna herself came north with the returning messenger to bring her own assurances of joy and satisfaction over the match, and to declare herself content at last to lay Baudouin's ghost to rest. Sadok had already sent word to her of March's approaching death, so on receipt of Alexander's letter she had (with some private ceremony, it was understood) burned the blood-stained shirt and buried its ashes at Craig Arian, which was now her home, as Castle Rose was to be Alexander's.

So Cornwall and its dark past were laid aside, and all was rejoicing. Another feast was held to welcome the Princess Anna, with nothing more alarming to follow than an exchange of gifts and compliments. The two ladies embraced, assessed one another carefully with the sweetest of smiles, and found that, with the one fixed at Craig Arian and the other at Castle Rose, they could be and remain the fastest of friends. And so it came about. Anna, truth to tell, would have grudged handing over the rule of Craig Arian to one she still saw—would probably always see—as an untried boy. She went back to it, and to the undemanding help and devotion of Barnabas and Theodora and their servants, and waited eagerly for the next news to come from Castle Rose.

Which it did, in time. But not until Alice and her father had made their last pilgrimage together.

It was early in November. By that time affairs were in good train at the castle; Alexander had come to know every farm, field and tenant on the place, whom to trust, whom to watch, when to move and when to be patient. Soon he was almost as much part of the place as Alice, and the duke, watching with deep contentment, could set out at last on his journey home.

Alice, nearly four months pregnant, insisted on going with him, and allowed the litter to be ordered mainly so that her father, should he tire, might be persuaded to ride in it. They set out quietly, as so often before, and if this time there were tears among the people assembled in the courtyard to watch them go, why, there had always been tears, even when their lord had been expected to come home again.

So they went, taking it easily, through the cool mists of a mild November day, and there at the convent Alice, between her father and her husband, prayed at her mother's tomb. Later, by that same tomb, she said good-bye to her father, and the two groups parted, the duke to be escorted to St. Martin's by his servants, and the young folk to ride home to take up their life together.

Soon after this the looked-for letter came from the High King.

The lovers were walking on the terrace in the faint warmth of the November sun. Below them, along the river's bank, the beeches blazed, magnificent in red and gold, among oaks still green, but edged and splashed with amber. The delicate birches, half their leaves already gone with the autumn winds, showed spangled with palest yellow. The hollies were rich with berries, and busy with blackbirds greedy for the first fruit. All the birds of summer had gone, but a heron flapped heavily to his fishing-place, and a charm of winter finches wrangled somewhere among the boughs. The river, full and smooth, slid past almost without sound among its reeds and sallows.

There were two letters. Alice, moving still lightly but with more careful grace than of old, sat down on a seat framed by the bare twining stems of roses and honeysuckle, and reached a hand to Beltrane, who came bustling up, full of importance.

"From my father?"

"Indeed, indeed, my lady. And this other has the royal seal. From the High King himself, it must be!" An anxious look. "My lord duke, he's well?"

"Yes." Alice was skimming the brief letter. "All is very well. Oh, and he has heard from Jeshua. He and Mariamne reached Jerusalem safely. She's to have a baby in May, the same as me! They'll stay with his family till the birth, then he wants to come back to Castle Rose. Since Queen Clotilda went into the convent there's no place for him there. Well, that's good news for us. You'll soon be able to take things more easily, Beltrane! And it will be good to have Mariamne here again. That's all, thank you. Tell the other servants, will you?"

Alexander was already deep in the other letter, which

was indeed from the High King. It was long, beautifully penned by Arthur's scribe. In it the King thanked Alexander for what he had done to defend his corner of the realm against treachery, and acquitted him of any blame over Madoc's death. He himself (he wrote) had for some time been watching the activities of the Young Celts; had even, in the person of his trusted nephew Mordred, infiltrated their counsels. So he had been forewarned. But now (he went on) with the possibility of Britain's involvement in the wars on the Continent, he must make his back safe. To this end he had caused Queen Morgan to be removed under guard to the remote fortress of Castell Aur in the Welsh mountains, where another nephew, Gawain of Orkney himself, was set to keep close watch on her. In any case her following would soon disperse. The fighting abroad would sufficiently divert the energies of the idle swords, and feed the ambition of the young men thirsting for action and glory. Meantime, if Prince Alexander ever rode south to Camelot, he would be assured of an honourable place among the High King's Companions . . .

"Camelot!" said Alexander, when they had both read the letter.

"Camelot!" sighed Alice. "I used to think I wanted to go there more than anything in the world!"

"And don't you now?"

She smiled, smoothing her hands down over the soft swell of her body. "Fine dresses, satins, jewels? They'd not fit me for long! No, it was a girl's dream. I have all I want here. And you?"

"A boy's dream, no more," he said. His hand went over to lie gently over hers. "All I want, all I shall ever want, is here, too."

* * *

It is a fact that Alexander never did get to Camelot. It was written later, by the chronicler, that "He lost his way, and wandered for a great while."

But he knew, and we know, that he had found it.

The Legend

(The tale of Sir Alisander le Orphelin and Alice la Beale Pilgrim, as related by Thomas Malory in *Le Morte d'Arthur*, Book X).

King Mark of Cornwall had a younger brother, Boudwin, whom the people loved. There came a time when the Saracens attempted to invade Cornwall from the sea, and Boudwin, raising the country against them, put wildfire in three of his own ships, and sent these among the enemy ships, destroying them, and killing the whole invading army of forty thousand men.

King Mark, already jealous of his brother's popularity, was angry at Boudwin's success, and planned to kill him. He sent for him to come to court with his wife Anglides and their infant son Alisander. At supper the king picked a quarrel with Boudwin and stabbed him to death. Queen Isoud sent to warn Anglides that her son was in grave danger, so, helped by Sir Tristram, she fled from Mark's castle, taking with her Boudwin's blood-stained shirt and doublet as a reminder of a murder which must be avenged.

Meanwhile Mark, raging through the castle and failing to find the child to kill him, sent a knight called Sadok to catch the fugitives and bring them back. But Sadok had been Boudwin's friend, so when he came up with Anglides and the child he let them go, only requiring her to promise that one day, when Alisander was grown, she would send him to avenge his father's murder. Then Sadok rode back to tell King Mark that he had drowned the boy himself. At which Mark rejoiced.

Anglides travelled on till she came to the castle of Arundel in Sussex, which belonged to a cousin. She was made welcome, and lived there in safety till Alisander was grown. Then, on Lady Day, when he with twenty others was made knight, she showed him the bloody shirt and doublet, and bade him avenge his father's murder.

When the feasting and jousting were over Alisander set out to ride to London, but, missing his way, journeyed on, fighting in one tournament after another, always overcoming his opponent, until eventually he was wounded in a fight undertaken for a damosel who owned a castle nearby. The damosel had the wounded Alisander carried into her castle, where Morgan le Fay (who suspected the damosel's motives, and who wanted him for herself) tended him for a while. At length, after drugging him, she carried him off to her own castle, where she promised to heal him on condition that he made no attempt to leave her lands for a year and a day. Perforce, he promised, and she did heal him.

But then one day a lady who was cousin to Morgan warned him privately that Morgan intended to keep him there as her lover, at which he was horrified. "I would liefer cut away my hangers than I would do her such pleasure," he cried, but because of his promise he could not leave the castle. Then one day the castle was attacked and burned down, so he was able, with the lady's help, to escape into the grounds, where he camped out, setting himself to defend the land (and presumably his virtue) from all comers for the required year and a day. His fame as a fighter soon spread through the kingdoms. It appears that Morgan did not pursue him.

There was a duke called Ansirus, who travelled every third year to Jerusalem, so that he was known as Ansirus the Pilgrim. He had a very beautiful daughter called Alice, whom men called Alice la Beale Pilgrim. She heard of Alisander's prowess, and gave it out that she would marry any knight who could make himself master of the piece of land which Alisander was holding. Since she was so lovely, and sole heiress of the duke's estates, many knights tried to dislodge Alisander, but failed to do so.

At last she decided to see him for herself, and reached the place in time to watch him defeat a notable knight, whereupon she ran to his horse's head and asked him to take off his helmet and let her see his face. He did so. "O sweet Jesu," said Alice. "Thee must I love, and never other."

"Then show me your visage," said Alisander. Then she unwimpled her visage, and when he saw her he said: "Here have I found my love and my lady."

So they were married, and lived in great joy. But it so happened that Alisander had never grace nor fortune to come to King Arthur's court, and he never did avenge his father's murder.

Author's Note

My story has two primary sources. One is a remark made to me by a friend: "Everybody has their own Grail." The other is a brief incident in my book *The Wicked Day*, where Mordred, alone in the forest, encounters a wandering priest and a young girl. I had Malory's "Alice la Beale Pilgrim" in mind—she had long fascinated me—but somehow she could not fit into that story. Here she is at last.

It will be seen from the "legend" summarised here that Malory's tale of Alisander le Orphelin and Alice la Beale Pilgrim was not easy to transpose into the "real Arthurian" or Dark Age setting. It is a mediaeval tale of action where kings, queens and knights move as conventionally as chess pieces, and, like chessmen, make the same moves over and over again. The main concern of the knights seems to be their jousting scores—the mediaeval equivalent of the batting average.

Malory's brief reference to Duke Ansirus the Pilgrim, combined with the idea of some kind of "grail quest," gave me the Jerusalem and Tours setting. Again, a reference from *The Wicked Day* remembered the murder of the young Merovingian princes, so I linked the pilgrims with the adventure of Chlodovald's rescue.

Here we move from legend to historical fact. The necessary source for any account of the Merovingian (Merwing) kings is Gregory of Tours' *History of the Franks*. In Book III he gives a vivid account of the murder of the young princes by their uncles, and the agonised grief of Queen Clotilda at the choice of "scissors or sword" that the murderers gave her. He tells us that the youngest boy, Chlodovald, escaped, "for those who guarded him were brave men." He cut his hair—the symbolic lion's mane of the Frankish kings—with his own hand, and devoted himself to God. He stayed for some time in hiding, but eventually returned to his own country, where he founded a monastery, which bore his name. This was St. Cloud, near Paris. For the purposes of my story I have had him taken to a hiding-place in Britain.

Gregory's history is one of battles, murders and sudden deaths, relieved by the deeds of holy men, but with very little in the way of description or social background. For an account of the Merovingian way of life—houses, occupations, countryside—I went to Gibbon's *Decline and Fall of the Roman Empire*.

Europe under the Merovingians. Clovis (482–511 AD) unified Gaul, and established Paris as his capital. At his death his lands were divided among his four sons. The eldest son, the bastard Theuderic, received lands around the Rhine, Moselle, and upper Meuse. Chlodomer was established in the regions along the Loire. To Childebert went the country of the English Channel, with Bordeaux and Saintes. The youngest, Lothar, was settled north of the Somme and in Aquitaine. These territories were supposed to be roughly of equal value, but this was obviously disputable, and, as the boundaries of the "kingdoms" were not well defined, the result of the partition was a constant quarrelling—what one commentator calls "bloody competition"—between the brothers.

Pilgrimages. By the first century AD there was a system of guest houses for pilgrims to Jerusalem, on traditional routes provided with watering-places. Pilgrimages became extremely popular. As Philo of Alexandria wrote: "It is a test of faith and an escape from everyday life." And Chaucer made gentle fun of the fact that when the good weather arrived, "than longen folk to goon on pilgrimages." The earliest known account of a Christian pilgrimage to Jerusalem was that of the so-called "pilgrim of Bordeaux" in the early fourth century.

The Legend of the Holy Grail. The Grail was the cup or chalice traditionally used by Christ at the Last Supper. According to one legend, Joseph of Arimathea, having preserved in it a few drops of Christ's blood, brought it to Britain, where it soon disappeared. There is a mass of literature about the quests for the lost Grail, which is associated with the spear that pierced Christ's side, and a sword. In my book *The Hollow Hills* I used the quest story, but with the sword as the object. That sword eventually came into Arthur's possession, as Caliburn (Excalibur), but the spear and Grail were given for safe keeping to Nimuë, Arthur's chief adviser, who had been the pupil and then the lover of Merlin the enchanter.

Morgan and Morgause. Morgause, according to legend, was Arthur's half-sister, the illegitimate daughter of his father King Uther Pendragon. She married King Lot of Lothian and Orkney, and had four sons by him. She also bore a son, Mordred, to her half-brother Arthur, whom she seduced into an incestuous union. She was murdered by one of her sons, Gaheris. Morgan, Arthur's legitimate sister, married King Urbgen of Rheged. She took a lover, Accolon, and persuaded him to steal the enchanted sword Caliburn and with it to usurp her brother's power. The plot failed, and she was put aside by Urbgen, and imprisoned (fairly comfortably) by Arthur.

March. This is King Mark of Cornwall, who in mediaeval Arthurian romances is uncle to Tristram (Drustan). He is usually depicted as cruel and treacherous. Mark's queen, Iseult the Fair, and Tristram were lovers.

Some Other Brief Notes

Place Names. I have followed a simple rule, which is to make the geography of the story as clear as possible for the reader to follow. Hence the use of some modern names alongside those of the Roman or Dark Age maps.

The Saxon Shore. This was a stretch of the south-east and south coastal regions of Britain, roughly from Norfolk to Hampshire, where Saxon incomers were allowed to settle.

The Saracen Longships. Malory's tale is of course mediaeval, but since we are here in the Dark Age of the early sixth century, the invaders are Saxon, and I have reduced their numbers to something a little more likely than forty thousand.

Castle Rose. This has nothing to do with Rose Castle, the seat of the bishops of Carlisle. It owes its name to the lovely New Red Sandstone of Cumbria (Rheged), of which it would probably have been built.

Don't miss a single book in Mary Stewart's
Arthurian Saga!
Published by Fawcett Books.
Available at your local bookstore.

THE CRYSTAL CAVE

Here begins the Arthurian legend. The passion, the intrigue, and in the middle—Merlin. Who was Merlin? A sinister, all-powerful being from another world? A Prince of Darkness? Or just a man with unique intelligence and unusual gifts? And just what makes the crystal cave so important to him?

THE HOLLOW HILLS

The spellbinding, suspenseful story of how Merlin, the Enchanter, helped Arthur beome king of all Britain. In fifth-century Britain, no life is safe and no law is stable. The prophetic voice of Merlin communicates the bristling atmosphere of the story's ancient setting and its profound relevance to our own time.

THE LAST ENCHANTMENT

In Camelot, Arthur is king. But other powers plot to destroy him. The witch Morgause, Arthur's half sister, ensnares him in an incestuous liaison as a fatal web of love, betrayal, and bloody vengeance is woven.

THE WICKED DAY

It is the final years of King Arthur's reign. Mordred, the son of King Arthur and Morgause, returns to Camelot as a young man and learns of his parentage. He becomes King Arthur's most trusted counselor, setting in motion the Fates and leading to the "wicked day of destiny."

And look for this enthralling novel of suspense and romance:

THE STORMY PETREL

Set against the arresting landscape of Scotland's fabled Western Islands, this is the story of Rose Fenemore, a teacher looking to awaken her dormant muse. But as the truth about the two men she meets unfolds, the stormy petrels—fragile, elusive birds who fly close to the waves—come to symbolize Rose's confusion and the mystery of her future.

THE STORMY PETREL
by Mary Stewart

Published by Fawcett Books.
Available in bookstores everywhere.

MARY STEWART

Published by Fawcett Books.
Available in your local bookstore.

Call toll free 1-800-793-BOOK (2665) to order by phone and use your major credit card. Or use this coupon to order by mail.

__AIRS ABOVE THE GROUND	449-21564-4	$5.99
__THE IVY TREE	449-21571-7	$5.99
__NINE COACHES WAITING	449-21572-5	$5.99
__THE STORMY PETREL	449-22085-0	$5.99
__THORNYHOLD	449-21712-4	$5.99
__A WALK IN WOLF WOOD	449-21422-2	$5.99

The Arthurian Saga:

__THE CRYSTAL CAVE	449-91161-6	$12.95
__THE HOLLOW HILLS	449-91173-X	$12.95
__THE LAST ENCHANTMENT	449-91176-4	$12.95
__THE WICKED DAY	449-91185-3	$12.95

Name _____

Address _____

City_____State_____Zip_____

Please send me the FAWCETT BOOKS I have checked above.
I am enclosing $_____
    plus
Postage & handling* $_____
Sales tax (where applicable) $_____
Total amount enclosed $_____

*Add $4 for the first book and $1 for each additional book.

Send check or money order (no cash or CODs) to:
Fawcett Mail Sales, 400 Hahn Road, Westminster, MD 21157.

Prices and numbers subject to change without notice.
Valid in the U.S. only.
All orders subject to availability.   STEWART